Welcome To Hickville High

Mary Karlik

GPK Publication LLC

Book Layout ©2013 BookDesignTemplates.com
Cover design by Jenny Zemanek. Cover art by Seedlings, LLC used under license.

Welcome to Hickville High — 1st ed.
ISBN: 978-0996155618

ACKNOWLEDGEMENTS

There are many people to thank who have helped along this journey. First, thank you to the Romance Writers of America for providing an amazing writing community. Thank you to the late Judi McCoy, my very first critique partner so many years ago. Thank you to the Flip-flop Sisters: Sherry Davis, Sandra Ferguson, Laura Martello, and Delores Shaffer. You lifted me up when I couldn't imagine how I'd survive the next day. Love you all. To Terry Southwick, thank you for being my friend, conference roomie, and mentor. To the Seton Hill University Writing Popular Fiction folks, I knew the minute I stepped on campus, I'd found my tribe. I'd had no idea I'd gain lifelong friends. Aileen Latcham, John McDevitt, Anita Miller, and so many others, thank you for helping me whip this book into shape. To my mentor, friend, and editor Shelley Bates, words cannot express how grateful I am for your guiding hand.

Last, thank you to my family. To my late husband, Greg, your wry sense of humor, dogged determination, and soul-filling love inspires my heroes. To my daughters, Kate Bazin and Amanda McDevitt, thank you for encouraging my constant chatter about books, plots, and characters. You are the light of my life. I am so proud of the women, wives, and mothers you have become.

1

The universe had completely crapped on Kelsey Quinn's life.

She dabbed at her eyes, blew her nose, and wadded up the tissue before dropping it to the pile on the seat next to her. Pressing her forehead against the car window, she watched the scenery fly by at seventy miles per hour. They passed Bob's Stay and Go combination gas station/fast food restaurant/hotel, followed by some weird concrete, starship-shaped pizza parlor. Next, three-foot fluorescent letters screamed about redemption across a junkyard fence surrounding rusted pieces of mangled metal. The few words of scripture painted there weren't going change her fate. Her dad was in the driver's seat and they were heading straight for the armpit of Texas.

With a sigh she slumped against the seat and tried not to think about the boyfriend who'd been ripped from her life, or the best friend she'd been forced to leave behind. But it wasn't just her forced exile from Drew and Zoe. She'd lost her identity. At St. Monica's, she knew who she was and where she fit in. It was her senior year, the year she'd looked forward to for as long as she'd been in school. They had taken it away with less thought than the car they'd sold one afternoon while she and Zoe were shopping. None of it was her fault. She was a victim of her dad's incompetence on one hand and her sister's immorality on the other.

Her dad exited onto a two-lane highway where they were greeted by a faded sign.

WELCOME TO HILLSIDE, TEXAS
POPULATION 5000

They slowed to a crawl as they entered the town. At a four-way stop her mom screeched, "Oh my God, Tom, look at the cute little diner. We're all starving. Let's stop before we go to the house."

"Sounds good to me. Jack's not expecting us for another couple of hours anyway." Dad angled the Infinity between two pickup trucks and turned off the engine.

The diner was nestled in the center of a row of dilapidated two-story buildings. EARLY BIRD CAFÉ was painted in bright blue letters across the glass. Kelsey pulled her compact mirror from her purse and studied her reflection. She'd been crying for two days—no amount of makeup magic would fix her swollen red eyes. It didn't matter. She didn't care about this place or these people. She sure as heck didn't care what they thought about her. She shoved the mirror back into her purse.

Her younger sister, Ryan, looked all wide-eyed and curious. And worse, she actually looked excited to investigate this hick little town. Why not? It was her fault they were in this mess in the first place. Her parents would have been justified in shipping Ryan off to some kind of school for troubled kids. But no—Quinns don't give up on their own. Everybody had to suffer because Ryan couldn't say no to drugs or boys.

Mackenzie, Kelsey's youngest sister, flipped her

compact gymnast's body from the third seat to the backseat, nailing Ryan in the shoulder with her foot.

"Watch it!" Ryan drew her fist back, but before she could get the hit off, Mackenzie flashed a cherub smile and released a powdered-sugar apology. *Yeah. That wasn't an accident.* Kelsey almost smiled when she saw foot impact with shoulder. Mackenzie had been fairly silent about the ruin Ryan's exploits had made of her life. Apparently, she had her limits too.

Kelsey reached for the door handle that offered freedom from her sixteen-hour prison. They had only been on this leg of the trip for six hours, but really, two days stuffed in an SUV with parents who had lost their minds, one sister she hated, and another who hardly spoke was about all Kelsey could stomach.

Cracking the door was like opening a portal to hell. Heat blasted in and snatched her breath. "God, this place should be called *Hellside*."

Dad coughed and said, "Welcome to Texas in July."

The Quinn family crawled from the confines of their cell-on-wheels, stretched their crunched bones and crinkled muscles, and tried not to pass out from heat stroke.

Kelsey's dad worked his neck from side to side. His classic super stressed move. Despite the stories he'd told about growing up on the farm, he sure didn't look excited about returning home after so many years away. But then again, Kelsey doubted his life plan included being fired from the investment firm he'd helped found.

He led the family up the steps to the sidewalk raised about two feet above the street and held the screen door open as they filed into the Early Bird Café. A waitress wearing blue jeans and a black "Cowgirl Up!" T-shirt zipped across the wood floors carrying a couple of plastic pitchers. "Howdy, folks. Sit wherever ya want."

Kelsey followed her mom to a large table in the corner situated between two roaring floor fans. Mom looked around the diner. "Isn't this cute?"

Kelsey took in the aluminum tables and chairs and the various occupants of those chairs and muttered, "I'm thinking, no."

Ryan grinned as she gawked at the framed football jerseys, photographs, and yellowed newspaper articles lining the walls over gray, chipped paint. "Look at this stuff. This is awesome!"

Trashy was the word Kelsey would have used, but she kept it to herself. How dared Ryan be so happy? Did she not have a freakn' clue that they'd given up everything because of her? They'd had it all in Chicago.

The cowgirl-up waitress scooted to their table and passed out plastic menus. "What would you folks like to drink? We have coke, water, and tea."

With the word *coke* Kelsey's throat went into a kind of get-me-wet-now spasm. "I'll have Coke."

The waitress pulled a pad from her apron pocket and smiled. "Okay, darlin', we have Seven-up, Dr. Pepper, and Pepsi."

"Oh, I thought you had Coke?"

The waitress's brain must have not cowgirled-up yet, because she looked at Kelsey like she was speaking gibberish and repeated, "We have Seven-up, Dr. Pepper, and Pepsi. Now which coke would you like?"

Kelsey sighed and looked at Dad.

A grin tugged at the corner of his mouth. "Coke and soda are the same here, Kel."

About the time Dad spoke, a grey-haired man sitting nearby stood and faced the family. "Well, who let the damn Yankees in Hillside?"

Kelsey held her breath. She'd heard about these rednecks. They hated all things not Texan. From the toothpick stuck between his teeth and the gut hanging over what Kelsey presumed was a western belt buckle, this guy could be the poster boy—until his weathered face cracked into a grin.

"Tom Quinn, welcome back to paradise."

Dad stood and reached for the man's hand. "Mr. Barksdale? It's been years. This is my wife Maggie and my daughters Kelsey, Ryan, and Mackenzie. Guys, this is Joe Barksdale. He was the Ag teacher when I was in school. Are you still teaching?"

"I got one year left." The man rocked back on his heels. "I understand you're taking over the feed store from your brother."

"Yes, Jack and Susan are ready to take it easy for a while."

"Well, I'll be…" Joe craned his neck toward his table and yelled, "Austin, git over here."

Austin unfolded from his chair and shuffled to stand next to their table. No wonder Texas was hot, with guys like Austin taking up space. He was taller than her six-foot dad. His hair was super short, almost buzzed, but it looked good, kind of natural. Like the navy blue T-shirt that matched his eyes and the jeans that stretched down to his worn brown boots. All outdoorsy and cowboy. The total opposite of her always-wears-khakis, five-foot-six boyfriend, Drew Montgomery.

Joe placed a hand on Austin's shoulder. "This here is my nephew. He's worked for your brother at the feed store since he was twelve." Turning to the boy he continued, "Austin, this is Tom Quinn."

Austin stuck out his hand. "Pleased to meet you, Mr. Quinn. Jack talks about you a lot."

Dad shook his hand and added, "Well, I hope you only believe the good stuff."

"Yes, sir." Something about the way he nodded when he spoke—or maybe it was the twang in his drawl—kept Kelsey focused on the conversation.

Dad crossed his arms. "Are you planning to stay on at the store?"

"Yes, sir."

"Good, I sure will need the help."

Cowgirl-up elbowed Joe in the ribs. "Are you gonna stay here yammering with my customers or are you gonna finish yer chicken fry so these nice people can eat?"

Joe grinned. "You got any good pie today?"

"I got lemon meringue and coconut."

"Coconut." He turned to the Quinn family. "I'll let y'all eat. Are y'all staying at Jack's new place in town?"

"No. We're moving straight into the old farmhouse," Dad answered with a smile that Kelsey recognized as the one he'd used over the past six months to avoid having to answer embarrassing questions about their finances.

"Well, welcome home."

Joe and Austin returned to their table and the Quinns ordered lunch. After the waitress walked off with their orders, Mom leaned across the table like she was about to spill a juicy secret. "See girls, it's going to all work out." She patted Ryan's hand. "This is exactly where we need to be."

"Seriously, Mom? A gross diner in the middle of nowhere is where we need to be?" Kelsey couldn't have hid the sarcasm in her voice if she'd wanted to. "Maybe this is good for Ryan—the rest of us are totally screwed."

Mom pressed her lips flat and swallowed before speaking. "We're family, we support each other—even if it means making a few sacrifices."

Mackenzie shoved her chair back. "Keep telling yourself that, Mom." She stood and stormed toward the posterboard RESTROOMS sign.

Stunned silence filled the table. Kelsey couldn't remember a single time she'd seen her youngest sister lose her temper, much less talk back to her parents.

Mom stood to go after her, but Dad placed a hand on her arm. "Let her go, Maggie."

Mom eased back into her seat. Ryan's eyes filled with tears and Dad rubbed his manicured hands across his face like he wondered what in the hell he was thinking by moving the family to Texas.

Cowgirl-up plunked a tray full of drinks on the end of the table and began passing them around. "Tom Quinn. I thought you looked familiar. Where've you been all these years?"

"Chicago," Dad answered.

"Chicago! No wonder you look like something the cat drug in. And you're taking over Jack's place." She looked at Kelsey and Ryan. "So you girls will be starting school here. What grade are y'all in?"

Dad answered for them. "Kelsey will be a senior, Ryan will be a junior, and Mackenzie—the one in the restroom—will be a freshman."

"Well I swanny, pretty little things like you girls are gonna set Hillside High on its ear. I'll be right back with your lunch." The waitress sashayed off toward the kitchen.

As soon as Cowgirl-up was out of earshot, Kelsey looked at her mom. "I swanny? Is she for real?"

"Isn't it cute, honey? This is a good change for the family."

This is a good change for the family. Giving up their friends, their house, and their lives? "The family doesn't need to change, Mom. Ryan is the one who's screwed up." Kelsey rose from the table before Mom could answer and headed to the restroom to find her sister.

Kelsey knocked on the door. "Mackenzie? You okay?"

She heard a lock click before the door cracked to reveal Mackenzie leaning against a rust-stained sink, blowing her nose. "I hate this place."

Kelsey entered the tiny room and closed the door behind her. She wrapped an arm around her sister. "I know. I kept thinking they'd back out, that they wouldn't go through with the move…"

"My gymnastics life is over." Tears streamed down her face.

Kelsey tore some tissue from the roll and handed it to her. "I know. While you and I were following all the rules, Ryan was out there breaking them. We're the ones suffering for it."

Mackenzie dabbed at her eyes. "Every time I hear Mom say 'isn't this cute' I want to scream."

"Yeah, there's nothing cute about this place. But we have to eat. Come on, let's get some lunch."

One thing for sure, Kelsey had never seen anything like the enormous chicken fried steak the Early Bird Café served. She stared at the plate of golden-brown-crust-covered meat soaked in cream gravy, and the mashed potatoes mounded next to it, and sighed. It was probably about a million calories. Just looking at it made her feel fat. "How am I going eat this?"

She looked up and caught Austin staring at her from the other table. He smiled and mouthed *Like this*. He exaggerated stabbing the meat with his fork and shoving a piece in his mouth. Her ears burned and she wanted to be mad but a smiled formed on her lips anyway. She ducked her head and dug into her meal. She had to admit it was delicious. So this was the first good thing she discovered about Hillside, Texas.

The second, she figured, would be the town shrinking in her rear view mirror.

2

In Texas, it is illegal to shoot buffalo from the second story of a hotel.

The narrow road that led from the Early Bird Café dead-ended at the county courthouse in the center of downtown. While they waited at the stop light, Kelsey studied the pinkish-red building. To say it looked out of place surrounded by the old-lady clothing stores would be an understatement. This wasn't the typical square building with a clock tower in the middle of downtown design she'd seen on this journey to hell. This building looked like something from a graphic novel. Turrets cornered the building, with gargoyles perched ominously on top of dormer windows nestled between the towers.

The light changed and Dad turned right and away from downtown, but something about the building tugged at Kelsey.

They headed down a two-lane road past a row of mobile homes. Most of the houses had wooden porches attached to the front and painted fences marking the yard. Life in a metallic cracker box—that had to suck. A couple of them had tires spread across the roof. The words *trailer trash* came to mind. Dad turned down a dirt drive, through an open double gate, to a somewhat rundown two-story farmhouse. Kelsey had been three the last time they'd visited the farm, but nothing about it seemed familiar.

She let out a long sigh. This was it. It had really happened. Her chest grew heavy as she regarded their new home. The house looked sad. She wasn't sure how a house could express an emotion, but it did. Perhaps it was the tired white paint or the neglected landscaping. Or maybe it was years of enduring the oppressive Texas heat.

Uncle Jack and Aunt Susan stood on the top step of the large front porch and next to them stood Austin. The tightness in Kelsey's chest ratcheted up a notch. She pulled a brush from her purse, ran it through her hair, and told herself it had nothing to do with the tall Texan on the porch.

Kelsey and her sisters filed out of the SUV to greet an uncle and aunt they barely knew while Austin melted into the background. After a round of awkward hugs, Uncle Jack clapped Austin on the shoulder and said, "This here is Austin McCoy. I believe y'all met him at the diner. He's gonna help out when the movers come. Tom, did they say what time they were coming?"

Dad glanced at his watch. "They said they should be here by three. It's two-thirty now, so I guess any minute."

"Sounds good. Y'all come on up and rest while you can."

Mom headed toward the front door. "Do you mind if I show the girls the house?"

Aunt Susan sat in the wicker settee nestled in the corner of the porch. "Not at all, Maggie. It's your house now."

Mom led the way through the front door and into a rectangular den with a fireplace on the far end of the room. The tan shag carpet looked as worn as the exterior. Mackenzie said what they were all thinking. "You've got to be kidding me. Coffee-pot wallpaper?"

"We can change that." Mom spoke nonchalantly, but the

white-knuckled grip on her purse said otherwise.

The stairs were to the left of the door, but the girls followed their mom through the den to the back of the house. They pushed through swinging doors to a large kitchen. Make that a large kitchen area, because while it was probably the same size as the den, beige counters beneath painted tan cabinets were crammed in the corner of the room between an avocado-green stove and refrigerator. How far they'd fallen from the Sub-Zero fridge and professional-grade gas stove they'd left behind.

Kelsey turned to her mom. "Are you sure about all of this?"

Mom straightened her back and set her chin. "It just needs a little fixing up—come on, let's check out what's waiting for us upstairs."

They wandered back through the living room to the stairs. Upstairs was as boring as the rest of the house. Four bedrooms and one bathroom. The slightly larger bedroom was the master.

Kelsey looked in the rooms next to the master. The first two were unimpressive. Square. Closet on one side, two windows facing the back of the house. The best room was the one at the end of the hall with two windows facing the back yard and two windows facing the side. Kelsey turned to her mom. "Can I have this room?"

Mom nodded. "You're the oldest, you should get first pick."

Ryan chimed in, "Well, the other rooms are exactly the same, so I don't care which one is mine."

Mackenzie echoed, "Me either."

Mom said, "Settled. We'll put your bags in your rooms later." With that, she jogged downstairs and out the front door.

Kelsey looked at her sisters. "I've seen enough of this dump. I'm getting out of here." She pulled her phone from her back pocket and ran downstairs to the front porch. She tapped the Facebook icon on her phone and looked for a place to sit.

Her parents were settled in the glider and Uncle Jack and Aunt Susan sat in rockers across from them. Austin leaned against the porch rail studying his phone. He looked up and his deep blue gaze held her for a couple of seconds before he returned to whatever he was reading. Was he checking her out? It wasn't like he'd looked her up and down. She didn't miss the mischievous glint in his eyes. Was he making fun of her?

She plastered an *I'm bored* look on her face and sat on the top step. A ceiling fan whirled overhead and a breeze wafted across the porch, but it did nothing to cool things down. The screen door screeched open as Ryan and Mackenzie stepped onto the porch. Mackenzie retreated to the corner near her parents. Ryan stood next to Austin. Typical. Mackenzie was the shadow, always fading into the background. Of course Ryan would stand next to Austin. If there was testosterone around, she was sure to follow.

Uncle Jack tipped his beer toward Austin. "Son, why don't you show the girls around the farm?"

"Yes, sir."

What needed to be shown? From what she could see, it was pretty simple. Farmhouse in need of repair, a barn that she supposed held some animal things, and lots and lots of nothing.

Ryan looked up at Austin and flashed him a smile.

"Hey." Austin gave a quick nod. "Come on, I'll show you the barn."

They stepped off the porch and into the heat. The ground seemed to pulse as the sun's rays beat down on them. Kelsey wiped sweat from her forehead as she watched Ryan chat up Austin. Of course Ryan would flirt with the new guy—he was a future notch on her guys-I've-slept-with belt.

Austin led them across the yard to the barn. "There's twenty acres behind the barn and a tank that has some pretty good fishing."

"Tank?" Kelsey asked the question, but she didn't want to understand. This farm, this town, was just a pit stop in her life—emphasis on *pit*. To learn about life here was to accept it, and that was never going to happen.

"It's the same as a pond." Austin led them through a doorway opening to a small room. "This is the tack room. Jack got rid of most of the animals before y'all came. He kept two of the horses—Harry and Buster—Winifred the pig, and the chickens."

The air was stifling. It was like walking into a giant oven. Four saddles lined the wall on one side of the room and a row of bridles hung across the opposite wall. Kelsey would have loved to inhale the scent of the leather, but the other less pleasant odors kept her from taking a deep breath. She shielded her nose and mouth with her hand. "How do you get used to the smell?"

Austin furrowed his brow. "What smell?"

Kelsey's eyes watered. "I think it would be animal excrement."

He shrugged. "I can't smell it. So come on, I'll introduce you to the animals."

He led them through a door and into an area with four stalls. The two horses poked their heads out of the stalls. "During the summer, we leave them inside under the fans during the day and turn them out at night."

Kelsey looked at the fans perched above the stalls blowing on the horses. She couldn't imagine they helped much, but the horses didn't seem to mind.

"This is Buster." Austin stroked the side of the animal's face.

Ryan stood next to Austin, almost touching his shoulder as she reached to pat the horse. "Look at the white stripe on his nose. Isn't he cute?"

Really, Ryan, already flirting? Kelsey wanted to push Ryan away from Austin. Not that she cared about him, but it was embarrassing the way her sister threw herself at guys.

Austin stepped back from the horse. "That stripe is called a blaze. Buster and Harry are both really nice geldings."

"Geldings?" Kelsey asked the question before she could stop herself.

"Horses that have been cut."

Ryan peeked over the top rail of the stall. "Cut?"

"You know, cut. Neutered. Jack thought they'd be good for y'all to learn to ride on."

"Is this a requirement to living in Texas?" Kelsey laced her voice with sarcasm.

Austin smirked. "It should be. Come closer, they won't bite."

Kelsey stepped closer and looked into Harry's stall. He was a pretty horse with brown and white splotches all over him. His mane and tail were half white and half brown.

As if reading her thoughts, Austin explained, "He's what we call a paint—he's a Tobiano. See how the brown extends over both flanks? Look at his legs. He has white socks. There is a pattern to his colors. Now, Buster is a buckskin dun."

Kelsey nodded like she understood. The truth was, she wasn't interested enough to understand. It was stupid. In her mind, one was a brown and white horse, the other tan.

Ryan stood next to Austin stroking Buster's nose. Mackenzie cowered against the wall with her arms folded across her chest, looking totally freaked out by the animals.

Austin motioned to Mackenzie with his head. "Don't you want to pet one?"

"Nope. The only horse I want to touch is the vault."

"Vault?"

"She's a gymnast," Kelsey supplied, although she had her doubts that Austin understood.

He nodded like he did anyway. "Okay. Come on, let's meet the chickens."

*

Austin led the girls through the barn to the chicken coop. God, what a bunch of greenhorns. No wonder Jack had asked him to help out.

He'd already figured the girls out. Kelsey was sexy as hell with dark hair that was just long enough to dance on her shoulders as she walked. She had cool blue eyes that matched an ice-queen-bitch attitude that said she was too good for this redneck town. Ryan, with her short spiky hair, was desperate for attention and would do anything to get it. He'd bet ten minutes alone with a guy and she'd be shedding her clothes, but that wasn't what he was about. The youngest—what's-her-name—wore long bangs that covered her face. She looked scared to death, but he reckoned she was too tough to admit it.

As they reached the eight-by-ten fence in front of the coop, he turned to the girls. "We have one rooster, The General, and eight hens." He cracked opened the gate and squeezed through. The girls followed.

The chickens ran toward them. The girls squealed and ran for the gate. Austin bent low and guided the birds back toward the coop. "They're not going to hurt you. They think I have feed. Come on, you're gonna have to learn how to fetch eggs someday."

Kelsey, Ryan, and the other one stood flat against the fence, wide-eyed and breathing hard. Kelsey spoke up. "Fetch eggs? Not today. Besides, we're wearing sandals." The other girls nodded in agreement.

Austin straightened and shook his head. "Hopeless."

One of the chickens broke from the group and charged the girls, flapping and squawking like she was telling them to get the hell out of her coop. The girls screamed and pushed through the gate.

Laughing, Austin picked up the bird and walked to the fence. "Here, pet Miss Emma. Make friends."

Kelsey eyed the bird suspiciously. "Don't they carry salmonella or something?"

"Only if they're slaughtered and the meat kept out too long."

The girls let out a collective, "Ewww."

Ryan stepped up. "I'll touch her." Gingerly, she reached through the wire of the fence and lightly stroked the chicken's back. The bird wriggled in Austin's hold and she jerked her hand back until it settled again. "Her feathers are so soft. Mackenzie, your turn."

Mackenzie. That was her name. She stepped closer and reached toward the fence but hesitated.

"Come on, Kenzie, don't be chicken." Ryan snorted at her joke.

"Not funny." Mackenzie rolled her eyes and shoved her hand through the octagon-shaped hole to touch the bird. Her hand got a little too close to the beak and Miss Emma managed to get a good peck into her index finger.

She jumped back and gave a little squeal. Austin lowered the bird to the ground. "Are you okay?"

"Yeah, it didn't break the skin."

"Okay. So we'll pick up on chicken handling one-oh-one later. Hang on." He jogged to the hen house and grabbed an egg before joining the girls outside the chicken yard. "Let's meet Winifred."

He led them to a fenced yard to the right of the henhouse.

"Winnie!"

A rotund white pig lumbered to the fence. "Hey girl, are you hungry?" He tossed the egg and the pig craned her neck just enough to snatch it out of the air. She crunched and yolk squeezed from her mouth and slid down her chin.

Kelsey gave a disgusted look. "That just might be the grossest thing I've ever seen."

He laughed. "It's good for her."

McKenzie held her stomach. "I'm never eating eggs

again. Can we go back to the house?"

"Sure." Austin knew the girls were from Chicago, but he'd had no idea they'd be completely clueless.

"Thank you," Mackenzie sighed.

As they walked up the steps to join the adults, Jack pulled a sip of beer and swallowed. "So did you teach the girls everything they need to know?"

Austin leaned against the porch railing. "Let's just say we got a start."

Kelsey plopped down on the vacant rocker. "I am not a country girl."

Jack winked, tipped his beer toward her and said, "You are now."

Mackenzie and Ryan joined Austin leaning against the railing.

Kelsey folded her arms across her chest and set her jaw before speaking. "Mom, did you know there are chickens— with eggs?"

Mrs. Quinn answered, "That's wonderful, dear. Farm fresh eggs!"

"Well, who's going to pick them?" Kelsey said.

Pick them? Austin bit his lower lip and studied the toes of his boots to keep from laughing. Mr. Quinn answered, "They're not picked, they're gathered. And the gatherer would be you and your sisters."

Austin raised his eyes enough to see the glare Kelsey shot Ryan.

Ryan answered the look. "What?"

"You know what," Kelsey spat.

Definitely something going on there.

Susan rose from her rocker. "Would you girls like some sweet tea? Or there's coke in the fridge."

Kelsey pulled the screen door open. "I'll get it, thanks."

The girls headed into the house.

Mrs. Quinn looked at Austin. "They're having a few adjustment issues."

A few adjustment issues? Like they've just landed on another planet adjustment issues. Austin nodded. "It's got to be a big change from Chicago."

"You have no idea." Mr. Quinn took a swig from his beer. The words were barely out of his mouth when yelling could be heard from within the house.

"I'd better go keep them from killing each other." Mrs. Quinn started to stand, but Mr. Quinn stopped her.

"Let them work it out. Besides, if they kill each other we won't have to deal with their bickering anymore."

Just then the door ripped open and the girls spilled onto the porch. Kelsey's and Ryan's faces were red, and they were both huffing, but neither said a word. Mackenzie looked utterly defeated, as if her whole world had been taken away. She sipped from her Coke and clunked down the steps and toward the backyard.

She'd barely cleared the corner of the house when Kelsey started in on Ryan. "This is all your fault."

Mr. Quinn stood. "Girls…"

Tears dripped from Ryan's eyes and rolled down her cheeks. "I know why we're here and I know you can't wait to tell the world either. So why don't you?"

Kelsey glared at her sister. "Don't go there, Ryan."

"Girls…" Mr. Quinn warned again.

Austin looked for an easy escape from the porch and the Quinn sisters' war, but they stood in the way. He leaned against the rail and listened, feeling awkward at being caught in the middle of the family drama.

Ryan brushed her cheeks dry with the palms of her hands and moved to stand inches away from him. "Do you want to know what I did?"

"Not really." *Christ, why is she dragging me into this?*

"Stop it, Ryan," Kelsey ordered.

Austin shifted left to step around Ryan, but she countered and blocked his path. Mr. and Mrs. Quinn both got to their feet. Jack and Susan looked as uncomfortable as

Austin felt.

Ryan ran her fingers through her spiky hair. "See, it's my fault. Everything is my fault."

He shot Kelsey a *help me* look.

She grabbed his elbow and pulled him away from Ryan. "Ignore her. She's crazy. Come on, let's find Mackenzie."

They headed down the steps and around to the back of the house. "So I take it you and your sisters don't get along."

"Ryan and I don't get along. Mackenzie is fine."

They rounded the corner of the house and saw Mackenzie standing at the edge of a swimming pool staring into the forest-green water.

Kelsey joined her sister. "Wow, that's supposed to be a pool?"

Mackenzie took a sip from her drink. "I can't believe this is happening to us."

Kelsey nodded slowly. "Me either."

Austin felt a little sorry for the girls. Their life had taken a complete one-eighty. Uprooted from the suburban life they knew, torn from their friends to move to a dinky little town in Texas … it had to suck for them. Unfortunately, it was probably going to get a whole lot suckier before it got better.

3

In Texas, if it grows, it sticks; if it crawls, it bites.

Exhausted, Kelsey stared at the boxes lining the walls of her new room. How was she going to squeeze all of her stuff into this broom closet? She flipped onto her back and stared at the popcorn texture on the ceiling. It didn't matter. This was a temporary assignment. One more year of school and she was off to college. Just like Dad, she was going to blow this hellhole. Only she wasn't coming back.

Her phone played her best friend's ring tone. "Zoe!"

"Have you made it to Texas yet?"

"Oh, yeah. I'm in the house of shag carpet and coffee-pot wallpaper now."

"Sounds—vintage."

"It's horrible. My room is half the size of my old one. There's only one bathroom in the whole freaking house. I have to share a bathroom with my parents! There's a pool, but it's lime green and smells like puke. And there's chickens, and horses, and a pig. We have a freaking pig."

"The horses sound kinda cool."

"I don't know. Zoe, if I start talking with an accent, just shoot me. Come down here and do me in."

"That's a little drastic, don't ya think?"

"You haven't heard these people talk."

"Speaking of people, have you met anybody yet?"

"There's a guy named Austin who's going to work for Dad."

"Is he cute?"

He has deep blue eyes that seem to be laughing. "Hmm, he's not Drew, that's for sure. I guess. He's tall, short hair…" *Makes me want to check my makeup.* "He's a cowboy— boots, jeans, hard body."

"So he's a T.H."

"T.H.?"

"Texas hottie. Facebook code."

Kelsey laughed. "You know most people figure out your codes."

"Nobody will know T.H. unless you tell them. So what's the town like?"

"Miniscule. And, believe it or not, I haven't seen much. We ate at the Early Bird Café."

"That sounds kind of cute."

"Cute? I guess, for a trailer trash hangout." It was the kind of place her parents wouldn't have set foot in back in Chicago.

Zoe snorted. "That bad?"

"Yeah, the huge floor fans were the first clue. Oh, and you should have seen our waitress. She could be a model for *Trailer Trash Monthly*. I already miss Chicago, and normal food, and normal people. I miss you."

"I miss you too. You'll be back for the gala though, right?"

"Are you kidding? This year I'm going as Drew Montgomery's girlfriend. I am not going to miss that." Her phone beeped. "Speaking of said boyfriend, he just texted me. Can I call you tomorrow?"

"Yeah, I'll talk to you later."

She read the text.

Drew: I miss you, babe.
Kelsey: Miss you too.

Drew was biking through Italy with his brother and they'd already been apart for a couple of weeks. He'd text or Facebook when he could, but she missed his voice. Her heart ached for him, for her friends, for her old life. How had her parents lost everything? How had they gone from having it all, to having nothing? She didn't try to stop the tears that slid from the corners of her eyes, or the pain that settled a little deeper in her chest.

Drew: I can't wait until my lips are on yours.
Kelsey: Me either.

She closed her eyes and tried to remember what his kisses felt like.

Kelsey: I'm dreaming of your arms around me.
Drew: I have to go. TTYL.

Kelsey hugged the phone to her chest as if she were somehow holding him. She thought about their last date together. They'd gone to the Adler Planetarium. The exhibit took them on a journey through space. The computer graphics were so amazing she could've almost reached out and touched the stars. They'd shared their last long kiss under the artificial night sky, but it was every bit as romantic as if he'd taken her to the heavens for real.

She played that night over in her mind until she drifted to sleep still cradling the phone.

*

She awoke to Mackenzie rustling around in the hall. The

first rays of the morning filtered through the blinds. From her bed, Kelsey saw Mackenzie slip into the bathroom wearing shorts and a tank top. The girl got up way too early to be normal. Even after a late night of unpacking boxes, she would go for a run.

Not Kelsey. She pulled the duvet over her head and settled back into sleep.

Until Dad stomped down the hall yelling like he was jacked up on way too much caffeine. "Get up, girls, rise and shine. Chores today."

The clock on her bedside table glowed six AM. "Is he serious?" she said into the air before nestling deeper into the covers.

She'd just about returned to slumber land when the blankets were ripped off her head, followed by the clatter of blinds being tugged open. She squinted against the light invading her room. A figure crossed in front of the window and stood over her.

"Go away, Ryan!" Kelsey yelled.

"We have to get up."

Kelsey sat up. "It's six in the morning!"

"Come on. We're supposed to learn how to gather eggs."

"How could you already be dressed?"

"Cuz Dad got to me first. Come on, Austin's already here and he brought a friend."

Kelsey groaned and crawled out of bed. God. Visitors. Not only did she have to get up early, she had to look decent. She dug through the clothes piled in her open suitcase and considered a pair of khaki walking shorts, but remembering the charging chickens of yesterday, tossed them aside for jeans. She layered two paper-thin tank tops and after twenty minutes comprised of face washing, teeth brushing, and makeup applying, felt ready to face her first full day in Hickville.

She trudged down the stairs to the kitchen for a cup of coffee, or as she called it, liquid heaven. She poured a mug of the black gold and headed toward laughter on the front porch.

As she pushed open the screen door, Uncle Jack tipped his coffee toward her. "Well, look who finally got up. I thought you were going to sleep all day."

She yawned. "It's like six-thirty on a Saturday morning."

Dad winked. "We decided to let you sleep late since it's your first day."

"I am not a morning person." Kelsey nestled in the glider.

Uncle Jack pushed out of his chair. "You'll learn."

Austin sat in the wicker rocker cradling a mug between his hands. He raised it to his mouth and Kelsey noticed how full his lips were. He peeked over the rim with those navy eyes and nailed her staring at him.

She managed not to jerk her gaze away as if she were embarrassed—that would make her look guilty. Instead, she allowed the corners of her mouth to turn up ever so slightly and casually shifted her gaze to the guy who stood across from Austin. He was about six feet tall and had sandy blond hair that hung almost to his shoulders, giving him a kind of rugged look. His build was skinnier than Austin's, but she guessed he was as solid.

He nodded toward her and said, "Hey. I'm Travis."

"Hi." Kelsey nodded.

Uncle Jack set his mug on the coffee table. "I'd better get to the feed store. The boys will do a good job for you, Tom." He stepped off the porch and turned back. "I'm supposed to remind you that Susan's expecting to see y'all for supper tonight."

"We'll be there," Dad said. "I'll come to the store when things get settled around here."

"Mighty fine. We can transfer the truck title this afternoon."

Kelsey felt her heart beat a little faster. "Truck title?" Surely he didn't mean the heap parked in front of the house.

"I bought Jack's Ford." He nodded toward the faded

green pickup with the dent in the side. "It'll be a great farm truck. You can use it to cart your sisters around."

Perfect. What else would go with a rundown farmhouse? The hooptie parked in front was like an exclamation point to the decline of the Quinn family's social status. They'd sold her Audi A4 without warning and now this?

"My friends are never to hear about this." She was serious, but her dad and uncle burst out laughing. She was sure she heard Austin and Travis chuckle too, but when she turned to look at them, they dropped their gazes to the porch floor and got quiet.

The screen door squeaked open and Mackenzie emerged drenched in sweat, sipping a glass of ice water.

Kelsey's demeanor softened toward her sister. "Hey, Kenzie. Where did you come from?"

"I came in through the back door." She edged toward her parents as if she were trying to gain distance from the strangers on the porch. "Mom, can I shower before I help?"

Mackenzie looked like she'd just as soon disappear than have to face talking to people—especially the two Texas boys occupying the porch.

"Honey, you're just going to get dirty doing chores," Mom answered.

Kelsey went into protective mode around her youngest sister. Outside the gym, Mackenzie was too timid and shy to take up for herself. "Mom, she's soaking wet—give her a break."

Mom looked at the soaked tank and shorts she wore and nodded. "Okay, but hurry."

As soon as Mackenzie got the go-ahead to defer chicken handling, she retreated back to the house.

Kelsey took a sip from her coffee. Did everything have to be such a battle? Her stomach answered with a growl. "So is there anything for breakfast?"

Mom said. "You get the eggs and I'll scramble them."

"You're kidding, right?"

Before Mom answered, Austin put his mug on the wicker-and-glass coffee table and stood. "Come on. It's not that bad. I'll help ya."

Kelsey was about to protest when Ryan jumped up and volunteered for the job. *Perfect—let her do the dirty work.* Pleased with the situation, Kelsey settled in the rocker Austin vacated.

Only before her butt got warm and her coffee turned cold, Dad gave her the look and said, "Go help your sister."

She slammed her mug down on the table and pretended she hadn't noticed the coffee splash over the edge. She set her jaw and gave Dad a dagger stare before she turned her back and jogged down the steps toward the henhouse. *I just have to make it until graduation* looped in her brain.

By the time Kelsey caught up with the others, Ryan was in full flirt mode. Kelsey's stomach tightened as she watch her sister grab Travis's bicep and cower behind him as they entered the chicken coop. Austin walked on the other side of Ryan and teased her about chicken phobia. Surely even these rednecks could see Ryan wasn't really afraid. But they played along anyway. What was it about her sister and guys? Why did Ryan seem to need their attention? Couldn't she see that it made her look desperate and weak? No girl should ever depend on a guy for self-esteem. Whatever. Kelsey just wanted to get the eggs so she could get back to her coffee.

She squeezed through the chicken yard gate, ignored the clucks of the feathered monsters, and walked right up to the henhouse. *Show no fear.* "So what do I do?"

A smile tugged at the corner of Austin's mouth. "Well, it's pretty basic. You stick your hand in the nest and take the egg."

Kelsey rolled her eyes. *Be in control.* "Is that all there is to it? Then what's the big deal?" She turned her back and reached toward the first nest.

"There is just one more thing."

She stopped with her hand in the air and looked over her

shoulder at Austin. "What?"

"The eggs will have chicken shit on them."

Her stomach knotted. *Be strong.* "I can handle it." She reached in and grabbed for a small oval shape. But the thing she held was rough. She pulled it from the nest and a scream blasted from her lungs.

A snake, big and ugly, dangled from her clutches. If she let it go, it would bite her. So she held the thing as far away from her body as possible, danced in place, and squealed, "Get it!"

"It's not gonna hurt you." Austin reached for the snake, but she saw it try to curl up toward her arm. Not good. She flailed it around in hopes it would change direction.

"Help me!"

Ryan ran from the chicken yard toward the barn. Chickens spilled out of the open gate. Travis took off after the chickens. Austin tried to get the snake, but his arm seemed to be one step behind Kelsey's.

Kelsey yelled again. "Help me!"

"Drop the snake!"

"No, he'll bite me."

"Then hold still." She did and the snake stretched its body toward her midriff. She gave one last yelp and dropped it—on her tennis shoe. Holding a snake in her hand was one thing; at least she had the illusion of controlling the situation. Having it slither on her feet was a whole new kind of terror.

Her lungs froze as a vision of the snake biting her ankle flashed through her mind. In that moment, time slowed and her world reduced to the snake on her shoe. She focused on the black and brown stripes coiling like a rope. A masculine hand entered her field of vision.

And then, the snake struck.

It grabbed his thumb and held on. The action unfroze Kelsey. She let out another blast from her lungs and kicked it off her foot, which might have been okay if it hadn't ripped the snake's fangs from the side of Austin's thumb.

The snake took off across the chicken yard but before it got far, the tip of a shovel pinned it to the ground. The snake wiggled on either side of the spade. Ryan gave the handle a twist, digging the tip deeper into the snake. When it quit moving, she raised the shovel a couple of feet before she slammed it down on its head and yelled, "Die, you bastard." Kelsey saw hatred in her sister's eyes as she slammed the shovel into the serpent a second and third time.

Austin dropped to his knees and held his hand, blood gushing from the bite.

"Oh, God, oh God. I'm sorry." Kelsey knelt next to Austin and yelled at Travis, who was trying to capture the last wayward chicken. "Travis, go get help!"

Austin sat down with his hand pressed to his chest. Blood ran down his wrist and forearm and soaked into his shirt.

Kelsey put an arm across his back. "Hang on, we'll get you to an emergency room."

"I'm okay."

Not the time to be tough, cowboy.

"You got bit by a snake. You're not okay."

"It wasn't poisonous." He took a deep breath. "Painful, but not poisonous."

Kelsey's parents rushed through the gate to Austin's side. Dad spoke first. "What kind of snake, son?" Kelsey stood and let her parents take over.

"Rat. Not poisonous." He pointed to where Ryan stood, shovel in hand, staring at the headless serpent as if she dared it to move.

Dad inspected the snake while Mom looked at Austin's thumb. "Poisonous or not, that's a nasty cut and I think you're going to need a couple of stitches. Let's get you to the hospital."

"Thanks, Mrs. Quinn, but I think I just need to wash it up and maybe a Band-Aid."

Kelsey looked at Austin. "Seriously? So does *cowboy*

equal *tough and stupid?* There's no way a Band-Aid is going to fix that."

Dad helped Austin to his feet. "She's right. I think you need to call your parents."

"I'm fine." Austin took a step and then fell to his knees. "I'm just a little woozy."

"That's it." Mom knelt next to him. "No arguments— you're going to the emergency room." She looked at Kelsey. "Go get the car."

Kelsey ran for the gate and as she opened it, Austin puked.

"Grab a kitchen towel. And hurry," Mom yelled.

By the time Kelsey pulled up to the gate, Dad and Travis held Austin up between them. They shoved him into the backseat. Dad slid into the front passenger seat while Mom sat next to Austin. Kelsey gripped the steering wheel and tore down the dirt road toward the highway. "I don't know where I'm going!"

"Turn left. I'll tell you where to go. Just be careful," Dad answered.

Kelsey pulled onto the highway and resisted the urge to floor it to town. Her heart pounded in her chest. She peeked in the rearview at Austin. He rested his head on the back of the seat with his eyes closed. His thumb bled through the towel wrapped around it, and he looked a little pale.

One day in Texas and she'd witnessed a snakebite. What kind of hellhole had her dad brought them to? If he hadn't screwed up and gotten fired, if Ryan hadn't screwed the boss's son and gotten caught, she'd be hanging out with her friends instead of racing a snake-bitten cowboy to the E.R.

She pulled up to the patient dropoff. Her parents helped Austin out of the SUV. The Cowgirl-up waitress from the trailer trash restaurant ran toward him. "Austin, baby. What happened?"

"Hey, Mom. I'm okay ... rat snake got me. How'd you know?"

"Travis called." She looked at the bloodstained wrap. "A rat snake did all that?"

Austin nodded. "Grabbed hold and wouldn't let go."

"Let's get you inside." She led him through the double doors, followed by Kelsey's parents.

Kelsey pulled through the drive to park the car. Travis and Ryan stepped out of a pickup truck as Kelsey pulled into a parking lot. And for once, her sister wasn't flirting.

Ryan and Travis waited for Kelsey and the three of them walked to the emergency waiting room together.

By the time they joined their parents, Austin and his mom had been escorted to triage. Kelsey shuddered. "I hate snakes. I don't think I'll ever be able to gather eggs."

Ryan folded her arms across her stomach. "That was so scary."

"You were amazing with that shovel," Kelsey said. "And a little freaky."

"I just wanted that snake dead."

Kelsey sat back. "Yeah. I gathered that when you yelled, 'Die, bastard' as you were making paste out of it."

Mom snapped, "Ryan Katherine. Language."

Ryan shrugged. "Sorry."

Travis leaned forward and rested his forearms on his knees. "The thing is, rat snakes aren't poisonous. They want to run from us as bad as we want to run from them. If you accidentally grab one, just let it go."

Dad rubbed the back of his neck. "Looks like we need a more extensive orientation to farm life."

But we shouldn't have to learn about farm life at all. Kelsey glared at her dad. "No wonder you left Hillside. I hate this place."

"There is a lot of beauty here too. You just have to open your eyes."

"The only thing I'll consider beautiful is the view of this place through my rearview mirror. Come May, I'm so out of here." Kelsey stood and crossed the room to stare out of the window.

Ryan followed and stood next to her. "God, Kelsey, what's your problem?"

"You are my problem. Dad is my problem. The fact that my whole freaking life has been turned upside down because of you and Dad is my problem." Kelsey took a deep breath and tried to let go of some of the anger that lived within her. "Go ahead, embrace this redneck life. Be happy with substandard everything. Me? I'm just hanging on until college."

Ryan gave an exasperated groan. "College? Really? For someone so smart, you just don't get it. How long do you think it'll be before they tap into our college funds?"

"They wouldn't do that."

Ryan leaned her shoulder against the window. "Get a grip. They sold your car. We are living in a broken-down farmhouse in the middle of Fumbuck, Texas. Do you seriously think there is any money left? You blame me for the move, but think about it. Would Dad really move us here if he had any choice? We're here because there's nowhere else to go."

Ryan pushed away from the glass and walked back to her family.

No money for college? But she'd planned to apply to Notre Dame—her parents' alma mater—and Boston College. Mom had said as soon as they settled in the new house they'd fill out the applications together. Ryan was right. If there had been any other way, they wouldn't have moved. But did that mean there was no college money? The months of Dad being unemployed had taken a toll on the family. She'd never have thought they'd be a one-car family eating sandwiches for dinner either. But they had. Tears spilled down her face as the reality of her situation settled in her chest. She took a deep breath and brushed her cheeks dry.

She heard Dad telling a story about the time Uncle Jack put a snake in her dad's bed when they were kids. The group was huddled around him, laughing, and Kelsey felt like a complete stranger to her family. She would never, could never, embrace this lifestyle. In a few weeks she'd return to Chicago for the gala, back to her life. And then, she would find a way out of Hillside. She'd get a job, apply for scholarships—whatever it took. She would never be a Texas girl.

4

In Texas, it is illegal to put graffiti on someone else's cow.

Austin followed his mom through the double doors to the waiting room. His blood soaked shirt stuck to his skin, mixed with sweat, dirt, and probably a little chicken shit. The numbing medicine was starting to wear off and he felt like hell.

Mrs. Quinn raced to his side. "Austin, are you okay?"

God, the high-pitched, nasal tone of her voice made his head throb. "Yeah. It's just a few stitches." He held out his bandaged thumb for her to inspect.

The Quinn clan gathered around him, all smiles and apologies—except Kelsey. She leaned against the windows on the opposite side of the room with her arms folded across her chest and her jaw clenched in a *don't freaking talk to me* kind of way.

What the hell. He didn't care.

Travis grabbed his injured arm and studied the bandage wrapped around his thumb down to his wrist. "Dude, that's gonna screw with your game. Coach is gonna freak."

"Yeah, unless I can throw left-handed."

His mom patted him on the shoulder. "Don't you worry

about football. Those stitches will come out next week. You'll be fine by your first game."

Kelsey pushed off the window and joined the others, looking at him with a coolness he figured was an integral part of her personality. "So you're not going to die."

"Nah. There's a small amount of venom in the snake's saliva. I had a reaction to that. I got four stitches and antibiotics. I'm okay."

Did he see relief ripple through her? Nah—had to have imagined it. She probably didn't give a rat's ass what happened to him.

His mom rubbed his back like he was a little kid. "I can get your prescriptions filled before I have to go back to the cafe. Don't you have work today?"

He stepped away from his mom's hand. "Jack wanted me to help with the farm."

"I've been away for a long time," Mr. Quinn said. "But I think that if you give me a list, I can handle what needs to be done."

Austin's hand throbbed and all he wanted to do was pop a pain pill and crash. But he couldn't leave the defenseless animals in the hands of these people. He'd have to suck it up and take care of business. "It's just my hand. What I can't do I'll show you how to do." He turned to his mom. "I can get the prescriptions filled. I need to change clothes anyway."

"I don't want you driving." His mom looked at Travis. "Can you drive him?"

"Yes, ma'am. I'll take care of him." He winked at her.

"Uh-huh. I just bet you will. You boys stay out of trouble." Her warning sounded stern, but Austin knew she trusted them. After all, they would never do anything to screw up their senior year on the football team.

"Okay, so Travis, you and Austin are going to get the prescription filled and meet us at the house. We'll start on the chores." Mr. Quinn clapped his hands together like he was breaking the huddle.

Austin couldn't believe this guy thought he was going to be able to just take over the farm. He'd bet Mr. Quinn was the kind of guy who paid somebody else to change the oil in his luxury car. And from the spindly arms sticking out of the short sleeves of his expensive-looking shirt, Austin figured Mr. Quinn probably couldn't lift a feed sack to save his life.

"It's okay, Mr. Quinn. It's only nine. I'll be there in plenty of time to finish up."

"Can we ple-e-e-ase get something to eat before we face the beasts?" Kelsey made a puppy-dog face at her dad. She was working him and he'd bet Mr. Quinn caved every time.

"Sure, honey." Mr. Quinn wrapped his arm around Kelsey and flashed a shit-eating grin. "As soon as we gather those eggs."

Okay, so maybe Mr. Quinn wasn't so bad after all.

*

Kelsey walked ahead of her parents toward the parking lot and watched Travis and Austin amble to their truck. Pickup trucks, untucked shirts, jeans and cowboy boots—she guessed that was standard for Texas boys.

Ryan bumped her shoulder. "They look pretty hot, don't they?"

"No. Don't any guys here dress normal?"

"Normal as in Drew? Are you kidding me? These guys are real, Kelsey. Open your eyes."

"My eyes are open and I don't like what I see." But she kept watching. He was so laid-back. She watched him climb into the passenger seat of the truck without banging the dirt off his boots. She straightened her back and decided that was another thing she didn't like about him. Drew was impeccable and never allowed dirty shoes in his car. Of course, he never had dirty shoes either. When he cleaned up after playing lacrosse, he sealed his dirty clothes in a bag before he got into the car.

"Kelsey, this way."

Crap. She'd walked right past their car. She ducked her head and turned around.

"Don't like what you see, huh?"

"Shut up, Ryan." Kelsey climbed into the car behind Dad.

She dreaded facing the chickens. Kelsey tried to utilize her debate-savvy persuasiveness to develop a logical argument against egg gathering. But she knew that once her dad had a task in mind, it was set. She wished she had Mackenzie's knack for fading into the background.

Mackenzie!

"Mom, did anybody tell Kenzie where we were going?"

"Oh my God, we forgot her again. Does anybody have their cell?" Mom craned her neck to look at the girls in the backseat.

Kelsey and Ryan shook their heads. Kelsey spoke up. "We didn't have time to get them."

"We'll be home in a few minutes," Dad said.

When they pulled up to the house, Mackenzie was sitting on the top step of the porch with the snake-blood-tipped shovel in one hand and her cell in the other.

When they got out, she stood up. "What happened? I got out of the shower and nobody was around. I went to the chicken coop and all I found was blood and a dead snake."

Mom placed an arm around Mackenzie. "I'm sorry. We left in such a rush we didn't think to tell you." She recounted the story of the snakebite. When her mom finished, Mackenzie nodded, handed the shovel to her, and without a word went into the house.

Poor Mackenzie. She was so easy to overlook. Unlike Kelsey and Ryan, Mackenzie seldom complained. She didn't have friends outside the gym, never went to parties, didn't talk about guys, or school, or much of anything, for that matter. Her life was gymnastics—and now that was gone.

The protective side of Kelsey kicked in and she followed

her sister. She found her sitting at the kitchen table and took the seat across from her. "You okay?"

"I was so scared. I didn't know what happened. I called everybody's cell and couldn't get anybody." She leaned back in her chair and a tear slipped down her cheek. "What is it about me?"

"What do you mean?" Kelsey knew exactly what she meant and had no idea how to answer her question.

"Why don't I matter?"

"God, Kenzie, don't think that. You're amazing. None of us could ever do the stuff you do."

"Is that why nine times out of ten I had to call to see if anybody was picking me up from the gym?"

"That was just scheduling mixups. You know how busy our lives were in Chicago." Guilt niggled at the back of Kelsey's mind. When she'd been with Drew or her friends, it was just so easy to let time get away and forget Kenzie. But it had really only happened a few times, hadn't it?

Mackenzie brushed tears from her face. "I guess we don't have to worry about that anymore. We're stuck in Hickville."

Kelsey's parents joined them at the table. Dad spoke first. "I don't blame you for being upset, but these things happen."

"I'm not upset, Dad. I understand. I was just a little freaked out, okay?"

He gave a curt nod. "Good girl."

Yeah, good girl. Don't make waves. Let's just pretend we're all hunky-dory and get on with life. Kelsey wanted to shake her sister. She should be furious with them for scaring her. If it had happened to Ryan or her, they'd have rattled the walls with their anger. Not Kenzie. Retreat from conflict was her MO.

"About those eggs." God, Dad wouldn't let it drop.

"You're kidding. I don't even want eggs, and I'm way past hunger." Kelsey got up and grabbed a can of Dr. Pepper from the refrigerator.

"I know I've been a city boy for more years than I was on the farm, but I do remember a few things. We're going to do this together."

Too tired to argue, Kelsey popped the top on the can and gave a shrug. "Whatever."

Dad looked at Mom. "That means, 'Sure, Dad, I'd love to face the chickens with you,' right?"

Mom nodded. "Something like that."

"In the interest of cooperation, I'll give you time to finish your soda." He glanced at his watch. "Meet me in front in ten minutes."

Before Kelsey could argue that she'd intended to take more than ten minutes to drink her Dr. Pepper, Dad passed through the mudroom and out the back door. Kelsey looked at her mom. "If I grab another snake, I'm running away from home."

Mom gave a weary smile. "Just don't take Ryan with you. I need a snake killer."

Ten minutes later, Dad met her on the porch holding a bucket and a pair of leather work gloves. He handed Kelsey the gloves and said, "I was never one for snakes either. Let me give you a couple of pointers." They stepped off the porch and headed for the chicken coop. "First, if the chicken is nesting, move her out of the way. She'll squawk, but at least you can see what you're taking. If you see a snake, don't mess with it."

God, how stupid does he think I am? "That's a no-brainer, Dad."

"You can usually get the egg without the snake getting riled up. The snakes are almost always rat snakes. And they're called rat snakes because they like rats. They're good to have around."

"I'm thinking not so much." Kelsey slid through the gate of the chicken yard, followed by Dad.

"I know this hasn't been easy, Kel. You've had a tough

start, but give it a chance."

"Okay, I'll get the stupid eggs."

"I wasn't talking about gathering eggs."

Kelsey looked at him. "I know."

She pulled on the gloves and carefully reached under a hen. At the bottom of the nest lay a small, light-blue egg—only slightly covered in chicken shit. She picked it up and handed it to Dad. "These don't look at all like the ones we see in the store."

"No, these aren't your average hens. They're called Ameraucanas."

"Whatever they are, the eggs are beautiful." She worked down the line, carefully taking the eggs and handing them to him. In less than ten minutes they were walking back toward the gate with eight eggs resting in the pail.

"That wasn't so bad, was it?"

"No." She shrugged. It was kind of cool the way the hens stood and let her get the eggs. "I guess I'm the official egg gatherer."

"I guess you are."

She stopped halfway to the house and handed him the bucket. "Wait, I almost forgot." She took an egg from the pail and ran to the fence that corralled the pig. "Winifred! Here, piggy!"

The pig lumbered up to the fence and tipped her snout toward Kelsey. Kelsey tossed the egg at her and she snatched it out of the air. The egg crunched and oozed down the swine's chin. Kelsey's stomach gave a slight lurch. She wasn't sure she'd ever get used to the pig-and-egg scenario.

Dad regarded her with raised brows.

"Don't get excited. It's just something Austin showed me. I am not embracing farm life."

"Understood."

"Good. Can I go text Zoe?"

"Until Austin gets here. There's a lot to be done and we're all going to the feed store this afternoon."

So this was to be her life in Hickville. Heat, chores, and family outings to the feed store. Life just didn't get much suckier.

God, she'd been up since six and her day wasn't half over. As she settled against the headboard of her bed, she thought about how good it would feel to snuggle into the covers and take a nap. But the PB and J sandwich she'd slapped together was calling her name.

She took a bite and texted Zoe. Wow, while Kelsey was learning about snakes and chickens, Zoe was sleeping in after an impromptu party at Reed Barton's parents' lake house. Reed's parents were always there and there was never alcohol, but it was okay, they were cool. Everybody sat around the fire pit on the patio and listened to Reed and a couple of other guys play guitars. Yep, that was the life Kelsey had had to give up.

She was almost relieved when Zoe had to go. It was torture reading about the life she'd lost. She tossed her phone on the bed, curled up with a pillow, and let her mind drift to Drew.

God, how she missed him. She'd had a crush on him since they were freshmen. Last year, they had English together. She couldn't believe it when he chose to sit next to her. At first, when he'd talk to her, she'd get all nervous and heart racy. But she managed to hold a conversation, which led to flirting. Their first date was prom. It was a perfect night. From the moment he'd picked her up in his dad's Mercedes 550, he'd treated her like a princess.

Sadness weighed her down, making her heart feel heavy in her chest. Her eyes welled. She was so tired of crying, but didn't have the energy to try to stop the tears, so they ran down her face and soaked her pillow. It wasn't until her nose became too full of snot to breathe that she gathered the energy to sit up.

She blew her nose, looked at the dirty white paint on the bare walls, and thought of the sage-green walls of her old room. The color combined with the plush champagne carpet created a clean, crisp feel. Never one for tacky posters hanging from her walls, she'd placed framed photos she'd taken around Chicago to enhance her décor.

Her life had been so perfect there. She had Drew, Zoe, a great room, a great house. And now? Chickens squawked in the distance. She cringed at the noise and her sadness turned to anger. She hated her dad. She hated Ryan. She hated her life.

Mom stood in the doorway and knocked on the frame.

"Go away." She slumped back on her pillow.

Mom sat on the bed. "Want to talk?"

Kelsey sniffed, trying to calm her sobs. "What's there to say? Dad screwed up and we're here."

"It's not that simple."

"It *is* that simple, Mom. I hate him!" She squeezed her eyes shut and pressed her face against her pillow as another round of sobs broke loose.

Mom brushed her hair away from her face. "I know you do, right now. But it was the right thing for him to refuse to make those investments."

Kelsey sat up. "Really, Mom? Was that the real reason he was fired? Or was it because Ryan screwed his boss's son?"

Mom sucked in a sharp breath. Kelsey knew her words had hurt her, and she was glad. "What happened between Ryan and that boy had nothing to do with this." Her mother spoke softly, but there was no mistaking the anger in her voice.

Dad appeared in the doorway, sweat trickling down his face as he took in the scene in front of him. Kelsey knew he wouldn't ask questions. He wouldn't want to know. "We finished feeding. I want to head to the feed store after lunch."

"I'll be down in a minute to fix you a sandwich." Mom brushed a tear from her cheek.

Dad looked at Kelsey. "We're all going to the store. You

got that?"

"Yes. I've got it."

"Good, and you can leave the smartass tone at home."

She glared at him, but kept her mouth shut.

"Go on, Tom. Kelsey and I will be down."

He hesitated, and for a second, she thought he might gripe at her. Instead, he turned and walked away.

Mom turned back to her. "We're all having to make adjustments. This is not easy. But sometimes you have to make sacrifices for the people you love. Right now, Kelsey, I need your help. You're the oldest and whether you realize it or not, Ryan and Kenzie look up to you. Are we clear?"

"Look, Mom. I'll do my chores, go to the feed store—whatever. But this is a means to an end. I'll find a way to pay for college and by May, I'm out of here. And if you think I'm going to hold hands and skip across the yard with Ryan and Dad, you're wrong. Are we clear?"

Mom stood and faced her. "You know I love you, Kelsey. But sometimes, you act like a real bitch."

She turned and walked out of the room.

Kelsey's cheeks burned as though she'd been slapped. Her mother had just called her a bitch. What kind of mom did that? She took a deep breath and let it out slowly, easing the hurt. Great. How many weeks until the gala? She plopped on to the seat in front of her vanity. Too many.

She looked at her reflection in the mirror. Mascara puddled at the corners of her eyes and beneath her lower lashes. She jerked a tissue from a half-smashed box and dabbed at the black stains. No way was she going to let anybody know she'd cried, but the makeup was not cooperating.

Tossing the tissue aside, Kelsey padded across the hall to the bathroom and scrubbed her face clean. She held the bottle of foundation in her hand and regarded her reflection again. She'd never let Drew see her without the benefit of even skin tones and lightly dusted cheeks and eyes. It was a time-consuming ritual. What about now, what about here? Who cared if she didn't wear makeup?

She cared.

The last thing she wanted was to look as though she belonged to this place, and she'd bet her forty-dollar bottle of foundation that the local girls didn't know the first thing about creating the natural look.

She brushed foundation across her skin, covering the imperfections. By the time she'd constructed the perfect face, she felt better. She was still angry with her parents, but at least now she could get through the rest of the day feeling good about herself. She fluffed her hair and noticed curls had begun to sneak back into her über-straight style. She shouldn't have missed the flatiron step this morning. She shook her head and looked in the mirror again. She kind of liked the way her hair bounced with the curl.

"Kelsey! Come on, it's time to load up for the feed store," Dad yelled from downstairs.

She flicked the bathroom light off and moved toward the stairs. "Seriously, Dad—load up?" When she turned the corner of the landing she stopped.

Austin stood on the threshold of the front door, staring up at her. The screen banged his back, but he didn't seem to notice.

She wanted to look aloof to the Texan hulking in the doorway, but a tiny smile forced itself to the surface anyway.

Dad said, "Can I help you, son?"

Austin closed his mouth and stepped the rest of the way into the house. "Oh, hey, Mr. Quinn. Travis has to go to work. I thought I'd drop him off at his truck and meet y'all at the store."

Dad shook his head. "I'd feel better if you didn't drive."

"Yes, sir, but what about Kelsey?" With a glance up at her, he gave a half shrug. "Do you think she could drive me?"

Dad looked up at her too. "It will give you a chance to learn Hillside, Kel."

"But I've never driven a truck." Kelsey trotted down to the bottom step. Bad idea. Austin seemed to fill the space between the stairs and the front door and those deep blue eyes were focused on her again.

"It's not much different than a car, just higher. You drive the SUV, right?"

"Yes." Austin's gaze made her feel uncomfortable, as though he were seeing the freckles beneath the foundation. She ducked her head hoping he'd look away.

He pulled keys from his jeans pocket and dangled them in front of her. "No different."

"Okay, so we'll meet you at the store." Dad said.

Kelsey shrugged. "I'll get my purse."

5

In Texas, it is illegal to curse in front of or indecently expose a corpse.

Kelsey took the keys from Austin and followed him out the front door. A wall of heat hit her as she stepped on to the porch. Austin didn't seem to notice the fire in the air and jogged to his truck parked close to the barn. Kelsey wasn't sure she could breathe, much less walk. Sweat trickled between her breasts and across her forehead and she hadn't even made it out of the shade of the porch.

Ryan sat on the tailgate of the truck talking to Travis. She wore a white lace tank and denim shorts. Judging by the smile on her sister's face, Kelsey figured the last thing on her mind was the heat, or at least of the atmospheric kind.

Travis laughed and bumped shoulders with Ryan. Kelsey felt slightly queasy. Didn't Ryan care that she had been caught doing the nasty a few weeks ago? Didn't she care that she had a reputation for pretty much hooking up with any guy? She was only sixteen! Kelsey was turning eighteen in a few months and hadn't come close to "doing it." Ryan gave a little flirty squeal-giggle and shoved Travis back.

Really? Kelsey stopped halfway to the truck. The heat

from the sun had nothing on the anger that boiled inside her. She could have been at Reed Barton's lake party. But because Ryan couldn't manage one freaking day without a testosterone fix, she'd lost that life.

"Ryan."

Her sister popped off the tailgate and stalked toward her. "What?"

"I'm driving Travis to his truck. You're supposed to go with Mom and Dad to the feed store." Kelsey couldn't keep the biting tone from her words.

"Okay. What's wrong with you?"

"Nothing's wrong with me. I'm not the one throwing myself at the guys around here."

Ryan glanced over her shoulder at Travis. "God, Kelsey, we were just talking."

"For now."

Ryan ducked her head and Kelsey knew her words had stung. An apology hovered somewhere in her brain, but the anger she felt was too deep to bring it to the surface.

Ryan shoved her hands in her back pockets and walked back to Travis. "I have to go. I'll see you later."

Travis jumped up. "Yeah, later."

Kelsey climbed behind the wheel. Austin sat in the passenger seat and Travis plopped on the backseat behind him. She couldn't believe she was going to drive a truck. Drew would say it was redneck. But so was everything else in Hickville.

This particular redneck vehicle was a faded blue. The front bumper hung a little lower on the left side than the right and the windshield had a crack resembling an evil grin. She put the key in the ignition and felt along the seat for the buttons to move it forward.

"It's not electric." Austin said.

He showed her how to adjust her seat. When she finished, she placed her hands at two and ten and said, "Anything else I need to do?"

"Yeah, turn the key. It runs better that way."

"Ha ha." Kelsey started the engine and put it in gear.

As they pulled onto the two-lane highway, her phone dinged. She fished it out of her purse and saw a text from Drew. Her heart felt lighter. Of all the crap that had happened, this was the first bright spot in her day. She propped her hand on top of the steering wheel to read the message and Austin snatched it from her. "Hey, what are you doing?"

"I want to live."

"I'm not going to wreck. Come on, it's from my boyfriend."

"You're not texting while you're driving my truck." He looked at the screen of her iPhone. "It says, *Sorry I missed your call, babe.*" He looked at her. "Babe?"

"That's private." Kelsey reached across the cab for the phone, but Austin held it out of her reach. "Give it."

"You'll get it when we stop—unless you want me to answer for you."

"No. But I probably only have a few minutes to talk to him. Come on, he's in Italy."

"Turn right at that water tower."

Kelsey noted the huge hornet painted on the water tower beneath the words HILLSIDE HORNETS before she turned onto a narrow two-lane road.

The phone dinged again. Austin looked at Kelsey. "Want me to see what it says?"

"Can't you just hand it to me?" Frustration burned in her. She was going to miss the few minutes she had to text Drew because this guy was afraid she was going to wreck his hooptie.

Travis leaned forward. "If you want it that bad, pull over and I'll drive the rest of the way. "

Kelsey gripped the steering wheel. "What's the big deal?"

Austin dropped her phone in his shirt pocket. "You're

gonna see a white pipe fence on the left. The driveway past the fence is ours."

Kelsey followed Austin's directions and turned on to a gravel drive leading to a rectangular trailer house with tires spread across the roof. "This is your house?"

"Yep. Pull next to Travis's truck."

She parked next to a maroon truck and Travis opened the door. "Thanks for the ride, man. I'll catch ya later."

Kelsey watched him climb into his truck. It was clean, dent free, and although Kelsey didn't know a thing about pickups, it was obvious Travis's was a luxury model. As Travis backed out, she gave a little wave and then extended her hand toward Austin.

He dug the phone out of his pocket, but hesitated before giving it to her. "You're not leaving until you finish texting."

"Okay, just let me see my messages."

She snatched the phone and read the screen.

Drew: Sorry I missed you. Facetime later?

Her heart sank. She'd missed him.

Kelsey: K, I miss you.

She tapped Send, set the phone in the cup holder, and started the engine. The phone dinged a message, but before she could read it, Austin snatched it again.

"What is it with you? I'm not even moving yet."

"I'm not kidding, Kelsey. I put my phone on vibrate when I drive." He held the phone so she could read the message.

Drew: Miss you too.

She slammed the truck in reverse. "Did you get a ticket or something?"

He looked at her and gave a slight nod—like he'd just made a decision. "I want to show you something."

She followed his directions to the east side of town, to the cemetery. It wasn't fenced off like the ones back home. Instead, it abutted the city park. It was beautiful, though. Every grave was adorned with fake flowers. Normally she'd hate the idea of plastic flowers, but here it was fitting—everlasting flowers for an eternal resting place.

Large trees shaded the older area of the cemetery, but there was no shade in the area Austin directed her to. The sun seemed to suck the energy from her as soon as she got out of the truck.

They walked to a tombstone with a large bouquet of plastic yellow roses. Next to the flowers, a straw cowboy hat dangled from a metal cross someone had stuck in the ground. A white plastic cross stood in front of the metal one. A weathered pair of drumsticks lay on the ledge of the monument next to a University of Texas keychain, a tarnished Select soccer trophy, and a battered pink cell phone. Kelsey read the name on the pink granite.

Lindsey Barnes.

"Who was she?" Whoever she was, she had been seventeen when her life had ended two years ago.

"Travis's older sister." He pointed to a grave a few rows away. "See the one with the red roses? That's Abigail Yates, and that one—the one three to the left—that's Chelsea Hayes. No alcohol. They were coming home from school. Chelsea was driving and texting…" His voice trailed off. He looked across the stone field and drew a deep breath. "…me."

It was one word, barely audible, but it carried the emotion of tragedy, guilt, and despair all rolled up into two letters. Kelsey raised her hand to touch his shoulder to tell him that she understood. But she didn't understand. She couldn't imagine losing one friend—much less three.

He coughed, blinked a couple of times as though he was trying to gain control of his emotions. "They were supposed to meet us at The Grind downtown. Somehow, when we heard the sirens we knew it was them." He shook his head. "Man, we never thought they'd be dead. She ran a stop light and was T-boned by a cement truck."

"I'm sorry." Crap, what should she say? What *could* she say?

She followed him to the grave with the red roses. Like Lindsey's, there were drum sticks and a cell phone on the ledge of her tombstone, along with a small brass cross lying on its side. Austin propped the cross upright and moved toward Chelsea's grave.

A bouquet of fresh white daisies filled the granite urn on the side of the stone. A picture of a smiling, brown-eyed girl was set in the center of the granite.

Kelsey stared at the picture. "She was beautiful."

"They all were."

"She doesn't have trinkets on her gravestone."

"Her mom comes every day and makes sure it's clean. I guess it's all she can do for her now." Austin walked to his truck. Kelsey followed. He hesitated before opening the door and looked at her. "We all signed a contract that we wouldn't text and drive. It could have been any of us, Kelsey."

She nodded slowly. "I get your point."

As Austin climbed onto the seat, Kelsey noticed he held his bandaged hand pressed against his chest. "You hurting?"

"Nothing I can't handle. So tell me about Drew." He said his name like it tasted bad. She hated when her sister did that, but it was kind of funny the way Austin said it.

"He's amazing. He's applied to Harvard. I'm sure he'll get in."

"Did you say he's biking through Italy?"

"Yeah, which is why I don't get to talk to him much. There's like a seven-hour time difference. We Facetime when he can find free Wi-Fi."

"Must be nice to be able to take the summer off for a bike ride." He leaned his head against the seat.

"It beats farm work." She thought of the way the chickens stood when she reached for their egg. It was like they were saying, *Here you go. I was just keeping it warm for you.* She didn't mean to smile, but a small one found its way to her lips anyway.

"Hey, this is an exciting life. I bet he hasn't done any snake wrangling in Italy." The sincerity mixed with the sarcasm in his voice made her smile into a grin.

"Whatever. Come on, tell me how to get to the feed store before I get into trouble."

Kelsey followed Austin's directions, but when she pulled into the parking lot, she briefly hoped he'd directed her to the wrong place. The parking lot was full of potholes and loose gravel. But that was nothing compared to the store. The place was a dump. It was a dilapidated metal barn-looking building with a beat-up aluminum awning hanging above a plate glass window.

"This is it?" Kelsey asked.

"Yep."

The Infinity parked in front was her dad's, but she had to ask anyway. "Are you sure?"

"It's the only feed store in town."

"So—are there a lot of people in need of feed?" Surely if they were the only game in town they could afford to fix the awning or at least the holes in the parking lot.

"Well, yeah."

Kelsey parked next to the SUV. Noting the absence of cars in the parking lot, she gave Austin a sideways glance. "It doesn't look like we're doing a booming business."

He opened the door. "That's 'cuz it's the afternoon. Most of the business is early in the morning." He stepped from the truck. "Come on, I'll show you around."

She followed him up narrow concrete steps and through a dirty screen door. The smell hit her as soon as she crossed the threshold. It was kind of a chemical barnyard stink. She caught a faint sweet scent mixed up with the other odors, but it was gone before she could appreciate it. Probably snuffed out by stronger smells.

Sacks of feed were stacked on wooden pallets lining the walls. There was a section for each of the farm animals. Shelves lined up in rows perpendicular to the feed sacks. Kelsey and Austin walked down the aisle separating the shelves from the feed. It was surreal to look at all the animal stuff and realize that it was a part of her life now.

Austin smiled and said, "You look a little dazed."

"It's like I'm in *Wonder-Oz-warts.* I'm Dorothy, Alice, and Harry all rolled up in one. I've been plucked from one world and tossed into another." She stopped in front of a display of ropes and chains. On another shelf were tags and giant jars of medicine. "I don't know what any of this stuff is." She picked up a nylon harness. "I mean, I know these are probably some kind of animal containment devices…"

"Animal containment devices?" He took the thing from her. "This is a halter. And this particular one is for a horse."

"How do you know it's for a horse?"

He cupped one of the straps in his hand and let the rest of the halter dangle. "It's shaped like a horse's head. But if you're not sure, read the tag."

Kelsey shook her head. "I can't believe Dad knows all this stuff."

"It's not that hard. You'll get it in no time."

She pulled a fluorescent tag from a hook. "What are these?"

"Ear tags. We use them on cows and such."

Kelsey gave a shudder. "You poke them in their ears?"

Austin shook his head. "It's not that bad. You wear dangle earrings, right? What's the diff?"

"But I knew what was I was doing."

"Crazy, isn't it? You put a hole in your ears on purpose."

Kelsey hung the tag back on the peg. "But I had a choice."

The screen door squeaked and Kelsey turned to see her

mom coming through carrying a push broom. Now there was a sight her friends would never believe. Maggie Quinn, former president of the Junior League, working in a feed store. Normally her mom wore her hair parted on the side, straight, just below the jaw—like every other mom at St. Monica's. Today, she had it tucked under a Hill Feed ball cap. J. Crew sweaters and pearls were her mom's style, but she was wearing an old T-shirt and faded jeans. Still, she had a way of looking sophisticated no matter what she wore.

Mom leaned the broom against the counter. "Hi, Kelsey, Austin. We we're just finishing up in the back room. We're going to Uncle Jack's for dinner. Austin, you're welcome to come."

He held his bandaged hand close to his chest. "Thank you, Mrs. Quinn, but I'd better pass. My mom will be expecting me." He glanced around the store. "Is Jack in the back?'

"Yes."

"I'll just go see what I can help with." Austin headed toward the back of the store.

Kelsey noticed dark circles under Mom's eyes. "Are you okay?"

"Just a little tired." She gave a weak smile, but Kelsey caught a slight quiver in her chin.

For the first time, Kelsey saw her mother's optimistic outlook waver. Maybe Mom wasn't as excited about the move as she seemed. After all, she'd had to give up Junior League, St. Monica's altar society, St. Vincent de Paul, and whatever else she did with her free time. "You look like you could use a break. What can I do for you?"

Mom raised her brows, no doubt in shock that Kelsey was being cooperative. "If you'd sweep the floor I can—"

"Sit down and rest." Kelsey picked up the broom. "Really, I've got it."

"Thanks. I'll go check on Ryan and McKenzie. They're tagging new inventory."

Kelsey had never used a push broom in her life, or any other broom for that matter, but how hard could it be?'

She pushed the broom across the floor. It took her about five minutes to figure out short, quick strokes worked much better to gather the dirt. By the time she'd finished she had several little piles of dirt throughout the store. She leaned the broom handle against the wall and went in search of a dustpan. Her arms felt like lead. Who'd have thought sweeping could be such a workout?

She wandered through a doorway at the rear of the store. A short hall opened to a warehouse area. Boxes and sacks were stored on industrial shelves. At the back, a garage door was open and a forklift was parked close to a loading dock.

Ryan, Mackenzie, and her mom sat at a rickety wooden table. Behind the table was a makeshift kitchen with a sink, microwave, and refrigerator. Austin leaned against the counter talking to her dad and uncle.

"Hey, is there a dustpan? I need to pick up my piles."

Dad looked at her. "You used a broom?"

"Yes, and I'll never be able to raise my arms above my head again."

Uncle Jack grabbed a regular broom and dustpan and handed them to her. "Empty the dirt into the large can at the front."

Kelsey was grimy by the time she finished. Sweat mixed with dirt caked her body. She couldn't wait to shower. She was glad Drew wasn't around to see how gross she looked.

Austin was there, though. He'd come into the room with a smirk plastered across his face as he watched her wipe her hands on her jeans.

She looked at him skeptically. "What?"

"Nothing. I was just thinking that you probably aren't used to having dirt smudged on your cheek." His smirk transformed into a smile and his dark blue eyes seemed to sparkle just a bit.

Kelsey was drawn to that sparkle and couldn't look

away. She wiped her cheek with her shoulder. "Not really."

"It suits you."

She shouldn't smile, but her face wasn't listening to her brain and went beyond smile to a full-out grin. "What's that supposed to mean?"

"Nothing. Just that you look kind of cute with dirt smudged over your makeup." He stepped close to her and brushed her cheek with his good thumb. "It's this side."

"Thanks." Her face felt flushed, as if someone had let the Texas heat into the building. "So-o-o. Is there anything else?"

"Yeah." He jerked his head toward the back room. "I'm supposed to get you. I guess your folks want you to drive me home and they'll pick you up. Is that okay?"

"Sure."

He turned to walk to the back room and she followed, touching her cheek where Austin had wiped the dirt off. It wasn't like she could still feel his touch or anything, but she could feel the aftereffects. There was crazy stuff going on inside her. It didn't make sense. Drew was everything she ever wanted. And Austin? Not even close.

6

In Mesquite, Texas, it is illegal for children to have unusual haircuts.

Kelsey decided she liked driving a pickup truck. It wasn't just that she sat up high—she did that in the SUV. It was the feeling she got. Like she was doing something none of her friends would believe or approve of—like she was doing something rebellious.

Austin leaned on the door with his injured hand pressed against his chest. "So what was life like for Kelsey Quinn in Chicago?"

"Seriously?"

"Yeah. I mean, you obviously didn't mess with animals." He held his bandaged hand away from his body as if to validate his statement. "What kind of havoc did you create there?"

"I didn't create havoc in Chicago. That would've been Ryan." Kelsey put a playful, sarcastic tone in her voice. "Besides, it's just a little snake bite."

Austin laughed. "Your concern is heartening."

"I do feel bad." Remembering the blood gushing from the bite, she added, "Horrified, really."

He gave her a sideways look. "It wasn't all your fault. I should have booted that thing across the chicken yard."

"I just hope day two isn't so exciting."

"Aww, this is Texas, baby—every day is excit'n." His exaggerated tone made her smile.

"Excit'n? Chicago is excit'n." Kelsey tried to mock his accent but couldn't quite get the hang of dragging her words out and chopping off the end.

Austin covered his face with his good hand and shook his head. "Don't even try."

"It was pretty bad."

"No. It was real bad." He leaned his head against the seat and closed his eyes. His face had a strained look and he cupped his bandaged hand with the good one.

"Hurting?"

He peeked at her from half-open lids. "Yes. Distract me. Tell me about Chicago."

A knot formed in Kelsey's chest. "My life was perfect. I had everything there."

"Yeah? Like what?"

"Like everything. Chicago is awesome. We have museums, art galleries, Millennium Park. The restaurants are to die for. The shopping is amazing."

"We have a museum."

"Seriously?"

"Yeah. It's across from the courthouse. There's got to be at least fifty-sixty things on display."

"Woo. Look out Chicago. What about galleries and shopping?"

"Not so much on art galleries. There is one, but I haven't been there in a long time." He closed his eyes and took a breath before opening them. "Chelsea, the girl whose grave you saw, was an artist. She worked at the gallery. She liked to paint about high school life. Every painting, every drawing told a story."

"Ryan is an artist. She went to the art magnet school in

Chicago. She can paint, draw, sculpt—whatever she touches turns to art. I can't color and stay in the lines."

"Staying in the lines is highly overrated." He kept his head pressed against the seat as he spoke and his speech was a little stilted, as though he was having trouble speaking through the pain.

Kelsey tried to keep the conversation going. "Metaphorically or for real?"

"Both." He smiled, but it looked tense.

"Do you have pain pills with you?"

"I'm good." He leaned forward and turned in his seat a little toward her. "I'm guessing you're a stay-in-the-lines kinda girl—metaphorically."

She laughed bitterly. "You would be correct. A lot of good it's done me. I still got exiled here."

"Exiled?" He smiled full-on this time, and although she caught his look in glances between him and the road, it was enough to make her heart beat a little faster. He shook his head. "We've got a Wal-Mart. Spring Creek has a Target and a Penney's. What more do you need?"

Austin's tone was teasing, with a mix of sarcasm, and that made Kelsey laugh a little. "Okay, cowboy, how far is the closest real mall?"

"That'd be about an hour from here."

"An hour?" Okay, better than two hours. "I can do that."

"I'm glad to know you won't totally wither away out here in the wilderness."

"Seriously, Austin. What is there to do here?"

"In the summer, not a lot. But in the fall there's football. How about your school?"

"I went to a Catholic school."

"All girls?"

"Co-ed, thank you very much, so no jokes."

"It never entered my mind. What did you do for fun at the co-ed Catholic school?"

"I mostly studied my brains out so I could get into a

good college. I'm going to apply to Notre Dame to make my parents happy. I want to go to Harvard with Drew, but I'm not sure I could get in even if my parents still could afford it. I've thought about Boston College. At least then I'd be close to Drew." A tear slipped from her right eye. She took a deep breath and let it out slowly. "I'm sorry."

He looked at her as though he was seeing the pain she felt. "It's got to be rough moving away in your senior year. I've never lived anywhere but here. Sometimes this town gets a little small, but I can't imagine living anywhere else. I think I'd be pissed off if I was forced to move to a strange place."

God, I look weak and pathetic. She swiped at the lone tear and pushed her sadness away. "So what makes Hillside wonderful? Besides the museum and the Wal-Mart?"

"I didn't say it was wonderful. First off, everybody knows your business. Second, if they don't know your business they'll find it out. It can get a little... intense." Austin shook his head. "My mom says it's a good thing. We kinda take care of each other around here. "

"I guess I'll find out just how well you take care of each other tomorrow."

"What's tomorrow?"

She gripped the steering wheel a little tighter. "I register for classes."

"You'll be fine. It's not like you have a huge choice."

"Yeah, that's what I'm afraid of."

"Just try not to get Mr. Shipley for AP English."

"Why?"

"He's crazy. He's a survivalist. He's always talking about how to get out of idiotic scenarios that only one in a billion people will ever see."

Oh great. Welcome to Texas. "Who should I get?"

"Mrs. White. She's the only other choice, but she's really good." He gave her the names of other good and bad teachers, but by the time she pulled into his drive, she wasn't sure which was which.

She put the truck in Park and Austin said, "Do you want to come in while you wait on your folks?"

"And get out of this heat? Sure." Besides, she was curious about what the inside of one of these metal crackerboxes looked like. She handed him the keys and followed him up the wooden steps leading to a deck in front of the house. But before he got his key in the doorknob, her parents pulled into the drive.

She watched Dad park behind Austin's truck. "So I guess I'll see you tomorrow?"

"Bright and early."

His eyes twinkled just enough to make her duck her head and hide the blush she felt crawling up her cheeks. "Okay, then."

She jogged down the steps. When she reached her parents, she turned and raised her hand to wave good-bye, but he was already in the house. A pang of disappointment traveled through her as she left the gesture unfinished and climbed into the car.

She plopped onto the seat next to Mackenzie. "So is anybody else as I tired as I am?"

Mackenzie stretched out her arms in front. "This is a whole different kind of tired than eight hours in the gym."

Ryan leaned her head back. "We must have moved a hundred boxes while we waited for you and Austin to show up."

"What are you saying, Ryan? Because I didn't see you out there picking up chicken-poop-covered eggs."

Dad glanced in the rearview mirror. "Everybody did their share of chores. You got that."

She got it, but Kelsey wanted to fight with Ryan. She had followed all of the rules, even the stupid ones. Not Ryan. She'd snuck out, done drugs, done guys, and everybody's life was tuned upside down and inside out because of it. Sure, Dad had been fired from the investment firm. But it was only after Ryan had been caught having sex with his former partner's son that they'd decided to move to Texas. All Mom talked about was how this move was good for the family. Remembering her quivering chin, Kelsey doubted even Mom believed that line of crap anymore.

*

Aunt Susan and Uncle Jack's house was not what Kelsey expected. It was a brick rancher on a street with little *doppelganger* houses on each side. Aunt Susan answered the doorbell and greeted them with a round of tight hugs. "Mercy me, y'all must be tired. Come in."

They stepped into a white tile foyer surrounded by whiter carpet. Mom pulled her shoes off and ordered the girls to do the same. As Kelsey slid her feet from her sneakers, she watched her mom go into Junior League mode. "Thank you for having us. Your house is lovely." Leave it to her mom. It didn't matter how crappy her day was, she always managed to observe the social graces. She was the epitome of class, even wearing a ball cap and jeans.

Aunt Susan smiled. "Thank you. Jack thinks I'm crazy for wanting all this white, but after thirty years on the farm I wanted something that felt clean."

The kitchen, den, and eating area kind of morphed into one big room. The back door was on the right side between the den and dining area, across from the kitchen.

Uncle Jack came in through the back door wielding a pair of barbecue tongs in one hand and a bottle of Shiner beer in the other. "Well, look what the cat drug in. Just in time too. I'm 'bout to throw the steaks on the grill. Beer's in the fridge, Tom."

Aunt Susan added, "For the girls, I have sweet tea or coke."

Not sure which flavor of coke she would get, Kelsey opted for the tea. She watched her aunt get drinks and thought about how different her parents were from her aunt and uncle.

It hardly seemed possible that Uncle Jack and Dad were brothers. Uncle Jack wore denim cargo shorts, a Hawaiian shirt that fit loosely enough to cover his gut, a straw cowboy hat, and flip-flops. He was laid-back and loud. Dad wore plaid shorts, a polo shirt, and leather sandals. He didn't need to wear a loose-fitting shirt because he worked out every day—or at least he had until they moved. And he seldom cracked a joke, probably because he was stressed out all the time. It was too bad Dad hadn't inherited at least a little of Uncle Jack's laid-back attitude.

Kelsey took the glass of tea and followed her aunt and sisters onto the back patio.

Twenty minutes later she bit into what was quite possibly the greatest thing about Texas—the juiciest, most tender rib-eye she'd ever experienced. That, coupled with a loaded baked potato and Aunt Susan's sweet tea, gave life to her tired body.

Uncle Jack told stories about growing up on the farm. He had a way of making everything sound like an adventure. As the family laughed at Uncle Jack, Kelsey watched her dad. At first, his smile was tight, like it was all he could do to force it on his face. But as the evening continued, Kelsey saw him change. He leaned back in his chair, the furrows in his brow relaxed, and he actually let out a laugh or two.

And for a moment, she wasn't angry with him and she didn't hate Ryan.

After dinner, Aunt Susan pulled out the 1984 Hornets yearbook and flipped through the pages until she found what she was searching for. She handed the book to Kelsey and her sisters. "This is your dad."

Kelsey held the book as Ryan and Mackenzie looked on from either side. She studied the picture labeled *Thomas Anthony Quinn*. This was her straight-laced, militant dad?

The girls broke out laughing and Kelsey shook her head. "Seriously, Dad? This is you?" His hair was almost to his shoulders and he wore a lavender T-shirt beneath a white jacket with wide lapels.

Her dad peeked over her shoulder. "Hey, I was a stud."

The girls broke out in a collective, "Ewww."

Aunt Susan said, "Here, let me see that."

Kelsey handed her the book and she flipped to other pages of Thomas Anthony Quinn: junior class president, quarterback, president of the Latin club, and treasurer of the Future Farmers of America.

Ryan looked at her dad. "You did all this and you were a junior? What was left over for your senior year?"

"I didn't do much after that."

Mackenzie asked, "What happened?"

He took a step back and tugged at his collar before mumbling, "I focused on my studies." He drew a long swig of beer and walked to the kitchen to toss the bottle.

Aunt Susan shook her head. "Cassidy Jones is what happened. She was a real piece of work."

"Who's Cassidy Jones?" Kelsey eyed her dad.

"Nobody." He leaned over her shoulder and flipped the pages to the senior class. "Look up your uncle. Now, there's class."

Kelsey thumbed through the pictures until she reached the page with the Qs. She barely recognized the kid staring back at her from the album. He had thick, blond shoulder-length hair, oversized horn-rimmed glasses, and he wore the same jacket as her dad had, only with a giant bow tie.

Aunt Susan leaned over and looked at the picture. "Lord have mercy. I forgot all about that bow tie. That tie about got Jack suspended from school."

Ryan looked up at her aunt. "For a bow tie?"

"Yes. Jack was always the class clown, bless his heart. He wore that ridiculous tie on picture day and about half the senior boys had their turn at it."

Kelsey flipped through the senior class and sure enough, most of the guys and a couple of girls wore the tie. "But why would they kick him out of school?"

"For having a little fun." Jack moved to stand around the table with the girls.

Aunt Susan dismissed Jack with a flick of her hand. "You know you were making fun of Mr. Deaver." She shook her head. "He taught Economics. Always wore a bow tie, bless his heart."

"He was a hundred years old and dyed his hair with cheap dye. When he got nervous, brown sweat would roll down his forehead." Uncle Jack could barely get the story out before he broke out laughing. He had one of those infectious laughs that made everybody else spontaneously join in.

Aunt Susan shook her head. "Still, ya'll shouldn't have made fun of him."

Kelsey watched her uncle throw his head back and laugh. Dad laughed too, but it looked unnatural on his face. They were as different as brothers could be. As different as she and Ryan. Did they fight like she and Ryan too? They seemed to get along now.

Mackenzie leaned further over the book. "Where are you, Aunt Susan?"

"Look under Susan Blakely."

Kelsey let Mackenzie turn the pages until they found the picture of their aunt. Kelsey could tell she had been one of the popular girls. She was beautiful, with long hair parted down the middle and a heart-shaped face. She wore an expression of confidence, like she owned the school. Kelsey knew the look; it was the one she'd worn in last year's St. Monica's yearbook. The one taken before Dad lost his job, before Ryan shamed the family.

Hurt and anger flooded back, and the room seemed about two sizes too small. Tears threatened to show themselves and she wasn't about to let that happen. She excused herself from the table and headed down the hall to find the bathroom.

Once safely behind the closed door, she choked back the urge to cry. If she let loose, she wouldn't be able to stop before her eyes swelled and turned red.

Once she tamped down her emotions, she took a couple of deep breaths and tried to plaster a smile on her face—but she just couldn't make it stick.

This was supposed to have been her year, damn it. Her senior year. She probably would have been valedictorian, was friends with pretty much everyone, had planned to run for senior class president. She should *own* St. Monica's this year. Damn Ryan for screwing it up. Damn Dad for screwing it up. And damn Drew for having fun in Italy.

She was being unfair. It wasn't like she expected him to stay home because she'd been exiled to Texas. But her heart ached for him. Where was his heart? Did he miss her? She yanked her cell from her hip pocket.

Kelsey: Do u miss me?

She stared at the message waiting to be sent. Did he love her? She retyped.

Kelsey: Do u love me?

The blue cursor blinked at her, waiting impatiently for her to hit Send. Should she? She'd never been brave enough to ask Drew about his feelings. If he said no, she would be left with nothing. No boyfriend to talk about, to dream about. No reason to go to college in the East. No reason to escape Hickville.

But if he answered yes, what would that mean? He loved her and she'd still be stuck in Texas without him.

She looked at the cursor again. It seemed to blink, *Come on, Kelsey, you know what you want to do. Hit Send.*

She took a deep breath. Her thumb hovered over the icon. Her heart pounded in her chest, pushing heat to her face. She was about to do it when her mother tapped on the door.

"Are you all right in there, honey?"

She let her breath out slowly. "Mom, could you be more embarrassing?"

"Well, hurry up. Dad is ready to go."

Kelsey pressed her thumb to the green square labeled Send, shoved the phone in her pocket, and headed out of the bathroom. The phone dinged a reply before she reached the foyer. She wanted to read it right then, but Uncle Jack and Aunt Susan were making the rounds giving hugs, so she figured she could wait until she was in the car.

Dad took the truck keys from Uncle Jack. "Who wants to ride with me?" When nobody spoke up he shrugged and said, "Okay. You don't know what you're missing."

Ryan looked at him and said, "Yeah we do, Dad. Trust me."

Once they were in the Infinity and Kelsey got a chance to look at the text, her heart sank just a little.

It was from Zoe.

"Mom, Zoe has invited me to stay with her for the Gala. She said her parents offered to pay for my airline ticket."

Mom glanced at her and back to the road. "We're not going let Zoe's parents buy you an airline ticket."

"Why? You know I have planned on going all summer."

"We'll talk about it later."

Yeah, we'll talk about it later. Her breath caught in her chest and she could feel her pulse pounding in her head. Basically, Mom meant no. Obviously, she didn't want to deal with the fallout of those two letters tonight.

Kelsey's mind raced. They weren't taking her last tie to Chicago away from her. She'd figure out a way. "What if I earn the money? I'll get a job."

"If you can pay for it, I can't see any reason not to let you go. But a job has to work around your responsibilities at home. And we'll have to work out transportation."

"I'll do whatever it takes." Anything to get a reprieve from chores, chickens, and the cowboy. Oh, the cowboy. Navy blue eyes that seemed to burn right through her. *Definitely need a reprieve from him.*

7

In Texas, it's against the law to carry fence cutters or a pair of pliers that could cut a fence.

Kelsey stood in the combination bathtub-shower and let herself cry. In here, she didn't have to be strong. Nobody would see the anguish she'd kept hidden. Nobody could hear the hiccupping sobs that erupted from her body. She didn't have to convince herself not to worry about Drew not answering her text. She didn't have to pretend that she wasn't worried about earning the money to fly to Chicago.

And then there was her conversation with Zoe. Kelsey wanted to scream. Shopping. Dancing in the park. She should have been with them instead of playing chicken and snake with Austin. Zoe and her other friends were making new memories—ones that didn't include her. The life she knew was gone like the water rushing down the drain. And as much as she wanted to pretend otherwise, there was nothing she could do to stop it.

She climbed out of the tub and checked her phone just in case she'd missed a message from Drew. She checked it again after blowing her hair dry, and fell asleep with it cradled in her hand—still waiting for Drew's reply.

On day two in Hickville, Kelsey stepped out onto the porch to find Austin sitting in the wicker rocker sipping from a mug. He smiled at her and set the cup on the coffee table. "Morning, Kelsey. Ready to work?"

"No, I'm ready to relax with my coffee." She took a sip and sat in the glider across from him.

He slung a bucket full of feed on the table. "Chickens are hungry."

She leaned back and let out a long sigh. "Mmm, this coffee is good."

The screen door screeched open and Dad stepped onto the porch. "Good morning, Kelsey, Austin." Kelsey sipped from her cup and watched him stretch and yawn. The man who always wore a suit and tie to work was dressed in khaki slacks and a golf shirt. Casual for him, but she wondered how much cred he'd have at the feed store with that embroidered penguin above the breast pocket. He looked at Kelsey. "I want you to work around the farm with Austin. He'll show you what to do. As soon as Kenzie and Ryan come down, we're heading to the store."

Kelsey peeked over the rim of her mug. "I thought we were registering for school today."

"After lunch," he said.

Kelsey cradled her cup in her hand. "Hey, Dad? Did Mom talk to you about my idea to get a job?"

He folded his arms across his chest and Kelsey just knew he was going to balk. Instead, he nodded. "Yes. I think it's a good idea—after we've settled in here a bit. And, provided we can work out timing and transportation."

"How much settling in do we need?"

"We haven't finished unpacking boxes. You still have a few things to learn about the animals. Give it a few weeks."

"A few weeks? Dad, the gala is six weeks away!" She knew the drill. He wasn't going to out-and-out say no, he was just going to make it impossible for her to earn enough money to go.

"Let's get the house unpacked, learn your chores, and we'll talk."

"So are you saying that if the house is put away and I learn how to take care of the animals, I can get a job?"

Dad scratched his chin. "I guess I'm saying that if you do those things, you can start looking for a job."

I can so do that. What else was she going to do during the day?

Austin sat forward in his chair. "Mom says they can always use help at the diner. I could talk to her if you want."

No way was Kelsey going to work as a waitress. "Thanks, but I'd rather work in a boutique."

He leaned back and took another sip from his mug. "Okay, let me know if you change your mind."

"Yeah." *That's not going to happen.* She sat her mug down and picked up the pail. "Come on, Austin, make me a farm girl."

Austin's bum hand left him pretty much useless as far as actually helping with the chores. But he could talk, and talk he did. Kelsey learned how to feed the chickens, Winifred the pig, and the horses. She cleaned the coop, mucked stalls, and swept the barn. Austin tried to get her to help him turn the horses out into the pasture, but she wasn't ready for contact with animals that were bigger than she was. She felt a little guilty about watching him struggle to buckle the halter around the horses, but she sure wasn't going near them. Being chased by chickens was bad enough.

They visited the school to register after lunch. Still no word from Drew. Kelsey tried not to dwell on his non-response by reminding herself he was traveling across Italy on a bike; his phone could be dead. But still, she couldn't untangle the giant knot that formed in her gut when she thought about it.

Instead, she focused on the school.

The school Dad had attended in the center of town had been converted to administrative offices a few years ago. This version of Hillside High was built on the north end of town to reflect growth in the area. Behind the school stood the concrete football stadium. THIS IS HORNET TERRITORY! stretched across the top of the entrance. Below the welcome was the warning, BEWARE THE STING! with an image of an angry hornet making the exclamation point.

As they turned the corner to the front of the school, Kelsey's heart sank a little. It was a sprawling, single-story brick building with few windows and about as much charm as a prison. A couple of spindly wannabe trees were staked and anchored upright near the entrance.

Anxious butterflies took flight in her stomach as they parked in a visitor's space. If Mom was nervous, she didn't show it. But then, she wore her Junior League attire: pearls, a cute but sophisticated summer dress, and an expensive pair of sandals. To most people it screamed money, but Kelsey knew the truth. Those things were just remnants of the fairy tale that had once been their life.

As they got out of the SUV, Kelsey wondered how the counselor would evaluate the Quinn sisters. Each of them wore a skirt and blouse, but they were as different as their personalities. Mackenzie wore a drop-waist white skirt that flared at the bottom, and a soft pink sleeveless top. The soft color of her blouse reflected color onto her normally pale face. And the white in her skirt seemed to accentuate her curly blond hair. Her look was put together with the same precision as her performance in competition. Ryan, on the other hand, was as thrown together and as her life. She was dressed in her hippie long cotton wrap skirt and layered tank tops. And, although Mom has specifically asked her to tone down the spikes in her super-short brown hair, she'd spiked it with the same abandon as her art. Kelsey smoothed her A-line khaki skirt and smiled. At least one of them had opted for a conservative but sophisticated polo.

They met with Mrs. Bettis, the counselor. She was a tall, willowy woman, younger than their mom. Her features were delicate and she looked like she might blow over if she were yelled at too hard. After the introductions, she picked up the folder containing their transcripts from Chicago. "It's so nice that we are getting three such fine young women at Hillside High. Let's start with you, Kelsey."

Kelsey sat forward on the plastic chair. "I'd like to take Latin four, Philosophy, and I know this is a public school, but I was wondering if you offered a Theology class."

Mrs. Bettis sat up a little straighter and cleared her throat. "We don't have Latin, Philosophy, or Theology. We tried to get a Latin teacher, but we just aren't budgeted for it." She handed Kelsey a sheet of paper. "Here's the list of classes you can take. I highlighted my suggestions."

Kelsey studied the list. "You highlighted Spanish, but I've had three years of German."

"Since we don't offer German, I thought Spanish made sense. Besides, you are in Texas—it would be helpful. You can take French, though. Look at it as a way to expand beyond German."

"French then. Definitely want to take AP English. I'd like Mrs. White."

"Yes, everybody else does too. Her class is full. I can put you in Mr. Shipley's class." She agreed and in the end she was also put in calculus and physics.

Ryan and Mackenzie fared worse. Ryan was devastated to find the art program did not extend beyond drawing and painting. She had been into wood sculpture in Chicago. The only way she could work with wood at this school was to join shop class.

Mackenzie sat quietly while the counselor planned her schedule. Once the required classes were plugged in, Mrs. Bettis pulled her readers low onto her nose, peeped over the top of the red rims, and said, "You look very fit. Do you play a sport?"

Mackenzie winced and shook her head. "No, not any more."

Her mom said, "Mackenzie was quite the gymnast in Chicago."

Mrs. Bettis tapped her pen on the folder. "Ah, that explains the biceps. We don't have gymnastics and it's too late to try out for cheerleading, but it's something to consider for next year. Tryouts are in the spring."

"Yes, ma'am." Mackenzie smiled at the counselor's suggestion, but asking a bona fide gymnast to try out for cheerleader was like asking a pro football player to join a flag football team. Kelsey doubted her sister would really consider it.

Mrs. Bettis dropped her pen and leaned back in her chair. "Meanwhile, since you're a freshman, the field is wide open, so to speak. Is there a sport you'd like to try?"

Kenzie gave a half shrug. "I like to run."

"Track it is." She smiled like she'd just negotiated a major sports deal. "Well, that concludes our meeting." She picked up the phone and pressed a button. "Raeanne, I'm finished with the Quinns. Would you mind giving them a little tour of the school?"

Mrs. Bettis set the phone back in the charger and folded her hands on top of the desk. "Raeanne will be right in. We're so glad you're joining our little Hornet family."

Kelsey watched her mom put on an almost masklike smile as she stood. "Thank you for your time."

When Raeanne entered the office, Kelsey thought Mom was going to choke. Their middle-aged, five-foot-tall tour guide was the epitome of big hair and boobs. Big hair because she had shoulder length, dark brown hair that was full of product and poofed to add maximum height. Boobs, because "the girls" were not happy to be confined by her bra and low-cut blouse.

"Well, howdy. I'm Raeanne. I hear y'all are from the north."

"I'm Maggie Quinn. These are my daughters Kelsey, Ryan, and Mackenzie."

The girls shook hands as they were introduced.

"Well come on, time's a-wasting." Raeanne led them out of the office to a hall lined on both sides with trophy cases. "This is the Hornet Hall of Fame." She spoke slowly, giving weight to the words *Hornet* and *fame*. "Now if you get lost, just find your way to the hall with the trophies. It will lead you to the office." Raeanne's platform heels clicked across the linoleum in quick steps as she led them down the hall. It crossed Kelsey's mind to ask her if anybody had ever been eternally lost in the school, but figured now was not the time to be a smartass.

Raeanne's boobs were practically dancing out of her blouse as she walked. When the woman stopped in front of a trophy case and turned to face the group, each boob gave a final *bump-bump* before settling into place. "It's quiz time. Who can tell me who was the highest scoring quarterback in a single game in Hornet history? It oughta be an easy one." She smiled and gave a little wink to Mrs. Quinn.

They stared back at her.

"You mean you don't know?" She rolled her eyes. "Oh my, only the handsomest guy to walk these halls back in nineteen eighty-four. The one and only Mr. Tom Quinn—and he was a junior when he did it." She stepped aside, revealing a picture of Kelsey's dad running across the goal line. The scoreboard in the background read HOME: 42 VISITORS: 0.

Raeanne looked directly at Kelsey as though she were speaking only to her. "Your daddy scored all of those points. All of them. It was a wonder to see."

Kelsey stepped close to the case and studied the picture. She didn't know squat about football, but it didn't seem quite fair to run over the other team. Besides, what kind of victory could it be if the team was so lousy they couldn't score a single point? She wondered how the town would feel about their hero when they found out he'd been fired from his job, had come home penniless, and was living on a loan from his brother.

"It must have been something." Her mom's eyes sparkled when she spoke, but Kelsey knew the look was an act of diplomacy, not sincerity. "I can't wait to see the rest of the school."

"Well, just come right this way to the science wing."

This school was way different from St. Monica's. First, St. Monica's was two-story and old. But it had character too. Its ancient metal lockers had to be kicked or pushed at just the right spot to open. These lockers looked new, devoid of dents and scratches. Instead of solid wood doors, these classrooms had metal doors with only a vertical window about six inches wide and three feet long.

Ryan stopped and peeked into one of the rooms. "Wow, they're not much for seeing in or out, are they?"

Raeanne looked at Ryan as though she were divulging very important information to a little kid. "That's part of our effort to make this school a safe zone. If we have an armed intruder we don't want to give him a big target, now, do we?"

Ryan looked back at Raeanne. Kelsey expected her sister to give a little head bob before firing off some smartass remark. But before Ryan had a chance to respond, Raeanne continued down the hall. "Be sure to look at the student handbook. This year we have instituted a strict zero-tolerance policy about firearms. Guns, even hunting rifles, cannot come on school property."

"Do you have a problem with guns?" Mackenzie asked.

Raeanne stiffened her back a little. "*I* don't have a problem with guns. But we've had a real problem in the past couple of years with kids leaving rifles in the gun racks of their trucks. It's just a potentially dangerous situation. So we decided to go zero tolerance this year."

"That's progressive of you."

Kelsey's mom spoke with a hint of sarcasm in her voice, but Raeanne apparently missed it because she leaned toward her and said, "I'll tell you what it is. It's proactive. We went to a seminar earlier in the summer and learned all about being proactive. Mr. Schaffer, the administrator, is a big believer in it, and now we are too."

The rest of the tour lasted about ten minutes. Once they climbed back in the car, Kelsey let her thoughts drift to Drew, the gala, and getting a job. She promised herself she wasn't going to obsess over his non-reply to the big question. And by *obsess* she meant *resist talking about it to Zoe*. But she knew she had to figure out a way to get there. First of all, it was the coolest fundraising event at St. Monica's—bigger than prom. Second, she was going with Drew Montgomery. He was one of those guys who was not only extremely hot, he was also nice. Every girl wanted to be with him, and he wanted to be with Kelsey.

She got a queasy feeling in her stomach. She hoped she hadn't blown it by sending that text. She needed to see him again, she had to get to the gala, and then everything would be okay.

The getting a job part was going to be a challenge. Not because she didn't think the good people of Hillside, Texas, would be willing to hire her. But because, although her parents had agreed to let her get a job, she wasn't feeling the commitment to allow her time to work at said job.

As her mom wove through town from the school to home, Kelsey tried to scope out possible places of employment. Old-lady boutiques, a hardware store, a junk/antique shop, a gift shop, a flower shop, and the café.

She had six weeks until the gala, three weeks until school started. Crap, three weeks! Once school started, her possible work hours would be severely limited. She didn't care what Dad said, she needed to start looking like yesterday. But with Dad driving the truck and Mom the SUV, how was she going to sneak away to job hunt?

Her phone dinged a text. Her heart pounded. Was this the answer to the question?

Disappointment replaced the thudding in her chest. It was from Austin.

Austin: How was registration?

Austin. If he took her job hunting, her parents wouldn't have to know a thing—until she snagged employment. But she'd deal with that later.

*

A week of egg gathering and working in the feed store later, she hadn't worked up the nerve to ask Austin to take her job hunting. And worse, Drew still hadn't answered her question. It was as if it hadn't been asked. She had to get to the gala.

She was unpacking like a crazy person. But finding places to put good-life stuff in a crap house was just depressing. Mom tried to hide it, but Kelsey saw tiny chin quivers just before she excused herself to the bathroom or to the porch. She wanted to hug her mom and cry with her. But Mom would have hated that. What was it she'd said? "Sometimes you have to make sacrifices for the ones you love." Mom's sacrifice was going to be in silence. Her dad and sisters, on the other hand, had apparently embraced the simple life.

Dad seemed a whole lot less stressed out, and she'd probably seen him smile more in the past week than she had her entire life. Both sisters had given up wearing makeup after the first day. Kelsey just couldn't. Maintaining her hair and makeup was her tie to her old life. Mackenzie continued her early-morning workout routine and then went to the store with Dad and Ryan. Ryan had a real knack for arranging and organizing things there, which left Kelsey with the farm chores.

Every morning she stepped out onto the porch to find Austin sitting in the wicker rocker sipping from a mug of coffee. He'd smile, set his cup on the coffee table and say,

"Morning Kelsey. Ready to work?"

She was never ready to work. She wanted to sit on the porch and drink several cups of coffee. But to do that, she'd have to get up literally before the chickens, and that just wasn't an option.

8

It is against the law to flirt or "mash" in Abilene, Texas.

Austin sat in the wicker rocker waiting for Kelsey. He could have gone ahead and started feeding the chickens, except the highlight of his day tended to be the moment she stepped on to the porch. In that instant, before she said hello, another side of her was revealed—a freer side. One that didn't see every second on the farm as a prison sentence.

Not that she was bitchy to him or anything. She did her work and then retreated to the house. But she was missing out on the beautiful aspect of farm life. Like the horses.

He couldn't get her to go near them. He worked with them after the feeding and cleaning chores were done. By that time, she was in the house, probably texting her boyfriend, Dan or Don or Drew or whatever the hell his name was.

Austin had had the stitches removed yesterday and now that he had full use of his hand, he hoped to change Kelsey's view of life on the farm.

The front door opened and his muscles tensed with anticipation. She stepped across the threshold, smiled, closed her eyes for a split second, and took a deep breath.

There, that was it.

That was the moment he'd been waiting for. The instant she was experiencing the—the—*splendor*. Yeah, the splendor of the country. And the best part was, she was totally unaware of it. As soon as she let the fresh air out of her lungs, her smile faded and the sadness returned to her eyes.

Austin wanted to grab that moment for her. He wanted to show her what she couldn't see. In the week she'd been in Texas, he hadn't even come close.

"Morning, Kelsey. Ready to work?"

"No." She sat across from him, like she did every morning, and drank her coffee.

"The chickens are hungry." He handed her the pail of feed.

"They'll live." She set it next to her chair and propped her feet on the coffee table.

It was a silly game they played every morning. But this morning she seemed different. There was something beyond the sadness. "What's up?"

"What do you mean?"

"I dunno. You just look different." He tapped the toe of her tennis shoe with his boot. "You're not all mad and 'I hate Texas' like usual."

"Yeah, well I've resigned myself to this year-long prison sentence."

"So—you want to talk about it?"

"Nope." She took a long sip of coffee.

Austin set his cup down and stood. "Well, I got my stitches out and can pick up more of the cleaning load so—I guess I'm gonna get started."

He grabbed for the pail, but before he could lift it, Kelsey laid her hand next to his on the handle. "I've got it."

He let go and took a step back. "Okay. I'd like to get started before it gets hot. It's already eighty-eight."

"I'm coming." She sat her mug next to his and followed him to the chicken yard. She scattered the chicken scratch across the ground. "I got a video from Zoe yesterday."

Austin cleaned and filled the chicken waterers and filled the feeders with lay crumble. "Yeah?"

"A bunch of my friends were at the park playing in the Crown Fountain. Ever hear of it?"

"No."

"It's pretty awesome. Here, look." She pulled her phone from her pocket and Austin leaned over her shoulder to watch the video.

There was a ginormous video screen with a picture of a face on it. The face was spitting real water onto the people below. Then the water stopped, the face closed its eyes, the screen turned off, and a waterfall cascaded from the top. It looked like it was at least three stories tall.

"Whoa. Now, that's cool."

Kelsey shoved her phone back into her pocket. "Yeah. They're going to be doing stuff like that all summer and they don't have a clue how lucky they are."

"Nah, this is lucky. They're missing out on rural America. Look at you. You're a pro at feeding chickens and gathering eggs. Just think, while they're playing in some E. Coli infested urban fountain, you are shoveling one-hundred-percent natural horse shit."

Kelsey shook her head. "When you put it like that…"

He slung his arm around her shoulder, careful to make sure it didn't look like he was trying to come on to her. They walked to the coop and Austin placed eggs in the empty chicken scratch pail that Kelsey held. "I mean, would Zoe have a clue how to pick up a warm, fresh-from-the-chicken-ass egg?"

"Unlike me, she probably would have grabbed the egg and not a snake."

"But then I wouldn't have had to have stitches and watch you do all the work for a week."

Kelsey spun away from Austin and pointed an accusing finger at him. "I knew it! It was your plan all along." Her eyes were bright with mischief and she was smiling, on the edge of laughing.

Austin slapped his hand over his heart. "You got me. I planted the snake there. If I'd only known you were such a greenhorn that I would still have to show you every little thing..."

He was a little worried he might have pushed the teasing too much, but Kelsey gave him the fake pout that girls tended to do when they were flirting and said, "Poor baby."

Wait. Was she flirting with him? Really?

She held up the pail of eggs. "I'll just run these little ol' chicken-shit-covered eggs to the house and you can start slopping Winifred." She batted her eyes at him dramatically.

Yes. She was definitely flirting.

"A Texas boy can't say no to a plea like that, even if it does come from a Yankee." This was new territory for him and he felt like he was walking across those eggs with spurs on. For once, Kelsey seemed to let go of the anger she held at her situation and have fun—they were having fun—and he didn't want it to go away.

She grinned a big cheesy grin and headed to the house, bucket of eggs in hand.

He was finishing filling Winifred's water trough when he saw Kelsey jogging down from the house. She was beautiful when she wasn't acting all surly. He was glad the smile hadn't left her face and couldn't help calling out to her, "Hey! I thought you'd probably spend the next couple of hours washing the eggs."

She stopped next to him. "Mom intercepted me. So I'm stuck with you a while longer."

"Stuck with me? Never say that to a man with a hose." He turned and nailed her in the gut with a stream of water.

She screamed and fought for the hose. He was taller and stronger and figured he could keep it mostly away from her, but the girl was quick and managed to get enough control over it to flip the stream of water into his face.

"Oh, it's on now, girl." They giggled as they wrestled

for the hose and eventually she was able to wrench it from his hands. They stood a couple of feet from each other, drenched, both a little out of breath. Austin dropped his hands to his sides. "Okay, take your best shot." He sucked in his gut and prepared for the blast of water.

She hesitated, then dropped the hose in the grass and turned the water off. "Nah. I think I'll save it for when you're not expecting it."

"Woo, I'm scared."

Water dripped off her eyelashes and nose and little curls formed around her face. She smiled up at him and said, "You should be."

Yeah, he should be. "These eyes are on you." He took a step back, stripped off his shirt, and wrung it out. "Do you want to change before we clean stalls?"

"No. This is the first time I've been cool since I've been in Texas."

He pulled the wet T-shirt over his head. "Maybe we need to add *water fight* to our daily routine."

"What we need to do is get the pool clean enough to swim in."

Kelsey headed toward the barn and Austin couldn't help but notice the way her damp tank top clung to her curves. His hands itched to explore those curves. He tried to think of something to erase the vision, like the chickens. But then he'd think of the way Kelsey's face softened and the smile that tugged at her lips as she tossed the chicken feed, and his blood threatened to run south again.

He shook his head to clear his imagination and caught up with Kelsey. "Wait before you go into the barn."

"Why?"

"I got here early and I have a surprise for you."

Kelsey stopped at the door to the tack room. "What do you mean, you have a surprise?"

"Now don't go all deer in the headlights on me. It's not bad. Go on, open the door."

She hesitated. "What did you do—rig a snake to jump out at me?"

"Yeah, that's it. No—it's a good thing." He pushed the door open and went in ahead of her.

She peeked inside the small area before entering. "So, give me a hint."

"You didn't notice?" He gave an exasperated sigh. "I swept and…" Austin opened the door leading to the stalls. He was afraid she'd balk when she saw what he'd done, so he grabbed her hand and dragged her to the concrete tie-up area.

She stared at the horses like she was looking at Godzilla. She pulled her hand from his and backed against the wall, just like Mackenzie had on their first day in Texas. "What are they doing out of their stalls?"

"It's okay, Kelsey. They're really nice guys and they'd like to meet you."

She wiggled her fingers at them and gave a weak, "Hi. Now that you've introduced us, you can put them away."

"You do live on a farm now. The horses live here too and if nothing else, you need to learn how to be safe around them."

"Can't I be safe with them in their stalls?"

He shook his head. "Not really. Come on. We'll take it slow." He tried to keep his voice soft and coaxing.

"I'm not real fond of animals that can squish me. Didn't you see *Jurassic Park*?"

"Those were dinosaurs. In case you haven't noticed, these guys are smaller and domesticated." He reached up to scratch Harry on the forehead. The horse closed its eyes.

"Maybe to you. To me, they might as well be ten feet tall."

"Come on. I promise Harry and Buster will not squish you." He took her hand. "Take a couple of steps closer to Harry. It's okay. I've got you and they're tied."

He liked the way her hand felt in his and wanted to pull her to him. Instead, he positioned her next to Harry. The gelding flared his nostrils, sending Kelsey reeling back. Austin caught her before she retreated more than a couple of steps, and led her back to the horse. "It's okay. He's just smelling you. Here, put out your hand."

"Will he bite?"

"Not unless you put your fingers in his mouth." He rubbed the flat of his fingers across the tip of Harry's nose. "See? It's okay. You try."

Carefully, she touched his nose between the nostrils. "It's so soft."

He caught a flash of a twinkle in her eye when she touched the horse's nose. She was on the brink of discovering a whole new world and if he played his cards right, it could be magical.

"Okay, we're going to stand at his shoulder." Austin moved to Harry's left side and guided Kelsey in front of him. "He won't kick you. Remember, the closer you are to the horse, the less impact he can have if he does kick. Scratch his neck, shoulders, belly—you're establishing a relationship."

Kelsey cocked her head. "What if I don't want one?"

"Then you'd miss a whole lot of fun." Austin reached around her and stroked Harry's back. "See, it's not so bad."

"It's okay." She sounded nonchalant, but she continued to pet the horse.

Austin grabbed a brush out of a grooming bucket and handed it to her. "Here, brush his back and stomach to his rump. But brush in the direction of the hair."

"Oh, now I see. This is a ploy to get me to do more work."

"You got me. Like Tom Sawyer, I'm going to have you do all of my chores so I can sit back and watch." He was joking when he said it, but that's exactly what he'd like to do. She was more than beautiful. She was graceful—poetry in motion. And he loved watching the micro expressions of pleasure play across her face. It was his little secret that the Quinn sister with an attitude hadn't figured out that she was half country, and that side of her was screaming to get out.

He spent the next half hour showing her how to move around the horse, where to stand, and how to pick up the feet. She did it all, too. But when he mentioned actually getting on the horse, she dug in her heels and said, "No."

"Come on, Kelsey. I promise I won't let go of the rope and you can just ride him around."

"A lot of good that rope will do if he takes off."

"First, he's not going to take off, and second, we'll be in the paddock so he can't go far."

"If he won't run off, why did you need 'second'?"

"Seriously? Okay, I said I wouldn't push you. But I will get you riding."

"I will not ride a horse." She stretched an arm across Harry's back and leaned against him.

Austin had to resist laughing out loud. She was going to be a natural. She was already developing an unconscious connection. "Come on, Kelsey. Aren't you a little interested?"

She reached up the horse's neck and scratched under his mane. "Nope. I will not ride a horse. Not in a box. Not with a fox. I will not ride a horse, Sam I am."

Austin released the laugh he'd been holding. "Do you remember how that book ends?"

"Yeah. But that was green eggs and ham—not giant four-legged animals." She looked him in the eyes and the air suddenly seemed charged. Austin took a step back and tried to tuck away the sizzle he felt.

He crossed the aisle to the other horse. "I'm going to brush Buster. You wanna help?"

"Sure, as long as I don't have to get on him."

Austin watched the way her body stretched as she made long, sweeping strokes across the horse's back. He was mesmerized by the way she set her mouth when she was concentrating on getting every inch of horsehair brushed.

She finished and handed the brush to Austin. "So, did I

pass?"

"Pass?"

"The way you were watching, I figured this had to be a test."

Busted. Crap. "No, you just looked so—calm. I didn't want to interfere." *Calm?* Did he really say *calm?* She was sexy as hell brushing that horse, but figured he really ought to keep that to himself. "I'd better get these horses turned out and get the stalls cleaned." He clipped a lead rope to Buster's halter and released the tie-ups.

Kelsey stood with her back against the far wall. "Don't get excited or anything, but I guess I should watch you do this, in case you can't. You know, like if you get bit by a snake or something."

9

In Texas, all criminals must give their victims 24-hour advance warning, either verbally or in writing.

After they turned the horses out into the paddock, they cleaned the stalls. When they finished, Kelsey retreated to the house. All but a few boxes had been unpacked and carted off. She'd mentioned job-hunting to Mom a couple of times, but she always put her off. Time was running out. Today was the day she was going to ask Austin to help her find a job.

She was antsy and found herself pacing around upstairs. From her parents' bedroom window, she could see Austin working with the horses. She watched him maneuver the tan horse, Buster, in small circles and large ones, changing gaits as he rode. At one point he stopped the horse and spun in small circles. She hated to admit it, but it did look a little fun.

Her phone chimed a text message—a video from Drew. She squealed and plopped onto her parents' bed to watch. Her heart pounded. This was the first video from him. Was he going to tell her he loved her? She held the phone against her heart, closed her eyes, and took a deep breath. Was this the moment she'd longed for?

She opened her eyes and pressed Play. Drew and his

brother Elliot sat next to each other in the grass, each holding a glass of white wine. "*Ciao*, Kelsey," they yelled.

A dark-haired girl with braided pigtails stuck her face in the picture. "*Ciao*, Kelsey."

The view switched back to the guys. Drew held up his glass. "Cheers, Kelsey. We're having a fabulous time. Meet our new friends, Sabine and Paul."

Drew took the camera and panned to pigtail girl and an almost buzz-cut guy. The girl held up her glass. *"Bonjour."*

Drew's voiced sounded again. "They're from Nice, France."

The girl took the camera and swung back to Drew and Elliot. "I'm sorry I haven't been able to Facetime much. It's paradise here. I wish you were with us. I miss you like crazy. I'll be home in a couple of weeks. *Ciao*."

The rest of the group echoed "*Ciao*," and the recording ended.

Kelsey played the video over and over. She studied Drew's image on the screen. His cycling shirt hugged the contours of his torso and his hair was a little shaggy, giving him sort of a reckless look that Kelsey found really sexy. God, she missed him. She tapped Play again and tried to imagine him holding her, but her mind flashed to Austin pulling off his wet T-shirt.

Talk about cut—he's ripped.

She got all tingly just thinking about their water fight. She probably shouldn't have let herself flirt with him, but it wasn't like they were going to hook up or anything. They were just having fun.

She stood and watched Austin, who was riding the other horse now. She could almost see the muscles flex in his back as he guided Harry around the paddock. He slowed to a walk and patted it on the neck. The heat, the dirt, the animals—this was Austin's paradise. She turned away from the window.

Zoe had her rich-kid life; Drew had Europe—and soon Harvard. Where did she fit in? *Nowhere* was the word that came to mind. She shuddered and headed downstairs to fix lunch.

Mom was in the kitchen packing sandwiches into a paper bag. "Hi, Kel. I'm taking sandwiches to the store for Dad and the girls."

"Do you mind if I offer a sandwich to Austin?"

"Of course not. But I'm kind of in a hurry. We have a truck coming in and I want to be there. Can you ride with him to the store this afternoon?"

Kelsey shrugged. "I'm sure I can. If not, I guess I'll just have to laze around here."

"Yeah. That's not going to happen." Mom creased a neat fold in the top of the bag. "I want you to know how much I appreciate your help. I'd never have gotten the house put together without you."

Kelsey gave a little shrug. "No problem." She was about to ask about the job again, but Mom was halfway out of the kitchen before she could get the words out. Instead, she said, "We'll head to the store right after lunch."

Mom stopped and turned. "Thanks, Kelsey. I know this isn't the life you want…"

She wanted to say that she hated it here, that it was just a means to an end, and that end was to leave Texas. But she saw the chin quiver. She didn't want to see her mom cry, not now. "But it's the life I have."

Mom nodded and gave a stiff smile. "I'll see you at the store."

Austin was eager to take her up on lunch. But instead of waiting for her to fix his sandwich like Drew always did, he fixed his own and offered to "slap one together" for her.

They sat across from each other at the kitchen table. Austin ate his sandwich in about three bites and munched on chips while he waited for Kelsey to finish hers. "You know I'm determined to get you on a horse."

"I don't think so."

"Come on, Kelsey. Nothing's gonna happen."

"Yeah. Because I'm not going to get on a horse."

"Okay, but you're missing out on a whole new world." Austin stood and gathered their plates. He practically had them washed and rinsed before Kelsey made it to the kitchen.

She rolled up the chip bag and clipped the end. "Thanks for your help."

He gave an aw-shucks grin and said, "My pleasure."

His easy manner made her smile. It was nice having him for a friend. "I guess we'd better get to the store."

"Yeah, I'll get my truck."

Kelsey rushed upstairs to freshen her makeup as much as possible. Her hair was a total disaster and she wished it were long enough to throw up into a ponytail. Instead, she clicked on her flat iron and tried to squeeze the curl out of it. When it was as good as it was going to get, she headed downstairs to the truck waiting for her in the drive.

When she stepped outside, she noticed the "happy-go-lucky" cowboy in the truck was yelling at someone on the phone. When she reached the truck, he swore and tossed his phone in the empty ashtray.

She opened the passenger door hesitantly. "Everything okay?"

"Yeah. I gotta run by the house on the way." She'd barely buckled her seatbelt before Austin whipped the truck around and tore down the gravel drive, spitting rocks behind them.

Kelsey was half-afraid to breathe, much less speak, so much anger hung in the air. On the radio, some country singer crooned about being like his dad and Austin jerked the radio off so fast Kelsey expected the knob to break off in his hand.

He flew down the farm-to-market road to his house, taking the turn by the water tower practically on two wheels. Kelsey kept a death grip on the door handle. "Austin, I don't know what's going on, but if we crash, you can't fix it."

"We're fine, Kelsey."

He kept going, foot on the accelerator, and she was

trapped. "Austin, slow down!"

He let off the accelerator, but the truck was still barreling down the highway. When they got to his house, he nearly spun out turning down the drive.

He pulled into the grass next to a beat-up red truck. Without saying a word, he jumped out of the cab and ran up the wooden steps and into his house.

Kelsey wasn't sure what to do. Should she wait in the truck? It was running, so it wasn't like she was going to roast in the heat. But what if something was wrong with his mom and he needed to call for help? He'd left his cell phone in the ashtray.

When he hadn't come out a few minutes later, Kelsey cut the engine, grabbed his cell phone, and decided to go after him. She could hear yelling as soon as she opened the passenger door. She edged to the bottom step and waited. Whatever was going on was not good. Angry words filtered through the screen door, adding weight to the heat hanging in the air.

She knew this was none of her business and she should retreat to the safety of the truck. But like watching a car wreck, she couldn't help but stay and listen.

"You sonofabitch! You don't tell me what to do!"

"Just leave, Dad."

"This is my goddamn home!"

"Leave or I'll call Jimmy. You know I will and he'll have to take you in this time."

"You good for nothin'—you'd do that, too. You ain't nothin' but a panty-ass wuss. You think you're such a man cuz you're quarterback. Tell me something, big man quarterback, who threw three interceptions in the playoff game last year? I've never been so ashamed to call you son in my life."

"That's enough, Bill. Get out." Austin's mom's voice quivered, with anger or tears, Kelsey wasn't sure.

The door burst open and a heavyset middle-aged man

stormed onto the porch. "You can't keep me away forever. This is my house."

Austin followed with his mom behind him. "The judge gave it to Mom."

The man reeled around to face Austin.

Kelsey's heart pounded. She backed toward the truck and wondered if she should call nine-one-one, or at least nine-one with her finger hovering over the other one.

Austin stood straight and tall, shielding his mom. His dad stood toe-to-toe with him and Kelsey was sure whatever was about to happen wouldn't be good.

"Go back to your apartment, Dad. There is nothing here for you."

"You got that right." His dad spat on the ground next to him and stormed down the steps. Austin didn't even flinch. His dad looked at Kelsey as he walked to his truck and yelled back at Austin, "At least this one's prettier than your last piece of ass."

Austin clenched his fist, but he didn't move. Nobody did, until the truck turned onto the highway. As soon as he was gone, a sigh of relief filled the air. Kelsey ran up the steps to Austin and his mom. She wanted to hug them both and tell them it was going to be okay. But when she reached the top of the steps, Austin backed up and stared at the ground in front of her. "Kelsey, I'm sorry. He shouldn't have said that. He's a jerk."

Kelsey shook her head. "Don't worry about me."

Austin turned to his mom. "Are you okay?"

"Yeah. Come on in. Let's get out of this heat."

Kelsey figured the inside of the trailer house would look like a rectangle chopped up into rooms. She couldn't have been more wrong. Wood floors, leather furniture, a rock fireplace, and beautiful, flowing aqua curtains—it looked like it had been cut from a design magazine.

Kelsey followed Austin to the kitchen. It was at least the size of their dilapidated one and had twice as many cabinets.

Ivy grew in pots along the tops of the cabinets. Large, medium, and small Mexican pots held plants of all sizes and shapes.

"Your home is beautiful, Mrs. McCoy."

"Thank you, darlin'. You want some tea?"

"No thanks." Kelsey followed Austin's lead and took a seat at the small oak table in the eating area.

Mrs. McCoy leaned against the counter. "Austin, I'm sorry I had to call you."

"Mom, if he comes again, call Jimmy. He can't hurt you if he's in jail."

"It's when he gets out that scares me. He has to damn near kill me to make it stick." She gave a ragged sigh. "I dunno. Maybe I should just let him have this place. It'd be worth it for peace of mind."

"He'd just want something else. It's not about the house, Mom. It's about control."

Mrs. McCoy nodded. "Yeah." She took a deep breath. "It's over now. He'll go home and drink himself into a stupor." She looked at Kelsey. "Sugar, I sure am sorry you had to see this."

Kelsey didn't know how to answer her, so she just nodded. She wanted to sink through the floor. She shouldn't be there listening to their family problems.

"Austin, you and Kelsey go on. I'm fine."

"Mom, if he comes back, you call Jimmy."

His mom nodded. "I'll call."

"Promise, Mom."

"I promise. If he comes back, I'll call Jimmy."

Austin and Kelsey stood, and Austin kissed his mom on the cheek. "Lock your doors. I have my phone if you need me."

"I'm fine, Austin."

Kelsey followed Austin to the truck, afraid to speak. She didn't want to know the ugly secret of his family any more than she wanted him to know about hers. She thought of the horrible words Austin's dad had said to him. Even with all the crap Ryan pulled, they always knew their dad loved them.

As they approached the outskirts of Hillside, Austin finally broke the silence. "I'm sorry, Kelsey."

"Is your mom going to be okay?"

"Yeah. He does this every couple of months. Mom has a restraining order against him, but she won't call the police."

"Is Jimmy the police?"

"One of them. He and Mom have been friends for a long time." Austin shook his head and laughed. "Is he the police? We're not Mayberry, you know. We do have a real police force with cop cars and everything."

"Well—I made you smile, didn't I?"

He nodded. "You do that a lot."

His words made her smile. "Sure, laugh at the urbanite learning the simple life." She poured sarcasm into her voice. "That's why I'm here, to provide you entertainment."

He rubbed the pink scar on his thumb. "That you do."

Austin stopped at a light across from the courthouse. The building still fascinated Kelsey, and she twisted her neck trying to look at the gargoyles perched on the gables.

"You want a tour of downtown?"

Anything to take his mind off what had just happened. Kelsey took a half a breath to answer. "Yes."

"Cool."

When the light changed, he turned left and pulled into a parking space in front of The Grind Coffee Shop across the street from the courthouse. "Do you want to try a Granada?"

"Does it hurt?"

"It's a drink. Come on, you have to try one."

"If I have to…" Kelsey jumped from the passenger side of the truck and waited for Austin to guide her through the door. If only it were Drew offering to buy her the drink.

10

When Texas was annexed in 1845, it retained the right to fly its flag at the same height as the national flag.

As soon as the screen door banged shut behind them, Austin smelled a mixture of coffee and perfume. A stereo "Oh my God, Austin," greeted him, followed by the source of the voices, Courtney Randall and Britney Boyd. They sat at a table near the door. The girls liked to hang on the football players, earning them the nicknames Take Me Now and Take Me Right Now. Austin hated those nicknames.

The girls rushed to his side. Courtney wrapped her hands around his bicep and positioned herself between him and Kelsey. "Austin, where have you been? We haven't seen you here in like forever."

Austin pulled from Courtney's grasp. "I've been really busy." He placed his hand on Kelsey's shoulder. "This is Kelsey Quinn. She's just moved here from Chicago."

Both girls took a step back to examine Kelsey. Britney spoke first. "Illinoise. Really. I've never been there."

Kelsey said, "Illi*noy*. The *s* is silent."

Britney flicked her hand and rolled her eyes. "Excuse me, *Ill-annoy*."

Courtney said, "So, *Ill-annoy*, why'd you move to Hillside?"

"My parents bought the feed store."

A plastic smile formed on Courtney's face. "Really. The feed store."

"Yeah." The tone in Kelsey's voice said *it sucks*. "So anyway, I'm a senior. How about you guys?"

"You guys?" Courtney looked around her mockingly and then back to Kelsey. "Oh, you mean Britney and me?"

Britney spoke up. "We're seniors." She turned to Austin. "Where have you been? We haven't seen you all summer."

"Working. Speaking of which, we've got to go." He placed a hand on the small of Kelsey's back and guided her to the counter. Leaving the girls standing in the middle of The Grind was probably a tactical error, but his tolerance for them was lower than usual. He just hoped it didn't come back to bite Kelsey on the ass. As it was, he figured they'd be twittering about Kelsey before she ordered and he'd bet his frappuccino it wouldn't be to plan a welcome reception.

"So are you ready to experience the best drink ever?"

"Sure. I'm always up for a little adventure." She flashed him a fake grin that exposed her teeth, but it was the smile behind the grin that nearly took Austin's breath away. The one where her eyes sparkled and her cheeks seemed to glow. It only lasted for a second, but he felt the impact all the way to his toes.

"May I help you?" Mrs. Hensen held an order pad in her hand. Austin looked at Kelsey, still reeling from the force of her smile. Mrs. Hensen rapped her knuckles on the counter. "Austin! You gonna order or are you gonna keep staring at that girl?"

He faced the counter and the portly woman standing behind it. "Two tall Grenadas."

Kelsey bent beneath the counter to look at the pastries inside the display case.

He reached over and touched her shoulder. "You

hungry?"

His touch surprised her and she jerked up and smacked her head on the counter. "*Oww*."

Austin felt he should hug her or pat her head or something. Instead he just sort of held his hands out toward her and hoped he didn't look too stupid. "I'm so sorry. Are you okay?"

She took a step back from him. "Yeah, fine." She rummaged through her purse and mumbled, "I have some money in here somewhere."

"Don't worry about it. My treat. After all, I injured you."

She looked up at him. "You didn't throw a snake at me."

Mrs. Hensen knocked on the counter again. "You gonna order anything else?"

Austin looked at Kelsey and waited for an answer.

"I'd like a slice of carrot cake."

Mrs. Hensen nodded. "Is that all?"

"Yes, ma'am." Austin pulled his wallet from his back pocket and handed the woman a twenty.

While they waited for their order, Austin looked around the crowded coffee shop. "There's a table next to Courtney and Britney."

"Hmm. I think you promised to show me downtown. How about if we take our drinks to go?"

"What about your carrot cake?"

"I can eat and walk."

Mrs. Hensen handed them their drinks and a slice of the cake. Kelsey slid the cake onto a napkin and followed Austin toward the exit.

As they approached the door and Courtney and Britney's table, Austin placed his hand low on Kelsey's back and ducked his head close to hers. "If I talk to you, we might get past them without being stopped." When they got to the door, he heard Courtney call to him. But instead of stopping, he rushed through, pushing Kelsey ahead of him. When they were safely outside he said, "I didn't hear anything, did you?"

"No, nothing." They headed down the sidewalk. She took a sip from her frozen drink and closed her eyes briefly. "Okay, this is amazing. It's like brown sugar and coffee. No, it's more like chocolate chip cookie dough before the flour and chocolate chips—only better."

"Wait until you taste Mrs. Hensen's carrot cake."

She balanced the slice of cake on the flat of her hand and bit off the corner. "Oh my God, this is amazing. Want some?"

"Yeah." He tore off a piece. It was good, but the feeling of her so close to him made him think crazy things, like what her lips might taste like.

With the drink in her right hand and the cake perched on her left, she struggled to take the next bite without getting cream cheese frosting all over her face. "I'm going to be a mess by the time I finish this."

"Hang on, follow me." He led her across the street to the two-foot wall surrounding the grounds of the courthouse.

They sat with their drinks next to them. Kelsey balanced the slice of cake on the flat of her hand and said, "Have some more." He pulled a bite from the cake, not because he wanted it, but because he liked the way he caught a whiff of her hair when he leaned close. She popped the last piece in her mouth and tried to wipe her hands. Bits of napkin stuck to her fingers and the more she wiped the worse it got.

She held her hands in front. "I feel like a little kid, I'm so sticky. Is there a bathroom where I can wash my hands?"

He was about to answer when her phone rang in her purse. "Will you get my phone?"

"Out of your purse?"

"Yes."

"But, that's like—no man's land."

"Come on, I can't get it."

She turned to give him access to the bag suspended from her shoulder. He gritted his teeth and reached into the purse until he felt the phone. He pulled it out and read aloud. "Call from your dad."

"Can you hold it to my ear?"

He tapped Answer and held the phone so she could talk. "Hi, Dad. What's up?" She sucked sugar off the tips of her fingers as she listened. "Austin is just showing me around town. Can we meet you in…" Kelsey looked at Austin. "…thirty minutes?" Austin nodded. "Thanks, Dad, see you then." She pulled her head away from the phone.

Austin tapped End, dropped it in her purse, and picked up her Granada. "Come on, there's a fountain on the other side."

They walked around the corner to the Fallen Heroes fountain centered in front of the west entrance of the courthouse. It was a simple design, a bronze representation of the American flag with the flags of the Army, Navy, Marines, and Coast Guard surrounding it. Water sprayed from the perimeter of the fountain toward the flags in the middle.

Austin led Kelsey down a path of engraved stones leading to the fountain. "The fountain was built after nine-eleven. The stones honor fallen soldiers dating back to the Alamo." They stopped in front of a granite stone next to the fountain. Austin read it aloud. "Edward Maccafferty. Defender of the Alamo. Died in battle March 6, 1836."

"Wow, and you want me to rinse my hands in this sacred water?"

Austin sat on the wall of the fountain and patted the seat next to him. "Come on, your hands might rot off, but other than that, it'll be fine."

Kelsey stuck her hands in the spray of water. She tried to stretch them far enough in front to avoid getting splashed, but the water ricocheted and nailed her right in the forehead. She squealed and jumped back, laughing. "Great. Now, I'm dripping wet." She dried her hands on her jeans and dabbed at her face with the sleeve of her shirt.

Austin grinned. "I didn't expect you to bathe in it."

She stuck her hand in the spray, directing it toward him. A small stream hit him in the arm but most of it deflected onto her face again. Through giggles she said, "I can't win."

He grabbed her free hand and pulled her to sit next to him. "Cut it out before you drown yourself."

She looked at him with water dripping from her bangs, down her cheeks, off her nose, and around her lips. "At least I'm not about to faint from heat exhaustion anymore."

He tried to think of something sarcastic to say but he couldn't drag his mind away from the way the water droplets sprinkled across her face made her look rejuvenated somehow, even with mascara smudged beneath her eyes. "Um, your eyes…"

Kelsey nodded. "I have raccoon eyes, don't I?"

Great, Austin, insult the girl. Way to score points. "A little, but they're not that bad." Her bangs began to curl across her forehead and he got the sense that the real Kelsey was hidden beneath the makeup and hair product. He definitely wanted to see more.

Kelsey wiped her eyes with her index finger. "I have an idea. Let's go back to The Grind and see your friends—I can really impress them now." Her tone was teasing, but her voice was laced with insecurity.

He brushed a wayward curl from the corner of her eye. "You look great to me."

She stood and looked up at the courthouse. "So tell me about this building. It seems so out of place."

Crap, I shouldn't have touched her. Austin stood next to her. "Think so?"

"Yeah, it's so—gothic."

"It's pretty cool." He pointed to the arched entrance on the corner of the building. "Do you see the faces carved in the stone?" *See? We're just friends having a boring conversation about architecture.*

"The faces on top of the columns?" She grabbed her drink and walked to the steps leading to the entrance.

Austin followed. "Yes. As we walk around the courthouse, you'll see them on all four entrances, but they change."

"Change how?"

"I'll show you. Here, Mabel—that's her name—is pretty. Now follow me." They walked to the next corner and stared up at the arched entrance. "See, Mabel is beginning to lose her good looks."

Kelsey looked in the direction Austin pointed. "Her eyes have a kind of eerie, deep-set look and her teeth are crooked."

"Yeah. The story goes that when the courthouse was built, they brought in an Italian sculptor who apparently fell in love with the daughter of the boarding-house landlady."

"Mabel."

"Right. Anyway, she didn't return his affection and as their relationship deteriorated, her likeness grew uglier and uglier."

"Really?"

"Yeah, come on." They headed down the sidewalk to the next corner.

Kelsey gazed at the stone building. "So as you walk around the building you see the fall of a relationship. Or is it that a beautiful woman is unmasked to reveal her real self?" They stopped and studied the next set of carvings. "Yikes, she's morphing into a witch."

"Just wait."

They walked to the fourth corner of the building. Austin watched Kelsey study the carvings. Soft curls fell around her face and he noticed freckles dotting her nose that he hadn't seen before. Her blue eyes were big and curious.

She looked closer. "Man, he must have really hated her. She's monstrous." Her gaze fell to him, and then jerked back to the building.

Damn. She'd caught him staring.

She stepped back from the entrance. "An immortal illustration of unrequited love. Harsh."

He hoped she wasn't making some weird veiled reference to him staring at her. She was cute, that was all. He moved next to her. "It depends on how you look at it."

"Huh?"

"The whole unrequited love thing." Austin led Kelsey back the direction they'd come. "I always wonder if legend has it wrong. Maybe she became more beautiful as he got to know her. It's all in how you look at it."

"And the path you take." Kelsey squinted at Austin. "I like that."

He gave a shrug. "I like happy endings."

Kelsey nodded. They were silent as they retraced their steps to the fountain, but as they walked, their arms brushed against each other. It was all Austin could do to keep from grabbing her hand. Instead, he looped a reminder in his brain that she had a boyfriend.

When they reached the fountain, her phone played a tune signaling a call. Her face lit up when she pulled it from her purse. "Drew! You called!"

She sat on the wall surrounding the fountain and Austin stepped away to give her privacy. He pretended to study the beautiful faces above the columns, but he had positioned himself to have a clear view of the sun-kissed girl perched on the fountain wall.

But the girl pulled a mirror from her purse and, with her cell balanced between her shoulder and ear, was messing with her hair and makeup. She did a lot of smiling and nodding but it looked about as real as the faces on the courthouse. The conversation didn't last long. She dropped the phone into her purse, pulled out a tube of lip gloss, and smoothed it across her mouth. Austin hated to kiss a girl with that stuff on her lips.

But he wasn't going to kiss this girl. She was taken.

*

Kelsey took a deep breath and stood. "I guess we should go to the feed store."

Austin wiped sweat from his forehead with his forearm. "Yeah, probably so." They headed for his truck. "So, your boyfriend called. Is he still in Europe?"

"Yes. But he's coming home early." She tried to look happy, like it was a good thing.

Austin nudged her with his shoulder. "He couldn't stay away, huh?"

"His parents have a lake house and are insisting they spend the rest of the summer together as a family. So—he won't be coming to Texas anytime soon." She shrugged as though it didn't matter, but it did. Drew was her tie to everything she wanted. He kept her focused on what mattered.

"That sucks."

"Yeah, well, that's pretty much my life, lately."

"You do mention that a lot."

Wow, she did mention it a lot. She was feeling sorry for herself and Austin was dealing with the dad from hell. "I do, don't I? I've been kind of a jerk. I just need to find a job so I can go to Chicago."

"No luck, huh?"

"Since I don't have a car, I don't have a way to get to town to look." *Please say you'll take me, please say you'll take me.*

"I can take you."

"Really? That would be so awesome."

"Sure. If we get an early start tomorrow, we can go before we have to be at the feed store."

"Thank, you!" She went in for a hug, but only made it halfway to full body contact because crazy sparks zinged between them. She let her arms fall to her sides and stepped back. "We'd better get to the store."

"Yeah. I don't want to get you in trouble."

Speaking of which... "Hey, Austin?"

"Yeah?"

"I don't exactly have permission to look for a job. I want

to surprise them."

"Okay." He clicked Unlock on his key fob. "I can keep a secret."

They were both quiet as they drove to the store. Normally, Kelsey would feel uncomfortable in the silence and try to fill the space with awkward conversation. She didn't feel that way with Austin. What she did feel scared the hell out of her.

Crazy stuff swirled inside her. All sorts of sparks were flying. Kelsey wasn't sure when she'd noticed the electricity. Maybe in the coffee house when he'd placed his hand on her back. Or maybe when she'd sprayed her face at the fountain. Whenever it started, she was fully into flirt mode before she realized it. And then, he walked so close to her, her arm hairs stood on end. What was that all about?

Drew was her boyfriend. He was everything she ever wanted in a guy. Drew gave her security and now Austin had come along and turned everything sideways.

11

In Port Arthur, Texas, obnoxious odors may not be emitted while in an elevator.

Austin parked in front of the Early Bird Café. Kelsey was half out of the truck before he had a chance to turn off the engine. The plan was for Austin to wait for her in the coffee shop while she popped into one of the boutiques and landed a job. In her head, getting a job would be a breeze. Surely the stores would jump at the chance to hire a young, fashionable salesperson.

In reality, not so much. She tried every old-lady store and a couple of junk shops posing as antique stores. The answer was pretty much the same everywhere. *We don't need any extra help, but if you want, you can leave your name and number in case something changes.* With twenty minutes left to get to the feed store, she'd run out of options.

The door to the café was propped open and the floor fans roared on high. Defeated and deflated, she crossed the threshold. Austin stood as soon as he saw her and said, "No luck, huh?"

"I tried pretty much every store on the square."

"There's always the diner."

Waitress in a redneck café? Could she do it? What choice did she have? Besides, she only needed about six hundred dollars for the airline ticket. The gala was still a little over a month away. She'd probably only have to work a few shifts to earn that kind of money. "Do you think they'll hire me?"

He shrugged. "I don't know. Let's find out."

Kelsey watched Mrs. McCoy fill coffee cups at a table of old men. She wore the same *Cowboy Up!* T-shirt she'd worn the first time Kelsey had seen her. Then she'd thought the woman looked like a trailer-trash waitress in a redneck café. Now, she was about to ask that woman for a job. This was her last option. If Mrs. McCoy turned her down, Kelsey could kiss Chicago good-bye.

After the last cup was topped off, Austin spoke up. "Mom, do you have a minute? Kelsey needs to talk to you."

"Sure, honey." Mrs. McCoy set the coffee pot on an empty table and walked to where they stood.

Kelsey took a deep breath. "I—I need a job. Austin said you might need some help."

Mrs. McCoy raised her brows. "I'll have to talk to the boss, but we can usually use an extra hand around here. Can you work the lunch rush?"

"Absolutely. When is it?"

"Eleven to two."

"That's perfect." *I hope.*

"Hang on, let me talk to T-bone." She grabbed the pot and disappeared through the kitchen door.

T-bone? Seriously?

Kelsey looked around the café. It had only been a little over a week since she'd been in here with her family, but it was if she were seeing it for the first time. It was more than a bunch of tacky decorations. Hillside's history was chronicled on the walls. She studied a yellowed newspaper that declared the war was over. "Reading this stuff is like a history lesson."

Austin nodded. "Look at this one."

She followed him to a black and white photo of three men standing at a bar. They looked like something from a western movie. They all had bushy mustaches, were dressed western, and had one boot resting on the rail around the base of the bar. "Who are they?"

"I don't know. But the bar is what is now The Grind—the place we had the Grenada."

"Oh, yeah. Wow, that's so cool."

"Sometimes when I go to The Grind, I try to imagine those men standing at the bar. I even gave them names. Billy, Sammy, and Tommy."

"Why those names?"

"I don't know—I was like five."

About a foot away from the men was a color photograph of a football player holding a giant trophy. "That's my dad." It was weird seeing pictures of her dad plastered around town. It was like looking at a stranger. A longing to know the boy in the picture tugged at her.

"Yeah, and that's the state champion trophy. It's crazy that he never told you about his football days."

"He never talked about Hillside at all—except for Uncle Jack and Aunt Susan. The only cousins we have are on Mom's side." Why hadn't he talked about his glory days? It had to have something to do with the girl Aunt Susan had mentioned. She was sure unearthing the mystery of Cassidy Jones would expose the skeletons in her dad's past. Was she willing to do that?

Oh yeah—more than willing.

In the front of the diner, near the cash register, she noticed laminated posters of Austin and Travis in their football jerseys. Each was headed with their name and position. The smile Austin usually wore was replaced by a stoic expression. It looked uncomfortable on his face and she wondered if he'd been told not to smile.

"Handsome boys, aren't they?"

Kelsey turned from the pictures and blushed. "I didn't

hear you come back."

Mrs. McCoy stood next to a wiry, gray-haired man wearing a white apron over a sleeveless T-shirt and jeans. He held a rag in his hands and an unlit cigarette drooped from the corner of his mouth.

"This here is T-bone. He owns the place. T, this is Kelsey Quinn."

He spoke around the cigarette. "When can you start?"

"Tomorrow?"

"Can you be here at ten?"

"Sure." *I think.*

"I'll try you two days a week, then we'll talk." He turned and walked back into the kitchen.

"Okay." Kelsey tried to give a casual chuckle but it got caught in the back of her throat and sounded more like she'd choked on a giant loogie or something.

Mrs. McCoy smiled at Kelsey. "Don't let him scare you. He don't talk much, but he won't bite."

"Is there anything I need to do before tomorrow?" *Besides talk my parents into letting me work?*

"Nah. Try to get here a little early so we can fill out paperwork and go over a few things." Mrs. McCoy looked at Austin. "I don't work late tonight, so I'll be fixing dinner."

"Okay. I get off at six. I'll see you then."

She nodded. "I'll see you tomorrow, Kelsey."

"I'll be here." She held her breath to keep from squealing and forced herself to take normal steps to the door. But as soon as she was on the sidewalk, she let a broad grin form and jumped from the sidewalk to the street two feet below.

Austin followed and opened the door for her. "That went well."

Kelsey was still grinning when she got into the truck. "And I start tomorrow. Chicago, here I come."

"Cool. Buckle up, we've got five minutes to get to the store."

*

"Tomorrow? What happened to making sure it works with our schedule?" Mom and Dad stood shoulder to shoulder—a united force, set on ruining her life.

"You said I could get a job. I got a job. It's only for a few hours a couple of days a week. What's the big deal? This morning we finished the chores by nine-thirty. Besides, what I don't get done before work, I'll finish when I get home."

Dad tossed his feed store cap on the rickety backroom table. "And when will you be available to help in the store?"

"You're being unfair. I'm the only one cleaning up after the animals. I'm the only one bringing in actual money, and you want me to work here too?"

Mom looked at Dad. "She has a point, Tom."

Kelsey took a deep breath and tried to release some of the anger she felt. "Dad, you're always saying I need to be more responsible. That's what I'm trying to do. Look, I'll do my chores in the morning, work at the café, and when you need an extra hand at the store, I'll do that too. It's not like I have a life here anyway." She shouldn't have thrown that last barb, but fortunately her parents ignored it.

"How are you going to get to work?"

"Mom could take me, or Austin could drop me off on his way to the store."

Dad looked at Mom. "Okay."

"Really?" Kelsey wanted to jump up and down, but instead smiled and nodded. "Thanks. I promise you won't regret it."

Austin wandered into the back room dragging the flatbed cart. "Mrs. Benson is picking up some cedar shavings."

"I'll help you load them." Kelsey looked at her dad. "See, I can do both."

He didn't say anything but gave her a *we'll see* look.

She practically skipped to Austin. He pulled a bag of

shavings from a shelf and smiled. "You look happy."

"Dad's okay with me starting tomorrow."

"Cool. Just don't let T-bone give you any crap." He reached for the next bag and his shoulder bumped hers, knocking her slightly off balance. She righted herself and playfully crashed into his. A game of who-can-shoulder-bump-the-hardest was born. He shoved her hard enough to make her lose her footing and she'd have fallen into the shavings if he hadn't caught her and pulled her upright.

He'd held her hand for a couple of seconds at most. But little zingers pulsed through her anyway. It didn't mean anything—it was just a reaction. She'd have been able to ignore it, pretend she'd imagined it—if she hadn't looked him in the eyes.

The second her gaze met his, those zingers went full force. She couldn't take her eyes away from his and wondered if he felt the same insane tingles.

And then he looked away and grabbed the next sack. "How many bags have we loaded so far?"

"Eight."

"I'll get the rest. I think Ryan might need some help up front."

Crap! He thinks I have a thing for him. "Okay. I want to text Drew anyway." *That'll show him.*

But before she texted Drew, she called Zoe. "Guess what?"

"You're moving back?"

"Only in my dreams. But I have almost as good news. I got a job."

"And that's good news how?"

"Because I'm earning money to come to the gala."

"Kelsey, I can give you money for tickets. You don't need to work."

"My parents would never allow you, or anybody else, to pay my way."

"We don't have to tell them."

"They're broke, not stupid. Besides, I like that I'm earning my own way. It makes me feel—I don't know—independent."

Zoe laughed like that was the funniest thing she'd heard in a long time. "I feel independent when I slide that plastic across the scanner."

Kelsey gave a fake chuckle back. "Yeah, I remember those days."

"Oh, Kelsey. I didn't mean it that way. I'm glad you're coming. It doesn't matter how you get here. So tell me about this job."

"Do you remember me telling you about the little café'?"

"The one with the trailer-trash waitress? Seriously? You're working there?"

"Yeah." She should have told her that the waitress was really nice, but she didn't. Zoe had already made her feel bad about having to work. She didn't want to give her any more ammo. "Call it a study in redneckness."

"That's epic. When do you start?"

"Tomorrow."

"I can't wait to hear about it."

*

Austin stopped at the light a block from the café. "You're quiet. Are you nervous?"

"No." She tried to sound casual, but her voice had a little quiver in it anyway.

"You're going to do great."

"I'm not worried." How hard could it be?

"I know, I'm just saying you've spun that phone around in your hand so much I'm surprised you haven't peeled the cover off."

She stopped in mid-turn and dropped the phone in her purse. "I'm just thinking about home. I can't wait to go back."

Austin parked in front of the café. "Text when you get off."

"Yes, Mom." She opened the door and took a deep breath. "Thanks for the ride."

"Sure. I'll see you later." Kelsey could feel his gaze on her as she climbed the steps to the diner. She hesitated at the door, took a deep breath, and headed in.

Mrs. McCoy stood with a coffee pot hanging from her hand talking to some old men. "There's our new girl now. This is Kelsey. Now, y'all be nice to her."

A tiny, freckle-faced man wearing a straw cowboy hat smiled at her. "I hope you do a better job than Sandy."

A red-faced man leaned back in his chair. "Just keep our cups full and the coffee hot and you'll be okay."

Mrs. McCoy swatted in the general direction of the red-faced man. "Shoot. You drink a pot of coffee before the rest of us get here."

"Somebody's got to get the place going." He smiled at Kelsey. "Half the town has a set of keys to this place. First one up starts the coffee."

"Oh, that's convenient."

Mrs. McCoy said, "Unless you forget to turn off the burglar alarm. Come on, Kelsey, let's get those papers filled out."

She led Kelsey to a tiny office nestled in the back of the kitchen, where she had her sign a W-something that had to do with taxes. *Taxes? I have to pay taxes?* After that, she handed her a white apron and took her back to an area adjacent to the kitchen. A long, stainless-steel counter was piled with dirty dishes. The counter emptied into a stainless-steel sink with a faucet that arched high above it. Next to that was a boxy-looking thing that Mrs. McCoy said was a dishwasher. "Come on, I'll give you a tour of the kitchen."

T-bone chopped onions at what she learned was called the prep table. Kelsey remembered Austin's advice about not letting the man intimidate her and took half a breath. "Good morning, T-bone."

He didn't look up, but sort of grunted and nodded. He looked at Mrs. McCoy and said, "Sandy, you got her washing those dishes yet?"

"Good grief, T, give her a chance to learn where things are first."

"She don't need to know nothing except where the dishwasher is."

They retreated to the cleanup area and she showed Kelsey how to rinse dishes and work the machine. "Okay, let me see you do a load before I turn you loose."

Kelsey squeezed the handle on the spray head hanging over the sink and rinsed bits of egg and some white stuff that looked like watered-down, gritty paste off a plate, and placed it in the rack below the box. When the rack was full, she pulled the box over it and pushed the button.

"Good. I'm going to check on my table. Grab that tub and see if there are any dishes that need clearing."

And that was the moment Kelsey realized that she was not going to be a *waitress* in a redneck diner, she was the *dishwasher* in a redneck diner. Her job was to pick up after people she didn't know, rinse their half-eaten food off the dishes, and throw away napkins that had been coughed, nose-blown, and spat in. Her stomach churned.

Chicago—gala—Drew. I can do this.

She grabbed the tub and followed Mrs. McCoy to the dining room.

Great. Britney Boyd and Courtney Randall were ordering from a menu. Maybe they wouldn't remember her from the coffee shop. She ducked her head and cleared plates from an empty table across from where the girls sat.

"Hey, Courtney, isn't that *Illanoise* bussing tables?"

Kelsey wanted to correct the mispronunciation, but continued to stack dishes-of-grossness in the tub.

Tables filled, customers ate, and then left disgusting dishes for her to clear and clean for the next two hours. She dodged a few more snarky comments from the girls, but was too busy trying to keep her breakfast down to think about it—until the girls finished their lunch.

They stood at the cash register receiving change from Mrs. McCoy and called to Kelsey, "Hey, we left you a special tip."

Yeah. I bet you did. She nodded and gave a sarcastic, "Thanks."

That *special tip* was a plate of mashed potatoes, ranch dressing, and ketchup mixed together. So what, she could handle that. The glasses stopped her. They were upside down, full of soda. She couldn't clear them without dumping coke all over the table.

Mrs. McCoy *tsk*ed from behind her. "I hate when kids do that. Sometimes you can hold your tub under the table ledge and scoot the glass over until it dumps."

"How do they do that?"

"They put cardboard over the top, turn it upside down, and slide out the cardboard. We quit using coasters because they're the perfect size for this stunt."

Kelsey tried the scoot-the-glass-to-the-edge trick, but the soda spilled anyway.

Mrs. McCoy shook her head. "Well, you've been initiated. Welcome to the Early Bird."

Kelsey cleaned up the mess. *Chicago—gala—Drew.*

The rest of the afternoon went by with the normal grossness of bussing tables. T-bone never spoke to her directly. Instead, he would yell directions at Mrs. McCoy for "the girl." That was fine with Kelsey. When the rush slowed and Kelsey finished loading the last round of dishes, Mrs. McCoy called her aside.

"You did real good, Kelsey. T wants to know if you can work Monday through Friday until school starts."

"I think so." *Or until I earn enough money to go to Chicago, but I'm not telling you that.*

"Well, ask your parents. You are working tomorrow,

right?"

"Yes, ma'm."

"Okay, we're good here if you want to text Austin."

"Thank you." Kelsey texted *I'm done* as she spoke.

T-bone poked his head around the corner of the kitchen and yelled, "Sandy, tell the girl her lunch is at the counter."

"She heard, T, along with half the town." She looked at Kelsey. "That's about as close to a pat on the back as you'll ever get."

Kelsey smiled. "I didn't realize I was hungry. Now I'm starving."

"Hang up your apron and go eat."

Kelsey found a hamburger and fries waiting for her. Mrs. McCoy brought her a Dr. Pepper, grabbed a salad, and sat next to her at the bar.

"Well, Miss Kelsey, what do you think of your first day at the diner?"

"It was good. I'll never leave a gross mess for the busboy again."

"Learned something, huh?"

"Yeah."

"I guess things are a mite bit different here than in Chicago."

"Oh, yes."

"Austin said you were catching on to the farm life. He said you were a real natural."

"Really?" *Cuz he told me that I gripe about it all the time.*

"He said you smile when you feed the chickens."

"I do?"

"Well, he'd probably kill me if he knew I shared that with you."

Awkward silence filled the air between them. Kelsey searched for conversation. "Mrs. McCoy…"

"Call me Sandy, honey."

"Okay, Sandy. Did you know my dad?"

"I was a few years younger than your dad. But I reckon everybody knew who he was—especially when he gave up football."

"Why did he give it up?"

"There were lots of rumors, but you know how school can be."

"My aunt said something about some girl—Cassidy Jones?"

Mrs. McCoy—Sandy—raised her brows and lowered the corners of her mouth in a *huh* kind of way. "Love can make the heart do crazy things. I guess your daddy is the best one to answer that question."

"Yeah. He doesn't talk about his school days. Before we moved here, I never really thought about what high school was like for my parents."

"You were probably too busy having your own experience. Do you like school?"

"I liked Saint Monica's. I can't believe I'm missing my senior year there."

"It's hard moving and leaving your friends behind, but it can be an adventure too. Your friends won't forget you."

"Yeah. I know. Mom says sometimes you make sacrifices for the ones you love. Is it really a sacrifice if you don't have a choice?"

"Maybe she wasn't talking about you."

That stopped Kelsey. She'd never considered that her mom was actually sacrificing anything. Sure, her mom had a few friends, but wasn't her life mostly the family? Other than wearing cute clothes to volunteer events, what had her mom given up?

She didn't have time to think about it for long because Austin came barreling through the door. "Hey, everybody."

Sandy turned toward the door. "Pull up a stool. We were just talking about school."

Austin sat next to Kelsey and snitched a fry from her plate. "I can't believe summer is almost over. Football practice starts next week." He bumped elbows with Kelsey. "Are you ready to become a Hillside Hornet?"

"Let's say I'm ready to get this year over with."

"Get it over with?" Sandy looked at her like she'd just insulted the flag or something. "You might want to be careful what you wish for—the next thing you know, you'll be crossing that stage wondering where it went."

Austin stood. "She's got a boyfriend waiting for her. I don't think she's too worried about her senior year."

Kelsey smacked him on the arm. "It's not just about Drew." *And do you really care?*

"Well you aren't gonna hurry up the year, so you might as well enjoy the ride." Sandy looked at Austin. "Are you two heading back to the feed store?"

"Yeah, why?"

"No reason. Jenny can't come in until six, so I'm working late tonight."

Kelsey finished her burger and stood to clear the plates, but Sandy stopped her. "I've got it. You go on."

Kelsey gathered her purse and left the diner behind Austin. *Enjoy the ride? What ride? I'm stuck in the middle of nowhere, with no friends.* She watched Austin jump off the sidewalk to the street. *Okay, one friend. But this isn't Chicago and he's not Drew.*

Kelsey didn't realize how tired she was until she sat in Austin's truck. She leaned her head against the back of the seat and closed her eyes.

He started the engine and said, "How was your first day?"

"Exhausting. I didn't know I was going to be a busboy. People are really gross."

"I've done that job before. I'd rather scoop shit than pick up what people leave on their plates. The worst is the ranch dressing floating in the tub."

"With ketchup and soggy bread." She peeped at him with one eye. "Okay, now I'm nauseous—thanks. I don't know how I'm going to heave feed sacks. I'm so tired. Carrying all those dishes gets heavy."

"That's what you've got me for. This is like strength training for football."

Football. School. Her stomach tightened. She opened her eyes and leaned her back against the door so she could face Austin. "Tell me about school here."

"Like what?"

"I don't know—anything."

"School is just school. But the football games are epic." Austin's whole face lit up. It reminded her of the way Ryan looked after finishing a sculpture she'd been working on, or Mackenzie when she nailed a new skill in gymnastics. Kelsey had never felt that passionate about anything. Sometimes she was a little jealous of her sisters, but the truth was, emotions just didn't run that deep with her.

"Epic? Really?" She couldn't help poking a little fun at Austin.

"The whole freaking town comes to our home games."

"I guess there's nothing else to do on Friday night."

"Nothing else?" He put his hand over his heart dramatically. "What more do you need?"

She laughed at his gesture. "Seriously, I am in Hickville."

"No, you are in heaven. You just haven't figured it out yet."

"So far I've seen snakes and crazy heat. Are you sure you've got that right?"

Austin looked at her with those eyes that always seemed to be smiling. "That's the way I see it."

She tried to come up with a snappy retort, but kind of got lost in his gaze and things got all wonky feeling in the truck. She stared out the window until she could speak coherently. "So the girls from the coffee shop came in today."

"Courtney and Britney?"

She closed her eyes briefly. *God, how can he sound so*

normal when my heart is racing? "Yeah. What's the story with them?" She glanced at him. A normal thing to do, except her heart was pounding in her chest.

"They like football players and hate girls that aren't in their group. Most of the girls are afraid of them. Why, something happen?"

"Not really." *Breathe. Don't look at him.* "They left me an upside-down glass of coke to clean up. No biggie."

"They can be real bitches. Don't worry, I've got your back."

"Do I look worried?"

"A little."

"Pshh, I can handle them." *It's you that scares me.*

12

In Texas, it is illegal to spit on the sidewalk.

Her parents agreed to Monday through Friday at the café. It didn't take her long to get into a routine. Chores in the morning, work the lunch rush, help at the store until time to close. Work, work, and more work. But it was okay because Austin was there.

She still had those awkward moments when her heart beat too fast, but it was obvious that he wasn't interested in more than friendship. And besides, she had Drew. He was her cure for Austinitis. All she had to do was text Drew. He'd answer with something sweet and she'd think about her goal and the money that was slowly building. If she was lucky, she'd have the money for airfare in plenty of time for the gala.

When Austin started football practice, things changed. He still came to the farm to work with the horses, but didn't get there until it was time for her to leave for work. Every morning, her mom and sisters rode to the store with her dad, leaving her with the clunker truck.

Most days, Austin stopped by the diner on his way to the feed store. She found herself watching the clock for him.

When he walked through the screen door, she couldn't help the smile that formed on her lips. They'd sit at the bar, share a plate of fries, and talk about nothing. And in the late afternoon, when they worked at the store, he teased with her sisters. He was the big brother they'd never had. He'd become a part of their family.

As football practice stepped up, Kelsey saw less of Austin and thought more about the impending first day of school. She didn't want to admit she was nervous. After all, she'd been to one of the top private schools in Chicago. She was bound to be eons ahead of these kids. But there was the other side of school, the part that had nothing to do with academics and everything to do with survival.

Normally, before the first day, her mom would take the girls shopping. They wore uniforms, but they still got to buy the latest fashions along with their needed supplies. It didn't matter that Kelsey was in high school; she loved the smell of the supplies. There was something about new spiral notebooks and packages of pens that made her feel like a kid opening a box of sixty-four crayons for the first time.

This year, there was no shopping for clothes. Instead of buying the spiral notebooks with the cool, colorful patterns on the cover and perforated pages, they bought the discount solid-color ones. Kelsey knew it shouldn't matter. It was just a place to take notes, no big deal. But instead of getting a fresh box of sixty-four crayons, it felt like she got the twenty-four pack of off-brand that never really colored right.

But her notebook trauma was nothing compared to the first day of school. August twenty-sixth had come way too early. Thank God Austin had offered to drive them to school; otherwise, they'd have to have their mom to take them in—not an option—or ride the bus—completely not an option.

Kelsey was excused from farm chores on the first day of school but she was up extra early anyway. They all were. And nerves ran high in the Quinn household.

Kelsey dug through her miniscule closet for the tenth

time looking for the perfect outfit. For eleven years her school clothes had been dictated to her and she'd hated it. Now that she had the freedom to choose, she didn't know how she was ever going to figure out what to wear.

She tried texting Zoe, but since the term at St. Monica's didn't start until September, she was probably still asleep and Kelsey wasn't surprised when she didn't answer. Kelsey had laid out a skirt and top the night before, but decided she didn't want to look like she'd put too much time into her outfit. This morning, she tried on three pairs of jeans and five tops and still hadn't come up with an answer.

She was about to try combo number six when Ryan came into her room. For the past two years Ryan had gone to an art magnet school and hadn't had to wear uniforms. She was used to figuring out what to wear.

"Do I look okay, Kel?"

Kelsey appraised her sister's attire. She wore sneakers, jeans, and a paint-splattered tee with sort of a Jackson Pollock look. Her super-short hair was more subdued than usual, but still had a trendy anime spiked look. Ryan didn't wear much makeup, but she didn't need to. She was blessed with perfect porcelain skin.

Kelsey shrugged. "You look cute. Not too dressed up, not too dressed down. I don't know what to wear. Everything I've put on either screams *I'm trying too hard* or *I'm not trying enough.*"

Ryan looked at the clothes strewn across the bed. "You can't figure out what to wear? Clothes are your favorite pastime."

"This isn't Chicago. What do they wear here?"

Ryan rolled her eyes. "It's still high school."

"I'm lost without my uniform."

Ryan picked a periwinkle blouse off Kelsey's bed and threw it at her. "Wear this. It will make the color in your eyes pop. Austin will love it."

"Austin?" She stood in her bra and panties holding the

blouse and trying not to feel the heat crawling up her body. "What do you mean, Austin?"

Ryan looked away from Kelsey and shrugged. "Just saying."

"We're just friends."

"Uh-huh."

"Ryan, I'd never cheat on Drew." She wanted to be mad at her sister, but a stupid smile kept her from it.

"Too bad—wear the blue anyway." Ryan left Kelsey staring at the blouse.

So what if she wore it? It didn't mean she was trying to impress Austin. It was the rest of the school that mattered to her. She wore the blouse and her favorite pair of jeans. Sophisticated, but not snobby. She flat-ironed her hair and applied her makeup to perfection—but not for Austin.

She met Mackenzie at the top of the stairs. Her sister wore a long-sleeved boyfriend shirt and a denim pencil skirt. "Long sleeves, Kenzie? Are you crazy? It's two hundred degrees out there."

Her sister blushed. "I—I know. This is what I want to wear."

Kelsey shrugged. "Okay. You look great—just hot."

Kenzie clunked down the stairs. "Let's just get this day over with."

*

Kelsey stepped on to the porch and smiled. Austin sat in the wicker chair sipping coffee, just as he'd done on those first few mornings they'd worked together.

He set his cup on the coffee table. "Morning, Kelsey. Ready for school?"

She took a deep breath. "As ready as I'll ever be."

She and her sisters followed him to his truck. He tapped the steering wheel with his fingers while Kelsey climbed into the passenger seat and her sisters sat in the back.

"Here we go." He backed out and headed toward the highway.

Ryan leaned forward. "Anything weird we should expect?"

"Nah. You can't go into the building until the ten-minute bell rings. Oh, and we have a closed campus, so you have to eat in the cafeteria."

Kelsey listened while Austin and Ryan talked about the horrors of school cafeteria rules. Even Mackenzie joined in the conversation. But Kelsey was too nervous to talk. She wouldn't admit that she wanted to be accepted by the girls in this school, but she did. She shuddered at the thought of being one of those kids in the lunchroom who sat at the loser table, or worse, by themselves. She wished she'd noticed how the girls here dressed, but she'd been too busy working since they'd arrived in Texas.

By the time they got to the school, the parking lot was almost full. Austin drove to a space in the first row and pulled in. Kelsey glanced at him. "You lucked out."

"We have assigned spots and senior football players get first pick."

"Seriously?" Kelsey shook her head.

"I know it's lame, but hey, I didn't make the rules. I just get to pick the best space."

When Austin shifted into Park, Kelsey felt her heart lurch into her throat. This was it. Her senior year. The year she was the new kid. The year her perfect world traveling along a perfect path wobbled out of control, landing her in the midst of a place with different people, customs, and language. And they would watch her. They'd analyze how she dressed—every move, every word—and an unspoken decision would be made dictating where she fit into their society.

She took a deep breath, let it out slowly, and opened the door of the truck.

She and her sisters walked together in a clump around

Austin. She was closest to him and secretly wanted to hang on to his arm. Not to make a claim on him, but for an added bit of security as she navigated these choppy waters. They hadn't walked far when several guys who, judging by their size, must be football players, yelled at Austin.

He mumbled to the girls, "I'll be right back," and jogged to his friends.

Kelsey stood in the parking lot with her sisters and waited. She turned to Mackenzie and Ryan and saw their wild-eyed look. She knew exactly how they felt. It was if they were rushing toward the rapids and their paddle had been taken away.

Kelsey swallowed and said, "Come on. We can find our classes, right?"

Ryan pulled her schedule out of her purse. "Yeah. I have Spanish. Mackenzie, you have history, right?"

"Yes. I think I know where it is."

Despite the uneasiness she felt, Kelsey adjusted her purse strap on her shoulder and faced the school. "Let's go."

"What about Austin?" Ryan asked.

Kelsey glanced over at him. "He's got friends to catch up with. Besides, we don't need him to babysit us."

The crowd of kids grew thicker as they neared the building and Kelsey felt their stares appraising the new girls in school. Her steps slowed and her sisters moved closer to her as they picked their way down the halls.

They came to an open area by the offices. Excited chatter laced with squeals of reunited friendships filled the air, and yet, amidst it all, Kelsey heard her heart pounding in her ears. For the first time in her life, she was the girl on the outside looking in. The Queen Bee had lost her crown and scepter.

She stopped next to a pillar and pulled her schedule from her notebook. "I go to room one-fourteen in C hall. How about y'all?"

Ryan's and Kenzie's classes were in B hall. Her sisters

split off in one direction and Kelsey the other.

She held her notebook close to her chest as she drifted through the river of kids. She didn't look at the ones standing by their lockers, but she felt their eyes—natives wary of the intruder. She struggled to find the perfect expression. Too smiley and she'd look desperate. Too serious equaled stuck up. And then there was the fact that she didn't really know where she was going. She didn't want to look like a loser staring at the numbers above the doors.

The five-minute bell sounded and everybody began to move into the classrooms. Kelsey was stuck in the hall, not sure which way to go.

"Hey, where are ya going?" A voice sounded from behind. Kelsey felt heat crawl up her neck to fill her face. Busted. She looked as lost as she felt.

She turned to a girl with a head full of curly red hair. A quick glance at the just-right amount of blush dusting her cheeks and the not-too-heavy eyeshadow and she knew this girl had to be one of the populars. Oh joy, Courtney and Ashley stood a few feet away watching. This was a test. How she handled this situation would have consequences that would extend to the lunchroom and beyond. She forced confidence into her voice and answered. "One-fourteen, AP English."

A slow smile spread across the girl's face. "Two doors down on the right."

Kelsey felt her shoulders relax. She'd passed. "Thanks."

"No problemo." The girl turned and walked back to her friends.

For a fleeting moment, Kelsey wished the girl had introduced herself, but she supposed it was too early in the game for that kind of approval. So she forced her feet to move in the direction of one-fourteen.

Just as she reached the doorway, Austin slid next to her. "Whoa, where are you going?"

"AP English."

"This is World Geography. See all the maps on the walls?"

Kelsey felt defeat all the way to her toes. She backed away from the door. "I was misinformed. Where is one-fourteen?"

"Across the hall."

Kelsey looked in time to see the redheaded girl disappear into the room Austin indicated. "Great."

Austin regarded her with a puzzled look. "You okay?"

"I'm good."

"Hey, I'm sorry about this morning. I didn't mean to leave y'all."

"It's no big deal. I found my way—ish."

"Wait for me after class and I'll show you where to go."

"I'll be here." She took a deep breath and headed into AP English. She scanned the seats and the faces that occupied them. There were two vacant seats. One by the redheaded girl and the other in the back row by some emo loser.

If she was going to win this power struggle, she couldn't back away from Red. She took a deep breath, stood a little taller, and headed to the seat next to Red. She forced a confident smile on her face and said, "Thanks for saving me a seat." She could almost see the girl mentally stumble. Red had no idea who she was playing with.

To her credit, she recovered quickly and said, "Actually, I was saving it for someone else."

"Too bad they're late, then."

Red jutted her lower jaw forward in a half-pissed, half-pout expression. She was waiting for the girl to think up a retort when Travis came in the room. Red jumped from her seat and gave him a hug. "Hey, Trav. I tried to save you a seat." She glared at Kelsey.

Travis turned to Kelsey and hugged her as best as he could, considering Kelsey had not jumped to her feet upon his arrival. "Hey, Kelsey." He indicated the redhead and said, "This is Sabrina Stevens. Hey, we'll talk after class." He looked around the room and took the seat next to the emo guy.

Kelsey let a soft smile form on her lips as she turned to face the front and listen to Mr. Shipley talk about the upcoming assignments. She had no idea what Sabrina thought, but hoped she was a little intimidated by Kelsey's fortitude.

13

In Texarkana, owners of horses may not ride them at night without taillights.

Mr. Shipley made all of the students say their names and tell one thing about themselves. Almost everybody was involved in either band or sports. Several were on the rodeo team. Rodeo team? Now that was something she'd never see at St. Monica's.

When it was Kelsey's turn she said, "I'm Kelsey Quinn. I moved here from Chicago." As soon as the first words left her mouth, every head in the room turned toward her. She'd hoped Mr. Shipley would move down the row to the boy who sat behind her. But no, he lingered on the new girl.

"Kelsey Quinn, from Chicago."

"Yes."

Mr. Shipley stood at the front of her row. Three desks separated her from the round little man with a mustache, but she felt like he was leaning over her with his face close to hers. "Well, Kelsey Quinn from Chicago, in my class it doesn't matter who your father is. Tom Quinn may have ruled the school in his day, but he's not here. You have to stand on your own merit."

"Okay." *Please, just move on. How did this get to be about my father?*

"Okay? This is not Chicago. Here, you answer with yes sir or no sir. Do you understand?"

"Yes, sir," she answered and resisted the urge to stand, click her heels together, and give the Nazi salute. Herr Shipley gave a curt nod and moved to the boy behind her.

After all of the introductions were made and he'd picked on a few other students, he stood at the front of the room and looked the class over. "We have a zero tolerance policy at this school. If you have a fight—you go to jail. If you come into my class high because you've smoked wacky weed in the parking lot—you go to jail. If you carry a hunting knife, a penknife, or a play knife on school property—you go to jail. Leave your hunting rifles at home. Are we clear?"

"Yes, sir," the class answered.

"We cannot, however, stop an intruder from bringing such paraphernalia into the building. I've devised a plan that will save your life. Listen closely." The man paced in front of the room as though he were delivering a speech to his troops. He pointed to Travis and said, "Barnes, you and the other young men will barricade the door and cover the window. Use whatever means you have, but you're going to have to be swift."

"Yes, sir," Travis answered.

Mr. Shipley addressed the class again. "In the event of an intruder, the rest of you will gather supplies to throw at him and lie prostrate on the floor. Do you know what *prostrate* is, Ms. Quinn?"

"Lying flat on your stomach?"

Mr. Shipley gave a half-smile that lifted one side of his mustache. "I see they taught vocabulary in Chicago. Welcome." He paced to the other side of the room. "As Ms. Quinn explained, you will drop to the floor and lie flat on your stomach. If he manages to penetrate—"

At the word *penetrate* snickers trickled through the

room. His sigh was so deep and hard that Kelsey imagined his skin rippling to his toes and back like a cartoon character. He began again. "If they find a hole and penetrate our defenses—" Most of the class broke out in laughter.

Mr. Shipley contracted his muscles so tightly Kelsey could swear she saw the cuffs of his khakis rise an inch or two above his loafers. It was like he'd wedgied himself.

"Ladies and gentlemen. Need I remind you of incidents at other schools? You may think we are immune at Hillside, but I assure you, there are crazy people everywhere."

The class quieted, but there was still a lot of eye rolling and snickering.

"As I was saying, if the shooter enters, you are to pelt him with the items you have gathered. The key is to knock him off balance and take him down. In the event of a drive-by, you will drop prostrate to the floor until you hear an all-clear signal. Do we need to practice?"

"No," drifted through the class.

"No what?"

"No, sir," the class answered.

"Very well. Let's move on to AP Literature." For the rest of the period, Mr. Shipley discussed how honored they should be to be in an AP class and that he expected more from them since they were college bound. Big woo. Kelsey had read most of the books he'd assigned anyway.

When class ended, Kelsey took her time gathering her things. After almost falling for Sabrina's misdirection, she was glad Austin was going to meet her. She wondered how her sisters were doing—especially Kenzie. If she wound up in the wrong class, she'd probably sit through it to avoid embarrassment.

*

Austin listened to Cody Biglow, tailback, talk nonstop as they walked to meet Kelsey. Austin had heard pretty much the same thing from the rest of the football team. "Have you s-s-seen the new girls? They are hot."

"Yeah. I work for their dad." The girls had been in the school for a little over an hour and already everybody was talking about them. Austin wondered how many guys had actually seen the Quinn sisters.

"Dude, introduce me. I heard the oldest is sw-e-et."

"Dude, she's taken."

Cody huffed. "M-maybe for now."

Austin shook his head. "Don't be a jerk."

"W-what? You got dibs?"

Austin didn't say anything. He didn't want to talk about Kelsey or her sisters—and didn't like the way the guys talked about them either. It was like hearing his friends talk about hooking up with a sister—if he had one.

Cody punched his shoulder. "That's it, isn't it? You g-g-got dibs."

"We're friends." Period. Besides, she'd placed Harvard-boy so high up in that Ivy League tower, he wouldn't have a chance even if he did go after Kelsey.

As they approached Mr. Shipley's room, Austin spotted Kelsey standing just inside the doorway. She had a wide-eyed look, sort of like an animal caught in a cage. When she saw him, her eyes softened and her lips formed a smile that he felt in his gut from ten feet away.

Cody hit his shoulder again. "D-damn, she's hot."

"Yeah." As beautiful as she was with her makeup on and her hair all fixed, he wanted to see the freckles sprinkled across her nose and the curls that refused to stay put. He was crazy about the girl who had an affinity for water fights and an aversion to large animals with four legs.

He greeted her with a friendly hug. "Hey, Kelsey. How was Shipley?"

"Crazy. We spent the first half of class reviewing intruder defense tactics."

"Not part of the curriculum in Chicago?" he teased.

"Are you kidding? We had metal detectors and campus police."

"Oh, you haven't met our campus cop, Mr. Tinny. You'll see him. He drives around in a golf cart with a hornet painted on the front."

"Seriously?"

Travis and Sabrina joined the group. Travis shook his head. "How can that guy still be teaching? He is whacked."

As they talked, Austin noticed that on one hand Sabrina seemed to be ignoring Kelsey's presence and on the other, Cody was openly ogling her. He was about to suggest they head toward their next class when Cody went into some kind of spastic oh-God-I'm-gonna-fumble gesture and wound up standing directly in front of Kelsey. Austin shot him a *what the hell?* look but Cody ignored it and stuck out his hand.

"Hey, I'm-m-m Cody Biglow."

She gave him a wary look as she shook his hand. "I'm Kelsey Quinn."

"I ju—I just wanted to m-m-m-meet you."

Austin had known Cody Biglow his entire life and knew Biglow had two modes. Loud-obnoxious and nervous-weirdo. He also knew Biglow had the back of him and every other man on the team.

Sabrina gave the bitch-eyeroll and said. "Let go of her hand, C-c-cody. You'll s-s-scare her."

Austin didn't care for Sabrina on a good day, but when she teased Cody about his stutter, he couldn't stand her.

Kelsey pulled her hand from Cody's and flashed him a grin. "My bad, I didn't let go."

In that moment, Austin knew Kelsey Quinn was about the best thing that'd happened to Hillside High.

"I've got to go." Sabrina huffed away from the group.

Austin checked the time on his cell. "We'd better go too, or we're going to be late." He looked at Travis and Cody and said, "We have econ together. Where are y'all going?"

Cody said, "I g-got econ too."

Travis stepped away from the group. "I have history. Catch y'all at lunch."

As they headed down the hall together, Austin saw Sabrina talking to Britney and Courtney. He could almost feel the daggers the girls were probably shooting at Kelsey's back. He leaned close to her. "Watch out for Sabrina."

Kelsey nodded. "I figured her out when she sent me to the wrong room."

"Seriously? She sent you to the wrong room?" Sabrina, Britney, and Courtney had a hold on most of the girls at school. Austin didn't understand why the girls would kowtow to them, but they did. Most of the guys put up with them, but he didn't have any use for them.

Kelsey looked back at Sabrina. "It's no big deal. I know her kind."

*

"I wonder if my sisters had any trouble this morning?" Kelsey surveyed the halls for friendly faces.

Austin said, "I saw Mackenzie on my way to meet you, but I haven't seen Ryan."

Kelsey tapped Austin's arm. "How was Mackenzie? She's so shy, I worry about her."

"Surrounded by other freshmen."

The thought of Mackenzie having to talk to people she didn't know made Kelsey's stomach tighten. "She must have been terrified."

"She seemed fine to me." Austin shrugged.

"I hope so." But Kelsey's stomach didn't feel it. Mackenzie just wasn't the type to make friends in new places.

Austin stopped and nodded toward a group standing across the hall from them. "Look, you can ask her yourself."

Mackenzie stood next to a locker with a group of girls around her and she was smiling as they talked. Kelsey called out, "Kenzie!"

Her sister said something to the group and trotted over to her. "Hi, Kelsey. How's your day going?"

Crappy. "Okay. How about you?"

"Good. There are some nice girls here."

Kelsey caught Cody elbowing Austin, and although Austin seemed oblivious, Kelsey was pretty sure Cody wanted to be introduced. She smiled at her sister and pointed to Cody. "This is Cody Biglow. He's on the football team with Austin."

Cody stuck his hand out to Mackenzie. "Nice to m-meet you. What year are you?"

"Thanks, you too. I'm a freshman. Are you a senior?"

Cody nodded.

Austin glanced at the hall clock. "We'd better go."

"Wait." Mackenzie looked at Kelsey. "Have you seen Ryan?"

"No. You?"

Mackenzie shook her head.

Austin put his hand on Kelsey's back. "We're gonna be late if we don't hurry."

Mackenzie returned to her friends and Kelsey, Cody, and Austin headed to economics. They slid into the room just as the bell rang.

Mrs. Moya's economics class was a lot less traumatic than Shipley's AP English. She was a normal teacher teaching a boring high school class. The big class assignment was to fictitiously purchase stock and follow it for the year. Kelsey had done the same project when she was a sophomore and wondered if she'd get to do anything new and exciting at this school.

The class dragged on and Kelsey thought about St. Monica's and her friends. They were going to spend the year taking fourth-year foreign languages, reading the equivalent of college sophomore literature, philosophy, Greek, and calculus. They'd celebrate when each of them got into their dream college.

And here she was, stuck in remedial everything because she was in Hickville, Texas—home of mediocrity. Probably not a bad school, but let's face it, St. Monica's was a prep school. Her grade point average should skyrocket here, but would the less than stellar course selection keep her from going to college with Drew?

Drew. She wished she'd never asked the *do you love me* question and at the same time, wished she had the guts to ask it again. When he got back from Europe, they'd talked for hours. He'd promised they'd Skype soon. But *soon* hadn't come. And lately, his calls and texts had been über short. She told herself it was because he was busy getting ready for school, but the truth was he was drifting away from her. She'd hoped he'd be at least a little jealous of Austin, but they didn't really talk about her life in Hillside. She wasn't sure he even knew about Austin.

Austin was another issue altogether. He was cute, funny, kind. He'd become a great friend. He was the kind of friend who made you feel better just being around him. But the feelings she'd had since that day at the courthouse freaked her out. It was too easy to flirt with him. All the talk about love and the changing faces probably hadn't helped. But if he'd wanted to kiss her—would she have let him?

No. She was just lonely for romance. It seemed like forever ago that she'd felt Drew's guiding hand on the small of her back. And it had been eons since he'd wrapped his arms around her, pulled her body against his, and had a major make-out session.

She looked at Austin sitting across from her writing notes in his spiral. She'd felt his hand on her back, guiding her. No. Not guiding, more like guarding, as though he were saying, "I'm right beside you, close enough to catch you if you fall, or protect you from harm."

She wanted to feel his hand on her back again. She closed her eyes and wondered what his lips would feel like on hers. She saw him moving closer, his grey-green eyes intent on her. His lips almost touched her…

"Kelsey…" Austin whispered.

She opened her eyes and saw the girl who sat in front holding a stack of papers for her to pass back. She took the papers and handed them to the boy who sat behind her.

What was she thinking? Austin had never even looked like he wanted to kiss her. He was a friend and never tried to be more. A few raised arm hairs at the courthouse and she was daydreaming about cheating on Drew.

She pulled her cell from her purse and snuck off a text to Drew.

Kelsey: I miss you. Hugs and kisses.

When the bell rang, Austin turned to Kelsey. "Are you okay? You looked pretty out of it."

Sure. I was just daydreaming about cheating on my perfect boyfriend with you. "I'm fine. I was just thinking about Drew."

"That would explain the smile on your lips."

Great, I must have looked like a complete moron. "Yeah. So—um—where to next? I have French." She handed her schedule to Austin.

The girl sitting in front of her turned around. "You have French? I do too, but not until this afternoon. You must not be in fourth year."

"No. I had three years of German at my old school."

"Oh, wow. So you'll be a senior with all the freshmen."

Kelsey nodded. Could this girl be a potential friend? She seemed nice.

Austin handed Kelsey her schedule and waved a hand at the girl. "This is Hannah Ellis."

Hannah stood and gathered her books. "So you're Kelsey, the new girl."

"That's me." Hannah was only a few inches taller than Kelsey, but her long arms and legs made her seem much taller. She had the kind of long, silky straight dark hair that Kelsey always envied on girls.

"Do you need help getting to French? I'm going that way. I can show you your class."

Was she trying to pull a Sabrina? She looked at Austin for a sign.

He gave a slight nod. "Don't worry, Hannah won't send you to the wrong class."

Hannah raised her dark brows. "Somebody did that?"

Kelsey shrugged. "It's no big deal. Which way?"

Cody caught up with them at the door and they headed down the hall. When they got to the main hallway, Austin said, "My class is the opposite direction. Lunch is next. Can I meet you by the cafeteria?"

"Sure." Kelsey nodded.

Austin and Cody peeled off and ran into other football-player-looking guys. Kelsey watched as he high-fived his way down the hall. Hannah looked at her. "He's pretty much the nicest guy in school."

"Yeah?"

Hannah led Kelsey down the hall in the opposite direction. "Yeah. He's had it pretty rough, but you'd never know—except this is a small town and everybody knows everything about everybody."

Kelsey gave her a sideways look. "Does that bother you?"

"I've never known anything else. I guess it's way different from Chicago."

"You have no idea."

14

In Texas there is a law that states: if two trains meet at a crossing, both must stop, and neither can proceed before the other has moved.

Austin shuffled through the stack of papers Mrs. White handed out and thought about Kelsey. *That would explain the smile on your lips? Really? Could I be more lame?* He hadn't been expecting her to say she was thinking about her boyfriend. Just hearing Drew's name made him want to puke. He couldn't stand the guy and he'd never met him. He was probably really nice and maybe he and Kelsey were meant to be together. It's just that Kelsey seemed to get all uptight when she talked to him.

She sure didn't look tense when she was thinking about Drew. When she'd closed her eyes, her face softened and she had a sexy kind of kiss-me-now look. That really bugged him. He had hoped Kelsey was on the verge of breaking up with Drew, not daydreaming about him. From what little he knew about Drew, the guy was a neat freak and would probably croak if he saw Kelsey working in the barn. Austin doubted Drew would appreciate the way she grumbled about her chores in complete contrast to the sparkle in her eyes, or the smile that played across her lips when she brushed the horses.

The horses. It was just a matter of time before she learned to ride. She said she was afraid of them, but she began to relax almost from the first brush stroke. And what about the water fight and that day at the courthouse? *There's loads of chemistry between us—isn't there?* He just had to make her see that the guy she wanted was the one in front of her, not the one she thought she wanted halfway across the country.

He stopped by his locker on his way to meet Kelsey at the cafeteria. Travis leaned against the locker next to his. A couple of other guys on the team stood in a half circle around him. Travis fist-bumped him. "Dude, we were just talking about the Quinn sisters."

Justin Hayes, wide receiver, smirked. "They're hot."

Austin was in a pissed-off mood and didn't want to hear them talk about the girls.

Justin moved a little closer. "Come on, Austin, you got any ass yet? I heard you were tight with the oldest one."

There'd been bad blood between Austin and Justin since they were sophomores. Hearing him reduce Kelsey to a piece of ass in the same tone his dad used sent Austin from pissed-off to total rage in a nanosecond.

He pushed Justin just hard enough to make him take a step back. "Watch your mouth, Hayes."

Justin pushed back. "What's wrong with you, man—you got the market cornered on Quinn ass?"

Austin slammed Justin against the locker and held his forearm across this throat. "I said, watch your mouth."

Travis grabbed Austin and pulled him off Justin. "Dude, chill."

Justin rubbed his neck. "Don't be getting all uppity. You know you want it same as the rest of us."

Travis stepped between them. "Let it go."

Austin knew Travis was right and turned back to his

locker.

But Justin couldn't let it go. "How does it feel, Barnes?"

Travis didn't say anything, he just gave him a *what* look.

Justin jutted his jaw before he spoke. "How does it feel to know your boy here killed your sister?"

Travis looked at Austin. "Don't let him get to you. You know he's full of crap."

Justin said, "Keep telling yourself that, Travis. We all know the truth here."

Austin took a step toward Justin, but Travis clapped a hand on his shoulder, stopping him. "Shake it off, dude."

Austin couldn't shake it off. Fury coursed through him, the only thought on his mind to take that son of a bitch down. He'd dropped his books, ready to launch into Justin, when Coach grabbed him by the arm and pulled him back.

"McCoy, Hayes, in my office. Now."

*

"Zero tolerance! What do you not understand about zero tolerance?"

Austin stood next to Justin. Back straight. Eyes forward.

"One punch and you'd be handcuffed. One punch and you'd be arrested. One punch and you'd be off my team. Do you want off my team! *Do you want off my team?"* Coach yelled into their faces like a drill sergeant.

"No, sir!" they shouted back.

Coach stood in front of them with his hands on his hips and worked his jaw like he was too angry to get the next words out. When he spoke, it was like he had to squeeze them through tight lips. "You disrespected what it means to be a Hornet. You disrespected the team. You got a problem, you take it out on the field, on the other guys. You're sidelined Friday."

Austin felt the blood drain from his face and his feet remained frozen where he stood.

Justin spoke up. "You're benching us, Coach? It's the first game."

"I didn't do squat. You lost your place when you decided to play smackdown in the hallway."

Justin took a step back. "You can't do that."

Coach narrowed his eyes. "I just did."

Austin sucked in a breath and said, "Coach, I know what we did was wrong. I want to earn my place back."

Coach crossed his arms. "What are you gonna do to earn your place?"

Austin answered, "Whatever it takes, Coach. I'm there. I want this. I'll earn it."

Coach moved in front of Justin. "What about you, Hayes? Do you want this?"

"Yes, sir."

"How bad, Hayes?"

"I'll do whatever you want, Coach."

"You wanna play, you'll work your ass off for me." Coach paced in front of the boys and rubbed his chin. He stopped and looked at the players. "Suit up to run. You've got five minutes to meet me on the field."

*

Kelsey waited outside of the cafeteria for Austin and watched groups file pass her. St. Monica's or Hillside High, the cliques were pretty much the same: jocks, band nerds, geeks, stoners, Barbies. She'd been one of the beautiful people at her old school and although she had first-day jitters, had been fairly confident she'd slide right into that group here. But so far, the students walked by her as if she didn't exist and not one person came close to saying hello.

The word *loser* formed in her mind.

L-O-S-E-R.
Lonely.
Outsider.

Social misfit.
Expendable.
Replaceable.
Loser. Loser-Loser-Loser stop it!

Girls like her didn't worry about being a loser. It was a matter of time before she was back on top. But everybody in "A" lunch had passed her by and still, no Austin. He'd told her he'd wait for her. What if he hadn't? Maybe he was sitting at a table laughing with Britney and Courtney about how stupid she looked standing all alone in the hall. The *L*-word loomed large in her mind again. Her eyes burned.

She hated this place, hated this school, and hated these people. She especially hated Austin for standing her up. Drew would have been there for her.

What was she going to do? Everybody in "A" lunch knew she was waiting for someone. If she walked in now, she might as well start wearing pigtails and a pocket protector because she'd never recover from the degradation. Austin had said it was a closed campus, so she couldn't leave, but that didn't mean she couldn't hide out during lunch.

She made her way away from the cafeteria toward the Hornet Hall of Honor. No losers there. She turned the word over in her mind. L-o-s-e-r. Place right hand on forehead with index finger pointing up and thumb to the left.

She stopped in front of the football trophy case with the homage to her dad. No big fat *L* on his forehead. He'd been Mr. Amazing—at least for a couple of years. Why had he quit football? Aunt Susan had mentioned some girl—Cassidy Jones. What could she have done to make him give all this up? His eyes were set with determination and he was smiling, but even then, he looked like he was carrying the weight of the world with him. But he had escaped this nothing town and so would she. She began disassembling the *L*-word looming in her mind.

L-O-S-E-R.
Leader.

Original.
Social trendsetter.
Exclusive.
Rebel.

I can do this. She backed away from the trophy case and turned toward the cafeteria. Her stomach growled, urging her on. *I can march back in there, grab a tray, and just sit somewhere. Alone.* Her stomach may have been begging, but her feet weren't moving. The word she'd ripped apart called to her again. She refused to listen. *Deep breath in, back straight, go.*

Go the other way, because no way was she going to sit by herself in the cafeteria. She turned around and walked down the hall in search of a place to hide out for the next thirty minutes or so. She made a right at the end of the hall and caught the scent of pizza. She followed it to one of the rooms where a group of students stood in line to get a slice. Above the pizza table, a banner stretched across the wall. Gold letters spelled out PURITY CLUB.

Ms. Bettis, the counselor, waved her in. "Welcome to our eat and greet."

Kelsey stepped into the room. That's when she noticed Ryan standing in the front of the line.

*

Austin stood on the goal line with Justin and waited for Coach Peterson. Whatever Coach had in store for them was going to be bad, but not as bad as missing the game Friday. It was so hot Austin could almost see waves of heat radiating from the ground. Sweat trickled down his forehead. If Kelsey were here, she'd probably say something about the stadium being hell's oven.

Kelsey. He hoped Travis would think to tell her why he hadn't met her at the cafeteria. She'd probably already met somebody to sit with anyway.

Justin hocked a loogie and spat on the ground. "Maybe he's just going to leave us out here to sweat to death."

Austin cut his eyes to Justin. He could be such a prick. A lot of guys talked crap about girls, but Justin and his buddy Eric were the biggest players in school. He hated the way they used girls. But the girls kept coming. And the rest of the guys were left to put the pieces together when they were finished with them.

Coach appeared from the stadium tunnel and headed toward them carrying a couple of sports bottles. Austin dreaded what was ahead. He shouldn't have let Justin rile him the way he had.

Coach Peterson looked even more pissed off than he had in his office. He stepped in front of Austin and Justin. "You don't fight on my team. You don't even *look* like you're gonna fight. You got that?"

"Yes, sir."

"Rules say if I'm gonna work you in heat, I gotta give you as much water as you want." He sat the bottles on the white chalked line and said, "Ball busters on my whistle. You got that?"

Before either of them could answer, he blew the whistle. Austin shoved his hands into the turf with his butt in the air and scrambled down the field. He hated these things. His shoulders burned from the weight and impact on them. And then there was the balancing act between his legs and arms. His legs were stronger and tended to get ahead of his arms, putting more weight on his shoulders.

When he reached the forty-yard line the whistle blew. He straightened and ran backward. The next whistle blew at the thirty and he turned and headed to the goal line. His shoulders thanked him all the way to the water bottle.

One squirt and he was on all fours again. This time Coach took them all the way to the fifty before blowing the whistle. It was a little harder to stand and his legs were heavier as he shuffled his feet backward. Sprinting was the easiest part, but he couldn't quite find the energy to explode into a full sprint.

By the sixth set, his shoulders were screaming for him to stop. A couple of times his hands slipped and his powerful legs drilled his face into the ground. As they bear-crawled past the fifty-yard line, Justin fell behind. Prick or no prick, he was still a team member and if Austin left him, there would be hell to pay.

He slowed his pace and yelled at Justin, "Come on, man. You can do this."

Justin groaned and almost stopped.

"Don't stop. We'll do it together. Come on. Come on. On my count. Right hand. Left." He didn't think Justin would join in, but he did. It was slow, but together, in sync, they made it down the field. They practically fell across the goal line before hearing the tweet ending this bit of the torture.

Austin stood on wobbly legs. They lined up next to each other before they backpedaled down the field. Fortunately, Coach only made them run backward for about ten yards before signaling the sprint. They turned and ran.

Normally, it took just a few seconds to run from one goal line to the other, but Austin's legs felt like two lead weights. Instead of eating up the earth, he felt like he was trying to sprint through waist-deep water. His lungs had that deep burn like he was turning over stagnant air from deep in the bases and his stomach roiled with nausea.

This was do or die time for him. He had to keep going to show Coach how bad he wanted to remain QB. Justin was faster than Austin and probably could have been drinking water by now, but he wasn't. He had moved to run closer to Austin and kept his pace even.

The nausea Austin felt grew and he got that pre-spew funny feeling in his throat. He stumbled.

Justin grabbed his elbow. "Don't go down on me, man." Together they made it to the water bottles.

Austin bent over and heaved. He heard Coach Peterson

bark, "Showers!" but couldn't move yet. When he finished puking up his guts, Justin handed him a water bottle and they headed for the field house.

He gave Justin a quick nod, a silent thank you for helping him survive the workout. But what had happened out there was a truce between football players who needed to work together for the sake of the team. Justin was still a prick.

15

Pigs who have sex at the Kingsville Airport are breaking the law.

Kelsey didn't waste time making it to the front of the room and the pizza. Ryan stood with her back to Kelsey loading up on the pepperoni.

"Hi, Ryan."

At the sound of Kelsey's voice, Ryan nearly dropped her pizza. She fumbled with the paper plate as she turned to face her sister. "Oh, hi."

Kelsey moved to the back of the line. "Save me a place?" *Wow, Ryan in the Purity Club. Zoe would get a kick out of this.*

"Sure." Ryan gave a weak smile and headed toward a seat in front of the teacher's desk.

Kelsey pulled a couple of slices on to a paper plate, grabbed a bottle of water, and took a seat next to Ryan. The food wasn't great but her stomach was happy and she didn't have to suffer the shame of being stood up. Everything was going to be all right.

A dark-haired, brown-eyed hottie sat next to Ryan and introduced himself as Eric Perez. Kelsey didn't miss the grin that spread all over Ryan's face when she spoke to him and it took a full nanosecond for Ryan to go into full-on flirt mode. Kelsey shook her head. This whole Purity Club thing was just a means to meet guys. Chicago or Hillside, Ryan hadn't changed. But as disgusting as she found her sister's actions, the irony of Ryan joining the club made Kelsey want to giggle.

Ms. Bettis waited for everyone to fill their plates and then took her place at the front of the room. She pointed to the banner and said, "Welcome to the Purity Club eat and greet." That's when Kelsey noticed the motto written across the banner in gold lettering: TRUE LOVE WAITS. The virginity pledge.

Kelsey avoided looking at her sister to keep from laughing.

Mrs. Bettis said, "Everybody, bow your heads. Father God, we just want to thank you for bringing all of these good kids together to share in their love for you and their desire to keep their bodies pure. And send a special welcome to our new members from up north, Ryan and Kelsey. And Father God, I just pray the third little Quinn... I can't seem to remember her name, but you know who she is. But Father, I just pray she follows in her sisters' footsteps and sees fit to join us in our purity journey."

Little giggles raced around inside Kelsey bursting to get out. Ryan had her eyes squeezed shut as if she were praying with all her might. Ryan was such a faker. A snort almost escaped Kelsey. If she let one loose, she was afraid she'd go into a full laughing meltdown. She faced forward and tried not to think about it.

Ms. Bettis continued with her prayer. "And Father God, thank you for bringing all these pure little bodies together to eat this wonderful pizza you provided for us today. And bless the hands that made the pizza for us and the driver who delivered it. And most of all Father, bless those who have lost this precious gift and help them to see they can be born again in purity. In Jesus' name we pray. Amen."

Amen filtered through the room as everyone dug in to the now blessed cold pizza.

When everybody finished their holy pizza, Mrs. Bettis made the group introduce themselves and asked for a volunteer to pass out white elastic bracelets stamped with the club motto. Ryan practically bolted out of her seat at the chance.

As Kelsey watched her sister hand out the bracelets, she figured out a couple of reasons why Ryan was in the club. It was either tall, lanky, blond, blue-eyed Colton Dodd, or buffed-out Eric Perez. They were both just her type—hot and male.

Ryan volunteered to be the secretary and gather all of the phone numbers and e-mail addresses. Kelsey shook her head. By the time Ryan finished with the guys, the group might as well be called the Impurity Club.

The bell sounded ten minutes to the end of lunch and the Purity Club was dismissed until next month. Kelsey tossed her plate and water bottle into the trash and found Ryan waiting for her at the door.

Ryan looked up with pleading eyes. "Kelsey, can I talk to you?"

Kelsey smirked. "What about? This little sham of yours?"

Ryan shook her head. "No, but…"

"Yes, but. I know what this is all about."

"You don't understand."

"Come on. Don't think I didn't see those future notches in your bed post."

Ryan grabbed Kelsey's arm and squeezed. "Kelsey, please. I'm your sister."

Kelsey looked at the fingers wrapped around her bicep. "Okay. Talk."

"Not here. We need to talk alone."

"I'm not missing class."

Ryan closed her eyes for a second and released Kelsey. "Okay, after school. Promise me."

"I promise. Jeez." She stepped into the hallway, but not before catching Ryan slamming her water bottle in the trashcan. What was up with her, anyway? When had she ever needed Kelsey for anything? Never. She was always the fun, pretty one. Kelsey might tell herself she ruled St. Monica's, but the truth was, if Ryan hadn't left for the fine arts magnet school, she would have been Queen Bee.

So what was going on with her now? Something about the desperation in her sister's tone made Kelsey think it wasn't about adding notches to her bedpost.

The bell sounded again and Kelsey pulled her schedule out of her pocket. No way was she going to find her next class in time.

Damn it, Austin. Where are you?

*

Coach Peterson met Austin and Justin in the locker room and handed them each a bottle of Gatorade. "Drink this and then drink water every chance you get. I can't have you fallin' out in practice this afternoon."

Austin wanted to smile, but he was too tired. Instead he mumbled, "Thanks, Coach."

"Just because you can run a few sorry-ass yards don't mean you're starting Friday. You're just warmin' up."

Austin showered, but he still felt like he could barely drag air into his lungs. He flopped against the metal locker across from where Justin sat on the bench. Justin shouldn't have mouthed off, but nobody deserved the brutal practice they'd survived. It had to have been a hundred and five on the heat index. He took a swig and decided it was time to end the feud. Like Coach said, they were a team. It was about time they acted like it. "I'm sorry, man."

Justin gave a smartass smirk. "Not as sorry as you're

gonna be if I get that Quinn ass before you."

Some guys just weren't worth the effort. He grabbed his drink and headed out of the locker room. If he hurried he might catch Kelsey before class.

He found her a few feet from her classroom door. "Kelsey."

She said, "Hey," but wasn't smiling.

"I'm sorry I missed you. I had a thing I had to do for Coach."

She gave a shrug. "No biggie. I found my way to the Purity Club eat and greet."

That took him back a step. "Really? You don't seem the Purity Club type."

"What's that supposed to mean?"

"I mean—it's just—most PC girls don't look like you." She raised her brows and he was fairly sure that was a meaningful expression and although he didn't know what it meant, figured it couldn't be good. "Not that you couldn't be a PC girl, you're just—you know."

She stepped closer—until she was just a few inches from him. Her lips formed a half smile. "I'm what?"

Her voice had a playful tone, and he wanted to tease back. But this close, with her sapphire eyes looking into his, his brain was empty. He felt himself blush and knew he'd turned bright red. He'd backed himself into a corner, but mostly he was red-faced because of the way her gaze made him want to grab her and kiss the PC out of her. He wanted more than anything to drop his mouth to hers. He wondered if she felt the same and leaned in—just out of kissing range. "You're too real for them."

His brain was seriously short-circuiting. She had a boyfriend. She was off limits—and perfect for the Purity Club.

She tucked her lips and took a step back. "I'm not sure if I've been complimented or insulted."

"Definitely a compliment."

"Okay, if you say so." The tardy bell rang and teachers up and down the halls closed their doors.

Kelsey turned and slid into her room just in time. Austin's class was on another hall completely. He was going to have to get a tardy slip, which would translate into running extra laps at football practice. Briefly he thought about skipping altogether, but that would make matters worse in the long run. He turned and headed for the office. This was the longest first day of school ever.

*

Kelsey went through the rest of the day in a daze. She must have relived that moment in the hall a million times. Standing in the pick-up line, it was a million-and-one. His eyes had danced as he looked at her. His lips had been mere inches from hers. All the signals said he was going to kiss her. Just thinking about it made her insides feel all squiggly. Her conscience reminded her that she had a boyfriend, but flirting was not the same as kissing. She refused to feel like she'd done anything wrong and chose to ignore the pangs of disappointment that he had football practice and she wouldn't see him after school.

When her mom pulled up, the girls piled into the SUV. The interrogation started before their seatbelts were even buckled. "How was school?"

Ryan and Mackenzie answered in unison. "Okay." For them maybe. For Kelsey, it pretty much sucked.

"Do you like your teachers?" Her sisters gave a pat yes so Kelsey didn't mention crazy Mr. Shipley.

"Do you have any homework?"

"Yes," they all said.

"Did you make friends?"

No one answered. Kelsey turned over the question in her mind. Friend? Zoe had been her best friend for as long as she could remember. They'd cut their knees together learning to shave their legs, giggled through experimenting with hairstyles and makeup, and supported each other through crushes and breakups. They had shared seventeen years of memories. How could she say she'd met a friend after one day?

She thought about the girl with the silky straight hair. Hannah could be someone to hang out with. Austin said she was nice, but she wasn't Zoe.

Her mom glanced across the seat to her. "You're awfully quiet, Kelsey. How did your day go?"

"It sucked."

"It can't have been that bad. Name one good thing that happened, even if it's small."

Kelsey's mind took her back to that moment in the hall with Austin. That shouldn't have been a good thing. She tried to push aside the excitement she felt when Austin was close, but her mind wanted to stay there.

"Kelsey?" her mom prodded.

"I'm trying. I met a girl named Hannah who seems okay."

"I'll take that. Ryan, your turn. One good thing."

"Well, I joined the Purity Club."

"Okay. What's the Purity Club?"

"It's kind of hard to explain. We all took a pledge to remain chaste until marriage." She said it with a hopeful tone. Like that ship hadn't already sailed.

Kelsey willed herself not to laugh, but heard Mackenzie snicker and let loose a snort. Tension filled the car. Kelsey looked back at Ryan and almost felt bad for her. Her face was red as though she was struggling not to cry.

Mom shot Kelsey a look and glanced in the rearview mirror. "I'm proud of you, Ryan."

Ryan took a deep breath and stared out of the passenger window. Guilt niggled at Kelsey's conscience, but she refused to acknowledge it. After all, Little Miss I've Turned my Life Around had had no trouble flirting with Eric Perez at the PC meeting.

Mom sighed. "Okay. Mackenzie, what about you? One good thing."

Mackenzie shrugged. "The kids talked to me—that was kind of weird."

Mom gave a satisfied nod. "So day one was a marginal success. Keep a positive attitude and tomorrow will be better. On another note, you don't have to go to the feed store today. Dad and I have a surprise waiting at the house."

16

It's against the law to throw banana peels on the streets of Waco.

As they drove up the gravel drive to the house, Kelsey tried not to feel excited. Sure, they were getting out of after-school work, but it wasn't anything as cool as *we're moving back to Chicago.* So what else was there? A back-to-school party? Who would they invite? Aunt Susan and Uncle Jack? Surely not. Her mom refused to give hints, even with her sisters' badgering.

When the SUV pulled to a stop, Mom turned to the girls. "You'll each find a bag on your bed—that's your clue."

Kelsey had to admit, this was kinda cool. She let excitement take over, scrambled out of the car ahead of her sisters, and bolted through the front door and up the stairs to her room. A navy and white canvas bag was perched on her pillow.

She pulled a matching beach towel and a red bikini from the bag. There weren't any beaches around but... the pool! She looked out of the back window. It was full of beautiful, pristine, moss-free water. She heard Mackenzie squeal, followed by Ryan.

They were changed and standing by the pool in less than fifteen minutes. Kelsey draped her towel over a chair of the iron patio set they'd brought from Chicago and noted the contrast between the elegant table and thick cushioned chairs against the peeling paint of the farmhouse. Another reminder of what they'd lost. She turned her back on the old house and jumped in. The water was cool and refreshing as it closed over her and shut out the world. She blew air out of her lungs and sank to the bottom.

When she was little, she swam at the country club and played mermaids with her friends. They would sink to the bottom and watch people swim above them. Whoever held their breath the longest got to be Queen Mermaid. Kelsey was always the queen. She ruled their world. And nobody worried about what the future or even the next hour held. They lived for the moment.

She pushed off the bottom toward the surface and for the first time in a long time, felt the freedom that came with living in the moment.

She came up at the deep end and trod water as she watched her mom ease down the steps. "Mom, this is awesome. When did you do this?"

"We've been working on it for a couple of days. I wasn't sure we were going to be able to keep it a surprise, but Dad said you guys avoided the backyard like the plague."

"Well, yeah—the smell alone was enough to keep us away." Kelsey's phone rested on the table. She heard it ding a text and thought about getting it, but the idea of leaving this little oasis gave her the strength to ignore it. Instead, she ducked under the water and swam to the shallow end, where Ryan and Mackenzie were having an underwater handstand contest.

When Kelsey broke the surface, she sat on a step next to her mom and put her arm around her. "Thanks, Mom. This was a really cool surprise. Literally."

Mom smiled and some of the fatigue in her face seemed

to disappear. "Dad is going to grill burgers tonight and I invited Austin and Travis over after football practice."

"Cool." Giddy excitement spread through Kelsey. Austin was coming over. It didn't matter that she saw him every day; she couldn't wait to see him again. She was tempted to run upstairs and fix her hair and makeup, but not enough to want to leave the water. Besides, (a) he'd already seen her at her worst and (b) they were just friends.

Her phone dinged again. It was probably Zoe wanting a first day report, but there was time for talk later. Now was the time to join her sisters in the center of the pool.

It was like they'd been transformed into little girls again. They had an underwater tea party, several handstand contests, and turned countless somersaults. Kelsey tried not to think about Austin coming over, but she couldn't help watching the house for signs of him.

By five, Dad had arrived home from work and fired up the grill—still no Austin. When her phone dinged three times in a row and then rang, she worried it was him canceling. She climbed out of the water, quick-dried her hands and face, and answered the call.

"Hey Kel." It was Drew. "Where have you been? I've texted a million times."

"I'm sorry…" She finished drying off with her free hand and plopped down in one of the cushiony patio chairs.

"How was your first day of school?"

"Horrible."

"Well, it is Texas."

"Yeah." She watched her sisters race across the pool and felt her muscles tense. She should never have climbed out of the pool to answer the phone. "Drew, I…"

"By the way, I sent you a package."

"Really?" She should have been excited, but somehow she was only mildly curious. "What is it?"

"A surprise."

"That's so sweet." She tried to focus her attention on

him, but the girls were jumping off the diving board.

"I know, but you're worth it. I bet you made tons of friends today."

Kelsey laughed. "I'll take that bet. Sadly, I have no friends." Austin and Travis appeared from the side of the house. She waved at them and pointed to the phone pressed to her ear.

"They just don't know you yet, babe."

Austin wore plaid swim trunks, flip-flops, sunglasses, and a towel draped around his neck—and her mouth went slightly dry as she watched him greet her family.

"Kelsey? Are you there?"

"Yeah. Sorry, you cut out for a second." Okay, so her brain had cut out for a second, but what girl's wouldn't with those two guys around?

"So what are you doing now that kept you from answering my text?"

"Swimming." Her tone was a little short, but she'd seen Austin and Travis squat next to the side of the pool to talk to Ryan and was anxious to join them.

"I thought you said the pool was gross." His tone sounded accusatory. Did he think she was lying?

"It was. Mom and Dad cleaned it up." *Why am I explaining this to you?*

"Did they drain it and everything?"

What? Why would you ask that? "I don't know, but it's clean." And she was ready to get wet again. "Hey, Drew? Mom could use some help with dinner…"

"Does she know you're talking to me? It's been so long since we've talked."

Yeah, and whose fault is that? "I know. Can I call you later?"

"I'm about to get busy, but I'll try to call you later."

They said good-bye and she tapped End and set her phone on the table. She felt only slightly guilty for cutting him off. Austin and Travis joined her at the table and all thoughts of Drew fled her brain as her face transformed into one big sloppy grin. "Hey!"

Travis shed his T-shirt and tossed it on the table. Austin set his towel next to Travis's shirt and dropped his keys on top. "How's the water?"

"Good," Kelsey squeaked. She felt self-conscious in her bikini. But maybe it was because his gaze seemed to dance from her head to her toes and back up. She stood and wrapped her towel around her waist.

Austin's smile fell slightly. "You aren't through swimming, are you?"

"No. I was just going to help Mom."

Her mom sat a couple of bags of chips on the table. "Enjoy your friends. This day is for you girls."

Kelsey tossed her wrap on the chair. "If you're sure."

Her mom nodded. "Go on."

Kelsey jumped into the pool behind Austin. When they surfaced, Kelsey stood in neck-deep water a few feet from him. "Remember when you squirted me with the hose?" She splashed Austin's face.

"Oh yeah? What about the fountain?" He splashed her back.

She laughed and splashed with both hands. Instead of returning fire, he powered through the water until he captured her. He twirled her in front of him and wrapped his arms around her, pinning her in place. "Splash me now," he teased.

The feeling of his body pressed to hers sent shivers down her back and she wanted more, like a deep, passionate kiss. But that was wrong. What kind of girl would she be to cheat on Drew less than five minutes after she'd spoken with him? "Okay, okay, you win."

He let go and she splashed him again. Austin grabbed her and threw her across the pool. Travis snatched Ryan and a game was born. The guys took turns launching the girls in the air. Mackenzie showed Travis how to cup his hands for her to step into. He tossed her in the air and she wowed everybody with a back flip.

They moved to the diving board next. Kelsey was used to seeing her sister twist her body into various flips and twists and was always amazed. Watching her flip off the board was no different. Back flip, layout, front flip—she executed each trick with ease.

Kelsey, Austin, and Travis sat on the side of the pool and cheered Mackenzie on. Ryan grabbed her cell phone and took pictures. Kelsey was proud of Mackenzie, but sad for her too. Even if there had been a gym in Hillside, she doubted her parents could afford it.

Ryan yelled at McKenzie, "Do another front."

Kelsey looked at Ryan and anger surfaced. Everybody had lost something with the move—except Ryan. She could do artwork anywhere. The only thing she'd left behind was a bad reputation and string of broken hearts.

She watched Mackenzie tread water in the deep end. She was breathing slightly hard, but her face glowed. Kelsey shoved the anger back below the surface. They were having fun for the first time in ages and she wasn't going to let anything spoil it.

Mackenzie swam to the side of the pool. "That was fun, but I'm done."

Travis shook his head. "Man, you should try out for cheerleader."

Mackenzie's smile faded a little. "Maybe."

"Burgers are up," Dad called.

They crawled out of the pool and dried off. Kelsey sat between Austin and Mackenzie and realized she was happy—really happy—and decided this was a great first day of school. In Chicago, she would have gone out with Zoe and her friends. It would never have occurred to her have dinner with her family.

When they'd finished eating, Kelsey turned to her mom. "I'll get the cleanup." She gathered the plates and carried them to the kitchen. Austin followed carrying the condiments.

She set the plates on the counter. "Thanks for helping."

He filled the sink with soapy water. "It's the least I can do after standing you up at lunch."

"Yeah, what was up with that? You were in a fight?"

His back stiffened. "It's a long story." He set the plates in the sink and began to wash them.

Kelsey was curious, but she got the feeling he didn't want to talk about it, so she let it go.

Austin wiped a soapy sponge across a plate. "I saw Eric Perez talking to Ryan today." He rinsed the plate and handed it to her to dry. "Kelsey, he's bad news. I tried to tell Ryan when you were on the phone, but I'm not sure she believed me."

Great—just the type she can't resist. "Yeah, she's not known for making great decisions." She started to say she'd talk to Ryan, but it would've been a lie. So they continued to work in silence and things got all wonky—like if her shoulder accidentally touched his, her insides would sizzle. Her hands trembled and she almost dropped the plate he handed her.

"Whoa, sorry, I must have left some soap on that one." He took the dish and rinsed it again. She dried it with a firm grip and set it down carefully.

When she grabbed the last plate, he held it and pulled back slightly. "Are you sure you've got it?"

"Give it." She tugged it away, but her hands still trembled. Worse, she couldn't stop grinning. Worse than that, it was the kind of grin that only comes from knowing a really hot guy is paying attention.

She carefully added the plate to the stack and concentrated on keeping her voice steady and casual. "So, other than missing lunch, how was your day?"

He fixed his gaze on hers and dried his hands on her dishtowel. Neither of them let go. "Parts of today were fantastic."

"Really? What parts?" Her gaze dropped to his lips and back to his eyes.

"The parts you were in." He pulled her closer with the towel and lowered his mouth to hers. As soon as their lips touched, the back door squeaked open and they both jumped back. They hadn't even made full contact. Still, Kelsey's heart pounded in her chest and her faced burned like she'd baked in the heat.

"I brought the rest of the stuff in." Ryan balanced a bag of chips, a basket of buns, and a plate of the leftover burgers.

Kelsey's hands shook as she took the chips from her sister. If Ryan had seen what had happened, she didn't show it. When Ryan retreated to the back yard, things got weird with Austin. He continued to help with the cleanup, but neither spoke.

The excitement that usually bounced between them turned to tension. Kelsey was aware of his every movement as if electrically charged particles sailed through the air with him.

Tremors zinged through her body when she bumped him. When he reached over her to put the plates in the cabinet, the feel of his chest behind her made her hold her breath as a shudder ran through her.

And she wasn't sure how she felt about it all. She wanted a real kiss from him, she wanted to feel his body pressed to hers. But what then? He was not her future any more than Texas was. And what about Drew? Were her feelings for him changing?

Austin broke the silence in the kitchen. "Hey, are you okay?"

"Yeah." She finished wiping the counter and folded the dishcloth across the sink.

"Kelsey, I know you're dating Drew… I'm sorry."

She looked into his eyes and then away. "It's okay."

"I shouldn't have—it's just—"

"It happened."

He placed his hands on her bare shoulders and she stiffened—not because she didn't want him to touch her, but because she wanted to fall against his chest and wrap her arms around him.

But she didn't.

And he withdrew his hands as though he'd been burned. "Are we good?"

"Yes, of course." She forced a casual smile. "Come on, let's join the others."

*

The sky was ablaze with an orange-red glow as the sun dipped below the horizon. Austin gripped the steering wheel as he drove toward the celestial inferno. Having Kelsey right there, but off limits, was killing him. He glanced at Travis. "I shouldn't have tried to kiss her, man."

"Dude, that's exactly what you should do. Make her forget that jerk-off."

"Kelsey's not like that. I made her feel like she'd done something wrong."

"Maybe you should convince her she should break up with him."

Austin shook his head at his friend. "Just convince her?"

"Yeah. Convince her."

"What, do I go up to her and say, 'Hey, Kelsey, I think Drew is a dip-wad and you should break up with him and date me?'"

Travis shrugged. "Sounds good to me."

"Yeah." Austin huffed.

"What?"

"It's not that easy. I just can't tell her to break up with him. What if she loves the guy? I mean, if I tell her to break up with him for me, and she really likes him, then not only will I have no chance with her, I'll lose her as a friend."

"So then you'll have no reason to talk about her all the time."

"I don't talk about her all the time."

"Dude, you're obsessed with her."

"I'm not."

"Yeah, you are. Justin made one comment about the Quinn sisters and you went ballistic and almost got kicked off the team. That, my friend, is obsessed."

"Justin is a prick."

"Yes, we all know that and nobody listens to his crap. But you did." Travis shook his head. "Man, he tossed that line out there and you took it. You know he gets off on stirring stuff up."

Travis was right. Pissing people off was a sport to Justin. And for all the sweat they'd poured out on the field today, he hadn't had the satisfaction of taking him down in the hall.

Austin turned in the drive of Travis's huge, single-story, red brick house and pulled to a stop. "Hey, man, I'll see you tomorrow."

Travis opened the door. "Yeah. Don't worry about Kelsey. She'll come around."

"Yeah, 'cuz who could resist me?"

"Well, now I'm gonna hurl. See ya." Travis climbed out of the truck and jogged to the door.

Travis's mom leaned out of the front door and waved to him. When he was younger, Austin had wished he could trade places with Travis for one day. He wanted to know what it was like to have a dad that didn't knock him across the room when he felt like it. He'd watch Travis's parents put their arms around each other and longed for parents who loved each other.

As he grew, he'd realized that having an asshole dad made him strong. He wouldn't trade his mom for anything. She was the toughest woman he knew, and she believed in Austin and was always on his side. Whatever good parts he had came from his mom. He thought of his dad and his stomach knotted. He hoped the bad parts had somehow bypassed him, because there was no way in hell he was gonna be like his dad.

17

In Texas it is illegal to sell your eyes.

Kelsey leaned against the headboard of her bed with her phone cradled in her hands. Her thumbs raced across the keys.

> *Drew: How was swimming?*
> *Kelsey: A blast.*
> *Drew: You didn't finish telling me about your bad day.*
> *Kelsey: It turned out great.*
> *Drew: What happened?*

Kelsey smiled to herself. *Yeah, what did happen?*

> *Drew: ??????*
> *Kelsey: Swimming and burgers.*

Ryan slipped into Kelsey's room and sat cross-legged on the end of the bed. "Can we talk?"

"Is this about the Purity Club thing?" Kelsey was fully prepared to give her a hard time, but her face looked like sadness had pulled it into one giant frown. As angry as she was at Ryan, she was still her sister.

Ryan nodded and took a deep breath, and when she let it out, a tear slid down her cheek. "I understand why you and Kenzie hate me…"

"We don't hate you." Kelsey set her phone on the bed beside her, ignoring a ding signaling Drew's reply.

"Come on, Kel, I'm not stupid."

Kelsey picked at a loose thread on her duvet. Okay, so she did hate her most of the time. "You make me mad, but…"

"You know our moving here didn't really have anything to do with me." Ryan huffed out the words.

"Are you kidding me? Yeah, Dad lost his job, but it wasn't until you got caught that they started talking to Uncle Jack." Kelsey raised her voice just short of yelling. She was not going to let Ryan get by without owning up to her part in all of this.

"Jeez, guys. Mom and Dad are going to hear you." Mackenzie stood at Kelsey's doorway as though she was afraid to cross the threshold. "Can I come in?"

Kelsey looked at Ryan. This was her sister talk; she should decide.

Ryan nodded. "You need to hear this too."

Mackenzie flipped the dressing-table chair to face the bed and sat.

"Okay. Maybe we moved here because of me." Ryan studied her hands. "Look, I made a lot of bad decisions in Chicago. I just kind of got swept up in a situation and I didn't know how to get out."

"Which situation was that? Screwing guys or smoking weed?" Kelsey spat out the words.

Ryan winced as if they had slapped her. "Just listen."

"Okay. I'm listening." Kelsey's phone dinged again and she clicked it over to vibrate.

"Did you know Alex Butler? He's older than you, Kelsey."

"Tall, dark curly hair. Drove an A4." Big player. "Yeah, I know him."

"Just after I started at The Art Academy, his sister, Lauren, had a party."

Mackenzie propped her feet on the mattress. "I remember. You begged Mom to let you go until you wore her down."

"That was my first major mistake," Ryan said. "I felt so cool. I was a special kid, in a special school, and I was going to my first real party. It was a sleepover. Mom made sure her parents were home, but they might as well have been on the moon. They had a keg."

Mackenzie curled her toes, popping them. "Their parents let them have beer?"

Kelsey looked at Mackenzie. "The Butlers were famous around school for their parties." She shook her head at Ryan. "You had to know it was going to be out of control."

Ryan nodded. "I couldn't wait to be a part of it either. Mom would have freaked if she knew. Lauren's mom insisted everybody spend the night and she took our keys, but that was the end of her chaperoning. Once the party got started, Lauren's parents went upstairs and we never saw them again. Everybody got so smashed. I wandered down to the basement. Alex was down there with a couple of guys. They had a bong."

Kelsey said, "You were only fifteen. He must have been at least—"

"Nineteen. Hot. And he flirted with me. They taught me how to use the bong. You know how they say you don't get high the first time you try pot? Big lie. I was whacked." Ryan pulled her knees to her chest and wrapped her arms around them. "The next thing I knew, we were alone in the basement and he was kissing me. Alex Butler was kissing *me*, Ryan Quinn. I barely remember him taking me to his bedroom. I didn't want to do it, but I didn't know how to make him stop. I mean, they tell you to say no, but he wouldn't listen. He just kept going. Besides, I wanted him to like me."

"But if he liked you, he'd stop. It wouldn't matter," said

Kelsey.

"Maybe in your world." Ryan closed her eyes briefly. "Think about it. I was drunk, high, and this gorgeous guy wanted to hook up. Reason flew out the window as soon as I arrived at that party. The worst part was the next morning. He woke me up at about four and told me I had to get out of his room. He just lay there and watched me dress. I was so humiliated. I found my way to the den where everybody else slept. There were so many kids that I couldn't find a place to lie down."

Mackenzie tilted her chair back on two legs. "What'd you do?"

"I cleaned up in the bathroom as best as I could and then sat in the dining room until everybody woke up. When Alex came downstairs, he acted like he'd never seen me."

Kelsey huffed. "What a jerk." He'd treated her sister like a whore. Got her high, used her, and kicked her out. The anger that Kelsey had kept burning toward Ryan turned to grief. "You never said anything. Why didn't you talk to me?"

"I was humiliated. I felt so stupid and I was scared. Forever I thought I was pregnant, and then I was sure I had HIV or something. I hung out at Lauren's house a couple of times after that, mostly because I wanted to see Alex. I saw him once—and he *introduced himself to me.*"

Mackenzie let the chair drop on all its legs. "Seriously?"

"Yeah. After that, some of the guys started paying attention to me. I thought I was suddenly popular because I'd been to a party at Lauren's. It didn't occur to me that it had anything to do with my sleeping with Alex. Then Ben Gibbs asked me out. We went out a few times before he tried anything. At first I said no. He kept trying—but not like he was physically forceful. I really liked him and he made me feel as though he really liked me. To say yes to him kind of made me feel better about what had happened with Alex. I mean, this time I was doing it with somebody I liked."

Kelsey said, "But you broke up with him."

Ryan nodded. "He told me that when he saw me go into Alex's room, he knew I'd be a good piece of ass. That's when I figured out why I was so popular."

"But you kept doing it." Kelsey didn't know if she should hug Ryan or shake her for being so stupid.

Ryan pulled on the ends of her pixie-cut hair. "I dated Bobby O'Malley after that. He was a trip. When he was in a good mood, he was funny and kind, but man, if his dad was on his case he could be mean. All he wanted to do was have sex."

Mackenzie had kind of a sick look on her face. Kelsey could totally relate. Knowing Ryan had slept around was one thing, but putting faces with the guys she'd slept with made Kelsey's stomach knot. "Ryan, why are you telling us all of this?"

"Because I want you to understand why I'm not sad that we left Chicago." She looked at Mackenzie. "I was your age and I'd had sex with three guys. My reputation was sealed. After that, I had a lot of dates and I just figured sex was going to happen. I didn't know how to make it *not* happen."

Mackenzie looked like she wanted to say something but couldn't. Finally, she took a breath and blurted, "I don't get it. Why date if you knew it was going to happen?"

Wow, Mackenzie expressing a strong opinion?

Ryan's wide-eyed expression said she was just as surprised. But she recovered quickly, shrugged, and said, "I don't know how to explain it. I'm not sure I understand myself. I kept thinking eventually one of them would like me for me. But they never did, and I felt like I was getting what I deserved." Ryan sniffed, but tears flowed freely down her face anyway.

Mackenzie handed her a box of tissue from Kelsey's dresser. "You didn't *deserve* anything."

"I wanted to get drunk. I wanted to get high. I let the rest happen."

Kelsey moved next to Ryan. "Okay, so you screwed up

at a party, but you didn't deserve date rape."

"I wasn't date raped, I let him."

Kelsey shook her head. "No. You were drunk and high. You really didn't have a choice. Didn't your shrink tell you this?"

"I never told her. I didn't tell her most things. All she knew about was the last time, when I got caught." Ryan dabbed her eyes and took a shaky breath. "This is my last chance. I don't want to be every guy's eff-buddy." Sobs erupted from her.

The crudeness of Ryan's words felt like a gut punch. Kelsey had had no idea of the pain her sister was experiencing. She wrapped her arms around Ryan and swallowed the dry lump in her throat. "Why didn't you talk to me?"

Ryan shrugged. "I don't know. You were always with Drew or Zoe. Besides, we haven't exactly been close."

"But we're sisters." And she'd been a crappy one to Ryan. The ugly truth was that she had seen the change in her sister after that party. She'd known Ryan was hurting about something, but was too busy with her friends to reach out. Guilty tears dripped down Kelsey's face. "I'm sorry I wasn't there for you."

"I thought I was handling it." Ryan sniffed. "I know it's stupid to try to go back, but the Purity Club is important to me. It's my chance to pretend I wasn't that girl."

"Nobody has to know." Kelsey hugged and rocked Ryan. As they cried, Kelsey could feel the hurt and mean words that had passed between them begin to disappear. She was going to be a better sister. She might hate it in Texas, but she didn't have to make it miserable for Ryan. She gave her a tight hug and released her.

Mackenzie shifted uneasily in her seat. "Well, you know I'm sure not going to say anything."

Kelsey and Ryan looked at each other and giggled. Ryan shook her head at Mackenzie. "Believe me, you're the last person I'd worry about spreading rumors."

Mackenzie shrugged and nodded. "Words are not my friends. So what's the Purity Club?"

Ryan flopped back on the mattress. "I'm not really sure. We took a True Love Waits pledge."

"All I know is that we prayed until our food got cold and then ate," Kelsey said.

Mackenzie smiled. "So far, you know that you take a pledge, pray, and eat cold food. And it's important to you?"

"Very," Ryan said, and they all started laughing.

Ryan sat up and faced Mackenzie. "We prayed for you, too."

"Me? What did I do?"

"Nothing," said Kelsey. "You just didn't come to the eat and greet. Mrs. Bettis prayed that you'd see fit to dedicate your body to purity or something like that."

"It sounds like they want to sacrifice me."

Kelsey shot back, "I think that's scheduled for next month." They all broke up again.

When they quieted, Ryan sat up and blew her nose. "Thanks, guys."

Kelsey picked up her phone. "Hey, if we're going to survive living in Hickville, we need to stick together." She looked at the text message she'd ignored earlier.

Austin: I had fun swimming.
Austin: Are we good?
Austin: ???

"Crap."

Kelsey: We're good. I had fun too.

Ryan said, "Is Drew mad at you again?"

"No. Austin thinks I'm mad at him."

"Because of the kiss?"

Kelsey eyed Mackenzie. "You saw that?"

Mackenzie chewed her lower lip. "You were standing in front of the window."

Kelsey felt her face turn red. "But it wasn't really a kiss."

Ryan volleyed her gaze between her sisters. "How did I miss all of this?"

"You were the reason we barely kissed." Kelsey scooted back to her headboard. "You came in carrying a bunch of junk from the table."

Ryan nodded. "That's why you were all awkward and stuff. I vote for him over Drew any day."

"There's no vote. But I have to admit, Drew got on my nerves when he called earlier."

"It took you long enough." Mackenzie stood and stretched. "I can't stand the way he orders you around. He's always telling you what to wear, or how to wear your hair, or worse, makeup. I remember that time you spent like forever in the bathroom making sure your hair was perfect and he came over and told you to go brush your hair. He screws with your mind, Kelsey."

Kelsey and Ryan stared at her.

"What? It's true."

Ryan said, "Words just became your friend."

Mackenzie ducked her head. "I'm sorry. I just got caught up in the moment."

"Don't stop now," Ryan said. "I've been telling Kelsey the same thing about Drew."

The last thing Kelsey wanted was to turn the day sour by getting into a Drew-versus-Austin discussion. So, she stood and said, "Guys, it's been fun, but I'm beat." She left her sisters and retreated to the bathroom to get ready for bed.

Teeth brushed and face washed, she climbed into bed and thought about the day. It had had a rough start, but a pretty fantastic finish. Her mind went to the almost kiss. This thing with Austin had her insides jumbled up. Drew/Austin.

Austin/Drew.

There was only one way to figure it out. She needed to see Drew. She punched his number.

"Hey, babe?"

"Hey, Drew. I'm sorry I couldn't talk earlier."

"No problem. What are you up to now?"

"Talking to you." She put a little flirt into her voice. "I miss you."

"I miss you too."

"I wish I could see you."

"I'm sorry, Kelsey. It's been a crazy summer."

"Yeah, I know." Silence hung between them. *Here it is—he's going to break up.* "Drew? Are you still there?"

"Yeah. Kelsey, it's going to be okay. Life is changing for both of us, but we're going to be okay." He sounded sad and defeated.

"Are you okay?"

"I'm great. It's our senior year." He sounded like he was trying to convince himself as much as she. "So Kelsey, who's this guy you're tagged with on Facebook?"

"What?"

"You're in a bikini, sitting on the side of the pool. He's plastered next to you."

Kelsey grabbed her laptop and clicked to her Facebook page. Crap. Ryan had posted a series of pictures. In this one, Austin was leaning back on his hands and his shoulder was touching hers.

"Oh, that." She tried to sound casual, but the truth was, looking at the picture gave her butterflies. "He's the guy working for Dad. We were watching Mackenzie do tricks off the diving board. I didn't realize he was sitting so close."

"Well, be careful. I don't like the way he's leaning on you—even if he is just a farm hand."

Kelsey clicked on the picture and enlarged it. Austin had an amazing smile and she loved the way his wet hair fell across his forehead. But mostly, she tried to remember the feel of his shoulder against hers.

"Kelsey? You there, babe?"

"Oh, yeah. Sorry." She yawned. "Drew, I'm beat. Can we talk tomorrow?"

"Yeah. Kelsey—I miss you."

"I miss you too. 'Night."

They hung up and she knew she should close her laptop and snuggle down to sleep, but she didn't want to close the picture. Not yet.

18

Peeping Toms are exempt from prosecution if they have one eye, are over 50 years old, or are a member of the Texas legislature.

Kelsey saw Austin's truck through the window and her heart beat a little faster. "He's here. Come on, guys."

Ryan and Mackenzie grabbed their backpacks and the three girls headed out the front door to his truck.

Austin smiled as they climbed into the cab. "Ready for day two?"

Kelsey huffed a half-laugh. "Yeah, I think I can find my classes today. What about you? Are you going to make it to lunch?"

He looked her in the eyes before shifting the truck into reverse. "Absolutely. No more almost fights before lunch."

Warmth spread through her. *What about almost kisses?* "Yeah, yeah. I'll believe it when I see it."

He glanced at her again before swinging the truck around. "I promise I'll be there for you."

Something in his tone said he wasn't talking about lunch. Tingles cascaded through her, followed by guilt. *Remember Drew?* In an effort to diffuse both sensations,

Kelsey teased, "Hmm. Maybe today I'll leave *you* waiting by the cafeteria."

He stopped before turning onto the highway and grinned at her. "However long it takes, I'll wait."

Kelsey told herself he was talking about lunch, but warmth spread through her anyway and she couldn't stop the stupid smile that spread across her face. She studied her hands and tried to calm her emotions. She wasn't in love with him. He was a friend, nothing more. But his closeness in the truck made her want to reach for his hand, or maybe snuggle up next to him on the seat, or really feel his lips on hers.

She bit her lip and tried to push those thoughts from her brain. *Drew. What do his kisses feel like?* She tried to remember the feel of his arms around her, but couldn't quite get there. And as the silence grew in the truck, so did the tension. The air was almost crackling with it. She could almost hear everybody trying to think of something to say to ease the awkwardness.

Ryan tried. "We get to use the saws in shop class today."

"That's really cool," exploded from Austin's lips, causing everybody in the truck to start.

Mackenzie spoke up. "What about your art teacher, Mr. Smith? Everybody says he's insane."

Ryan said, "He's a blast. He really gets art." The rest of the way to school, Ryan and Mackenzie talked about their classes. Kelsey and Austin exchanged a few awkward glances, but neither contributed to the conversation.

*

When lunch rolled around, Kelsey had barely stepped out of the classroom when she saw Austin. He leaned on a row of lockers across the hall, hands in pockets, eyes on her. Warmth spread through her and a sappy grin snapped on to her face.

He pushed off the lockers and crossed the hall to her.

"Hey, I told you I'd walk you to lunch."

Her face practically hurt, she was smiling so big, and she was sure she looked like a complete moron, but she had no control over her facial muscles at the moment. "No fights?"

"Not today." His eyes kind of twinkled as he spoke, making her heart beat a little faster.

When they turned to walk to the cafeteria, she was able to relax her face. They walked side by side but didn't really talk, at least not to each other. Pretty much everybody said hello to Austin and not only did he greet them back, he introduced them to Kelsey. Clearly he was the Drew of this school. Except Drew didn't go out of his way to speak to anybody. He didn't have to; he was the ruler of that world. Money gave him power.

Austin was just friendly. He seemed to like everybody and they liked him back. He fist-bumped a couple of football-player looking guys, and she wondered how much his status was tied to the sport. If he quit the team or couldn't play, would he still be king of the school?

She thought about her dad. He had been Mr. Football and then quit. Why? And what had that done to him?

As soon as they exited the food line, a group of guys and girls called Austin to their table. Kelsey sat next to him, plastered on her best Junior-League-in-training smile, and graciously greeted everyone. He immediately got lost in sports talk with Caleb James. She scanned the table and tried to remember the names of the people around her.

Britney, Sabrina, and Courtney sat at the far end of the table. They didn't speak to Kelsey and she didn't waste her breath saying hello to them, but she did catch the expressions that passed between them. It was mean-girl code for *What is she doing at our table?*

Hannah and another girl set their trays down across from Kelsey. Hannah introduced the girl as Shelby Cox. Shelby was a contrast to Hannah's long limbs and dark silky hair. She was a redhead. Not auburn, but orange-red, and it framed her round face in soft curls. She wasn't skinny like the girls Kelsey was friends with in Chicago, but she wasn't huge either—just sort of curvy.

Kelsey said hello and hoped the conversation wouldn't die after the introductions. She pushed the wilted lettuce around on her salad plate and tried to think of something to say.

Shelby took up the slack in the conversation. "So everybody says you're from Chicago, right?"

"Yeah."

"Wow, you must feel like you're on another planet."

Kelsey smiled. "It is different here."

"Are you bored out of your mind?" Shelby stabbed her salad with her fork.

"I wish. Instead, I've been busy learning about chickens and pigs and stuff."

"Seriously?" Hannah smiled. "Nothing stereotypical about that."

Kelsey gave up on finding a crisp piece of lettuce and set down her fork. "What do you mean?"

Hannah said, "Just that not everybody in Hillside plays Farmville. Do you like it? The pigs, chickens, and such?"

"Honestly, at first I thought I'd been sent straight to hell. But other than the heat, I'm getting used to it. It's not that bad. What about you guys? What do you do for fun?"

Shelby's eyes lit up. "Get out of Hillside. Spring Creek is pretty cool. They just got an Applebee's and I've heard they're getting a Chick-fil-A."

Hannah elbowed her. "You started the Chick-fil-A rumor."

"I did?"

"Yes. Remember? We were at The Grind and you said that if Spring Creek got a Chick-fil-A and a Target, there would never be a reason to drive to Dallas."

"Oh yeah, we decided if we told everybody it was coming, maybe it'd come true." Shelby raised her eyebrows at Kelsey. "I guess I'm pretty convincing."

The girls laughed and Kelsey wondered if she'd found her Texas friends. Then Hannah said to Kelsey, "Hey, do you want to go to Spring Creek after school? There's a really cool coffee shop. It's only twenty minutes from here. Your sisters can come too."

"Sounds fun, but we probably have to work at the feed store. I can text my mom and ask."

Hannah pulled her cell out of her purse. "Text me when you find out. I can drive."

Kelsey grabbed her phone too. "Cool. Call me so I can put your number in my phone." The three girls exchanged numbers and Kelsey felt giddy. She'd made friends. And if things went well, maybe she could invite them to swim on Saturday after she got off work. She thought about asking them right then and there, but didn't want to seem pushy.

Kelsey texted her sisters and her mom.

The rest of lunch went by with Shelby and Hannah telling stories about growing up in Hillside. Pretty much the whole table listened to their tales, adding details the girls left out. Kelsey decided Shelby and Hannah were two of the funniest people she'd ever met and couldn't wait to get to know them better.

Kelsey kept her phone in her hand, waiting to feel the familiar buzz. It was probably too much to hope to get out of work two days in a row. When the text came, defeat was swift. Kelsey read the message and looked at Hannah. "My mom said a truck is coming in and she needs us until close."

"Maybe we can go after. What time do you close?" Hannah stood to take her tray.

"Six." Kelsey and Shelby stood too, followed by the rest of the table.

Hannah said, "We'll pick you up at six."

Austin leaned toward the girls. "Where are y'all going?"

Sarah answered. "Spring Creek. We're going to Latte Da. Do you and Travis want to go?"

"Maybe. It depends on when we get out of practice."

Kelsey walked with the girls to the tray return. "Do you know where our store is?"

Shelby wrinkled her brow at Kelsey. "You do realize this is Hillside, right? We know everything."

"Duh." Kelsey set her tray on the belt just as the bell signaled that "A" lunch was over. She grabbed her backpack and headed out of the cafeteria. Ryan walked up with a girl Kelsey recognized from the Purity Club named Macey Brown. "Hey Ryan, did you get my text?"

"Yeah, I haven't had a chance to answer. I have tons of homework. Macey asked me over to study. I'll probably do that after the store closes."

"Okay. I'll see you after school."

"Cool."

Kelsey hurried back to the group, who stood in a circle waiting for her. Austin laughed at something the girls said and looked over them to her. Her insides went to tingle mode again. She took a deep breath and reminded herself that they were just friends.

When she reached them, they headed down the hall together. And just like that, Kelsey found her group at Hillside High.

*

Kelsey and her sisters loaded fifty-pound sacks of feed onto flat carts and rolled them from the back storage area to the shelves in the front of the store. The first few times they'd stocked the feed, Kelsey and Ryan could barely toss a bag together. Now, they lobbed the bags solo. Not as easily as Mackenzie, but they managed to get the bags where they needed to be.

Kelsey wore a wheat-colored Hillside Feed apron to protect her clothes from the dust on the bags, but it didn't matter because sweat trickled between her shoulder blades, down her back, and around her bra. It glued her bangs against her forehead like a stringy fringe. *Gross* didn't come close to describing how she felt, and at any minute her new friends were going to come through the door.

At five after six, Kelsey heaved the last of her load onto a pile and tried to fluff her bangs away from her face. "I'd give anything for a blow dryer and flat iron right now."

"And a shower." Mackenzie tossed the last bag from her cart onto a stack of horse feed. "I'm going to hit the pool as soon as we get home."

"You don't want to come with us? Hannah and Shelby invited you too."

Mackenzie shook her head. "No. I just want to go home."

"Okay." The bell on the door jingled as Hannah and Shelby entered the store. "Great, they're here and I look like crap." Kelsey untied her apron and brushed at her clothes.

"Hey, Kelsey," Shelby called, waving.

Kelsey walked toward the front of the store. "Hi." Shelby wore a paper-thin lavender tee, a gray gauzy tiered skirt printed with little peace signs all over it, and black flip-flops. Hannah was just as cute in cuffed denim shorts that hugged her thighs and an orange and navy polka-dot tee. And their hair and make-up had been refreshed since school.

Kelsey looked at her dusty jeans and sweat-soaked tee. "You guys look cute. What I wouldn't give to have a pair of shorts and flip-flops tucked away somewhere."

Hannah shrugged. "We can run by your house on our way."

"Seriously? You know I live out of town."

Hannah said, "It's no biggie. Besides, nobody gets to Latte Da until around seven."

"Okay, let me tell my parents I'm leaving. I'll be right back." Kelsey jogged to the back room of the store. As she crossed the threshold into the warehouse area, it hit her that this family was not the same family she'd known in Chicago.

Ryan stowed the carts near the loading dock as Mackenzie hung her apron on a hook in the kitchen. Her parents sat together at the table. Her dad plinked stuff on a laptop as her mom called out numbers from a packing sheet. Wow. Back home, Dad would have still been at work, Mackenzie would have been at the gym, she and Ryan would have been out with friends, and who knew what her mom did? But they were seldom together.

Her mom looked up from her paper. "I thought you were going out with your friends."

"I am. I just wanted to tell you I was leaving."

Her mom stood. "Did they come in? I'd like to meet them."

"Yeah, I'll get them."

Kelsey found the girls loitering in the horse area playing with the whips. "Hey, my parents want to meet you."

Shelby smacked the whip against her palm. "I could have fun with this thing."

Hannah took the whip and hung it back on its peg. "Come on, we're here to make a good impression."

The girls followed Kelsey to the back and greeted her parents. Her mom started to go into twenty-question mode—Where do you live? What do your parents do?—when Kelsey interrupted her. "If you really want me home by eleven, then we need to get going. I'm going by the house to change."

Mackenzie twisted her hands and took a deep breath. "Since you're going by the house, do you think I could have a ride—if there's room? If not, it's okay."

Hannah nodded, "Sure, come on."

Dad stood and took a ten out of his billfold. "Here. Don't spend it all in one place."

"Thanks, Dad." Kelsey held on to the bill like she'd won the lottery. Ten dollars was nothing in her old life. It wouldn't have lasted through the first ten minutes of a night out with her friends. But now, it was precious and she was determined to squeeze every penny out of it.

Macey arrived to pick up Ryan as they were leaving. This girl was the complete opposite of the girls Ryan had hung out with in Chicago. Fashion was definitely not her middle name. Not that her clothes were bad—jeans and a T-shirt—but somehow they didn't fit quite right. Or maybe it was the way she tied her stringy brown hair in a low ponytail. She probably didn't really need the support of the PC to remain chaste. Not that she didn't have potential to be cute, but a guy would have to have superpowers to find the girl beneath those baggy clothes.

Kelsey's stomach knotted as she gave Hannah directions to the house. Her family's financial status was about to be revealed. In Chicago, she wouldn't have wanted to hang out with somebody who couldn't afford to keep up with her lifestyle. It would be embarrassing to go shopping with someone who could only stand by and watch as she dropped cash on a cute outfit. Would they feel the same? She wouldn't blame them. Who would ever have thought she'd be that girl on the outside looking in?

And speaking of cute outfits, she had no idea what she was going to wear. This was her big debut into Hickville and she didn't want to blow it. She looked at Mackenzie sitting across from her, staring out the window. She could ask her sister, but noting that she'd worn long sleeves to school again, decided Mackenzie was not the best fashion advisor.

By the time they pulled into the long drive leading to the house, Kelsey had decided on a pale blue T-shirt dress and sandals. As they climbed out of Hannah's RAV4, she was sure that khaki shorts and a printed blouse would be better. As she opened the door to the house and led the girls into the den, she settled on ankle jeans and a tank. Remembering the heat, she amended the decision to shorts and a tank.

Mackenzie headed for the kitchen as soon as they entered the house. "Do you guys want a soda? I'm grabbing a Coke."

"Sure." Hannah followed Mackenzie.

"None for me." Shelby stood in the den and looked around.

Kelsey knew what Shelby was thinking: *Expensive leather furniture in this dump?* She thought the same thing often enough. "Hey, do you guys want to help me pick something to wear?"

"Of course," Shelby answered.

Hannah walked back into the room sipping a Coke. Shelby grabbed the can from her and took a drink.

Hannah reached for the can. "Hey, get your own."

Shelby ignored Hannah's comment and took another sip. "Come on, we're going to help Kelsey."

Hannah took her drink back from Shelby. "Can I have this upstairs?"

Kelsey raised her brows. "Seriously?"

Hannah followed Kelsey upstairs. "Seriously. My mom is OCD about our house."

"Well, nothing could hurt this dump." Kelsey turned right at the top of the stairs and led the girls to her room.

Shelby said, "Dump? If this place is a dump, I'd love to see where you lived in Chicago. Our house is half this size and I have four brothers."

Open mouth, insert foot. Must think fast. Kelsey dropped her purse on her bed. "Ah, but do you have coffee-pot wallpaper in your den?"

Hannah plopped on Kelsey's mattress like she'd been there a thousand times. "She's right, Shelby—that wallpaper is worse than that flowery crap your mom has all over the walls."

Shelby watched Kelsey flip through the hangers in her closet. "And that's saying a lot. Damn, girl, you got some clothes. Who are you?"

Kelsey turned her back on her closet and faced her new friends. *Awkward.* "Things were different in Chicago."

Shelby pulled a red silk sleeveless ruffle-neck blouse out of the closet and held it out for Hannah to see. "Yeah. Your furniture is like out of a catalog and your clothes are to die for—are you like in wit-pro or something?"

Kelsey pulled a gauzy V-neck shirt from her closet. "What's wit-pro?"

Shelby shook her head and grabbed a navy sleeveless button-down.

Hannah said, "Witness protection. Shelby has an overactive imagination. What's that bright orange thing?"

Kelsey pulled a T-shirt dress from her closet. "This? It's a racer-back."

"Love it." Shelby inspected the dress. "It's almost as bright as my hair, but it'll look awesome with yours."

Kelsey decided on the racer-back and sandals. She wasn't usually shy in front of her friends, but she'd just met these girls. So, she grabbed the dress and padded across the hall to change and refresh her makeup.

She checked herself out in the bathroom mirror. Shelby was right—the color of the dress looked great with her dark brown hair. But not so much with the funky tan she'd acquired. Her arms were dark brown from weeks of farm chores, but her shoulders and back were a light shade of pink from yesterday's pool time.

She crossed back to her room. "I can't wear this."

Hannah sat up. "Why?"

Kelsey turned to show her back. "I have a major farmer's tan."

Shelby shook her red curls. "Grab a sweater or jacket or something. They'll have the air cranked up anyway. Let's go."

Hannah stood. "Shelby's right. Besides, nobody's gonna be looking at your tan lines."

Kelsey pulled a gray zip hoodie from her closet. "What do you think?"

Shelby said, "Perfect. Let's go."

The girls waved good-bye to Mackenzie floating in the pool and piled back into Hannah's car. Hannah had just pulled on to the farm-to-market road when Kelsey's phone rang.

"Hey, can y'all pick me up?" said a familiar voice.

"Hang on, let me ask." Kelsey leaned forward. "Austin wants us to pick him up."

Hannah nodded. "Okay, but tell him to meet me at the end of his drive. Hey, ask him if Travis is meeting us there."

Kelsey spoke into her cell. "Meet us at the end of your drive and Hannah wants to know if Travis is coming."

Hannah smacked the seat back. "You didn't have to tell him I wanted to know."

Austin said, "Travis said he'd try, but he had stuff he had to do for his dad. Tell Hannah I'm standing on the side of the road. All she has to do is slow down."

Kelsey laughed. "Okay, be ready to jump in."

"I'm always ready—just waiting for the right moment."

Kelsey felt heat prickle in her face. "I don't know what that means, but I'll open the door for you."

"That's all I need. I'll see you in a few."

Kelsey ended the call and flopped back on the seat. Had he meant to tease her with double entendres? She was probably reading too much into it. But she had a feeling his words had nothing to do with getting into the car.

19

In Leffors, Texas, it is illegal to take more than three swallows of beer at any time while standing.

Shelby peeked around the headrest at Kelsey. "Did I hear some flirting going on?"

Was it that obvious? "We're just friends. You know he works for my dad."

Hannah made the turn by the water tower and down Austin's road. "Well, he basically dropped off the face of the earth after y'all moved here. He didn't even come to the trestle parties."

"Trestle parties?" As they neared his house, Austin stepped to the middle of the road and heat prickled through Kelsey. He was dead sexy wearing those aviators. And the way his maroon Texas Aggies T-shirt stretched across his chest reminded her of the water fight they'd had. Her mouth went slightly dry. *Stop thinking like that, Kelsey. He's just a friend.* She closed her eyes for just a second and tried to picture Drew, but couldn't make it stick.

"Yeah. Trestle parties are a summer tradition." Hannah slowed and Austin reached for the handle on the side opposite Kelsey. Just as he clicked the latch, Hannah gunned the engine, shooting the car forward out of his hand.

He folded his arms across his chest and yelled, "Ha ha. Very funny."

Hannah backed up until she was even with him. Again he reached for the door handle, and again she gunned it, backing the car out of his reach. The girls giggled as Austin backed away. Hannah pulled up next to him, but this time he didn't touch the door.

Hannah lowered the passenger window and yelled, "Come on, Austin. I won't do it again."

He shook his head. "Kelsey has to open the door."

Kelsey scooted across the seat and pushed the door open. He grabbed the car frame and jumped in. Hannah accelerated and his body slammed against Kelsey's, splaying her across the backseat and sending his sunglasses flying. If they hadn't been laughing so hard, Kelsey might not have been able to resist the urge to wrap her arms around his waist and hold him against her. As it was, they were all arms and legs, flailing like a bug on its back.

Hannah stopped the car and Austin lifted himself off Kelsey. But for a brief second, he pushed up on his forearms and hesitated. His gaze locked on hers and she felt it all the way to her core. Now she had to figure out how to pretend that her brain could still function and normal words could still come out of her mouth.

Shelby turned to Austin. "Glad you could join us. And why didn't you bring Kelsey to the trestle this summer?"

*

Austin hadn't thought much about the trestle since the Quinns had arrived in Hillside. Introducing Kelsey to farm life was a whole lot more fun than swimming with an occasional water moccasin.

"What's the trestle?" Kelsey fished his aviators off the floor and handed them to him. Her face was flushed and she was still a little out of breath from laughing. He tried not to focus on the way her chest moved as she caught her breath.

Down, boy. Look away. But he didn't. "It's where the train used to cross the river. It's halfway between here and Spring Creek. Everybody hangs out there in the summer."

Shelby said, "Somebody tied a rope from the trestle. It's a blast to swing out to the middle and drop into the river."

"So why haven't you taken me there, Austin?"

The way Kelsey's hair brushed her shoulders as she turned from looking at Shelby to him made him hold his breath for half a second. "I dunno. I guess between snake bites and water fights, we haven't had much time."

"Hey, that snake bite was weeks ago." She backhanded his thigh and he wanted to grab her hands and pull her into his lap.

"I heard about that." Shelby reached across the seat. "Let me see." Austin held out his hand so she could inspect it. "It doesn't look too bad."

"Naw, just a few stitches. I think it might even have improved my throw."

Kelsey grabbed his hand and ran her finger across the pink scar on his thumb. "So you should thank me."

"Let's see how I play Friday." He pulled his hand away. Sitting this close to her, feeling her little touches, was driving him crazy. If they'd been alone, he might not have been able to resist pulling her into his arms and begging her to touch him all over. He tried to divert his attention to the girls in the front seat. "So why Tuesday night at Latte Da?"

Hannah said, "They have back-to-school stuff going on all week. Besides, Kelsey hasn't been to Spring Creek, so we figured, why not. And since we're showing Kelsey all the cool stuff about Hillside, I think we should take her to the trestle after the game Friday."

Austin shook his head. "Can't. Coach already told us he's gonna drive out there to check on us. Anybody caught drinking is off the team and he said he'll assume anybody out there has to be drinking."

"That sucks." Shelby grinned at him. "But we can go, and we can take Kelsey."

"I don't know…" Kelsey gave him a *help me out of this* look.

He winked at her. "I have a better idea. Let's just go to Pepperonis after the game. Everybody will be there anyway."

Shelby shrugged. "Crappy pizza and an even crappier salad bar? I'm in."

Hannah punched the air with her fist. "I'm in."

"Kelsey?" Austin asked.

"I love crappy pizza. Of course I'll go."

Hannah and Shelby spent the rest of the drive educating Kelsey about the kids in their school, which was perfect for Austin. He nestled in the corner of the seat, folded his arms across his chest, watched, and listened. Well, mostly watched. With his dark sunglasses on, they couldn't tell where he was looking.

Not that he was staring in an obsessive stalker creepy sort of way. He was noticing things. Like the way Kelsey's whole face seemed to sparkle when she laughed, or the shape of her ankles. He'd never thought about ankles before, but he liked hers and the little dangly anklet she wore around one of them today.

By the time Hannah pulled her little red RAV4 into the parking lot, he was beginning to feel a little stalker obsessive. He focused his attention on everything else, or tried to. But darn, those cute little ankles kept calling him back.

The parking lot was packed. Country music played from a small stage on the patio outside. It seemed like everybody from Spring Creek and Hillside High had had the same idea. Austin walked slightly behind the girls as they headed for the door. When a group of guys sitting on the patio checked out the girls as they passed, Austin resisted the urge to claim Kelsey with a hand at the small of her back.

The line to order was at least ten deep. Austin scanned

for a place to sit, but every chair and sofa had a butt attached to it. Unfortunately, one of those butts belonged to a major ass: Justin Hayes. "Aw, crap." Hayes sat on one of those squishy chairs that are somewhere between a loveseat and a big chair. Britney Boyd sat next to him with her legs stretched across his lap. Courtney Randall and Sabrina Stevens sat on either end of a sofa with Eric Perez between them.

Austin leaned forward and spoke in Kelsey's ear. "It looks like the pricks and their chicks are here."

Kelsey looked in the direction Austin indicated and rolled her eyes. "Seriously? They had to come here."

Hanna and Shelby saw the group and both gave a half-wave. Hannah smiled at Kelsey. "I do not want to get on their bad side."

Kelsey sighed. "Well, being with me probably just put you there."

Shelby pulled back a step and looked at Kelsey. "One day in school and they hate you. Damn, girl, what'd you do?"

"Exist. We met at the coffee shop on the square and I didn't make a good impression."

"Were you with him?" Hannah pointed at Austin.

"Yeah." Kelsey smiled. "They didn't like that much."

Austin fluttered his lashes. "Can I help it if I'm dead sexy?"

Kelsey laughed and said, "Maybe to the skank sisters."

Austin captured Kelsey and pulled her tight against him, pinning her arms to her sides. "Come on, you know you can't resist me."

She giggled against his chest. "In your dreams."

He released her, but their gazes locked. Kelsey brushed her bangs from her eyes. Austin cleared his throat. And the air crackled between them.

Shelby clapped her hands. "Okay, getting a little sizzly here. Let's order and cool you two down."

Kelsey bit her bottom lip—which did nothing to cool

Austin off—and turned from him.

    Austin smirked. "God, Shelby, just put it out there."

    "I call 'em like I see 'em, Cowboy."

*

    Hannah maneuvered next to Kelsey and spoke almost in a whisper. "Don't mind Shelby. She and Austin are like brother and sister."

    "Why do you think I'd mind?"

    "I don't know. I just thought you might think she had a thing for him."

    "Oh. No. It's okay. Wait—do you think *I* have a thing for him?" *Crap, is it that obvious?*

    Shelby rolled her eyes. "Ah, yeah. The chemistry between you two is like—wow."

    Hannah smiled. "If Austin McCoy looked at me the way he looks at you... girl, I say go for it. He's the hottest, nicest guy in the whole school."

    Kelsey started to tell Hannah about Drew, but then she felt Austin's hand on her waist and inhaled the clean citrus scent of his aftershave and it didn't seem urgent anymore. He leaned close to her ear as though he was going to tell her a secret. "Do you want a frozen latte?"

    She nodded and tried to remain cool on the outside because things on the inside were a mess. He gave her waist a little squeeze and she had to bite her lip to keep from sighing. They ordered and he offered to treat. When he moved his hand from her side to pay, the spot where it had been felt cold and empty.

    After they got their drinks, Hannah and Shelby led them between the tables and away from Pricks and Chicks to the back of the coffee shop. Every spot was occupied. Hannah shouted over her shoulder, "Let's try outside."

    They wove through the crowd in the back room and out onto the patio. They didn't find any seats, but half the senior class seemed to be gathered around the small stage. Shelby tapped Kelsey's arm. "Hey, we're going to go talk to some guys from Spring Creek."

"Okay. Have fun." Kelsey pushed through the crowd and led Austin to the rail surrounding the patio. They barely had room to stand, but at least they could set their drinks on the ledge. The next song started and Kelsey turned to Austin. "Really? A Jason Mraz tune? In Hickville?"

Austin cocked his head, crossed his eyes, and said, "We got radio all the way down here."

"Okay. I deserved that. But this really is a cool place."

"Yeah. I can't believe it's so crowded on a Tuesday night." He leaned his elbows on the rail and faced her. She smiled and let herself get a tiny bit lost in the way his eyes danced when he looked at her.

He tucked a strand of hair behind her ear. "Kelsey…"

She didn't want to know what he was about to say. She just wanted to enjoy the night. She closed her eyes briefly and swayed with the music. "I love this song. Come on, feel it with me."

Austin laughed. "I can't dance like that. I'm pretty country."

She moved in front of him. "I'm not dancing. I'm swaying." When the song ended, she turned toward the stage and clapped.

The crowd seemed to swell and Kelsey got knocked into a couple of times. Austin moved behind her and rested his hands on her shoulders. It was a protective gesture and Kelsey should have kept it that way. She should have thought about Drew and resisted Austin's touch. But she didn't. Instead, she leaned against his chest. He slid his arms around her waist and held her against him. She laced her fingers with his, he rocked her with the music, and it felt like she'd stepped into a dream.

After about the third song, Hannah ran to them. "Austin, can I ask you a huge favor?"

"What is it?"

"We got invited to a party at the trestle."

Austin winced. "Hannah, I can't risk going—"

"No, you don't have to. Just take my car. We have a ride." She looked over her shoulder at Shelby standing with a group Kelsey didn't recognize—which wasn't saying much.

"Are you sure?"

"Yes." She dangled her car keys from her hand.

He took the keys with one hand, but left the other wrapped around Kelsey's waist. "But how will you get your car back?"

"I'll pick it up at your house. Don't worry, it'll be fine."

"I don't know…"

"Look, it's done." She cocked her head at Kelsey and said, "You're welcome to come if you want."

"I think I'll pass."

"Well, have fun, you two." Hannah wriggled her fingers at them and took off across the patio.

He looked at the enormous pink flower key ring and held it out to Kelsey. "Can you put this in your purse? I don't think it'll fit in my pocket."

She nodded and dropped the keys into her bag.

Austin checked the time on his phone. "It's like eight o'clock. Do you want to do something else?"

"Sure."

*

He took her hand and led her through the coffee shop and out to the parking lot.

"So where are you taking me?" She pulled away from him but didn't let go of his hand, so he tugged her back, and she giggled.

"You'll see." Excitement coursed through him. She'd leaned against him, laced her fingers with his, and now they were holding hands—like they were a couple. And no one had mentioned the boyfriend. It was turning out to be a perfect evening, and if he didn't screw it up, it was going to get better.

A warm breeze washed over him as he led her between rows of cars. He could sense a change in the air and hoped that it meant the he and Kelsey were getting closer. Footsteps sounded from behind. He turned toward the noise, but didn't have time to brace himself before Justin Hayes hit him like he was defending the line on the field. They both hit the ground. He saw Kelsey stumble, but she managed to keep from hitting the pavement.

Justin straddled Austin and pulled back his fist. But Austin was bigger and stronger, and in a blink, he'd pinned Justin to the blacktop. "What the hell is wrong with you?"

Justin didn't answer, but he wasn't trying to hit Austin either. A crowd had gathered and it wouldn't be long before someone called the cops. Austin released Justin and stood.

Justin stood too, but something was off. He had a wild look in his eyes.

Austin took a step back. "Are you freaking crazy?"

He started for Austin again, but Eric Perez held him back.

Kelsey pulled up in Hannah's car and opened the door. "Get in!" Austin dove for the car. As soon as he was mostly in, Kelsey took off. He managed to get the door closed and his seat belt on before they were out of the parking lot. "Damn, Kelsey. Who knew you had NASCAR talent?"

"What was that all about?"

"Who knows? Justin has a few screws loose."

She pulled up to a red light and they both took a deep breath. She leaned her head against the headrest and looked at him. "Are you okay?"

"Yeah. Just a little bruised from the fall."

The light turned green and she pulled forward. "Crap, Austin, I don't even know where I'm going."

"Turn around and head back to Hillside." A slow smile spread across his lips. "There's a special place I want to show you."

20

In Texas, it is illegal to milk another person's cow.

Kelsey parked Hannah's car close to the road. "What do I do with her keys?"

"Just toss them on the floor mat. They'll be safe. Come on."

"Seriously? If I did that in Chicago, the car would be gone in thirty seconds."

"Yeah, but this is Hickville, remember?"

"Okay, but if the one thief in Hillside jacks her car, it's your fault." Kelsey chucked the keys on the floor mat and slammed the door. They walked side by side, they way they had at the courthouse when they'd been so close their arm hairs touched—only this time he took her hand. A small part of her brain, way in the back, hinted that she was treading close to cheating on Drew. But she wasn't going there. Austin was a friend and they were having fun, that was all.

Kelsey headed toward his truck, but Austin tugged her toward the house. "We're not taking my truck."

She followed, but slowly enough to pull on his hand. "Okay. Where are you taking me?"

"Ever ride a four-wheeler?"

Her feet stopped moving. "What do you think?"

He grinned. "Come on, you're going to love it."

She stood her ground, but her insides were revving for an adventure. "It's almost dark."

"The sky's barely pink, and besides, it has lights." He checked his phone. "It's just eight thirty." He led her to the carport and the machine. "Climb on."

"But I'm in a dress."

"I won't peek."

She straddled the engine. "Don't these things flip?"

"I'll go slow. Besides, it's the best way to take you where I want to go."

He grabbed a blanket from a shelf, climbed on behind her, and showed her where to hold the handlebars. He placed his hands behind hers and spoke into her ear. "Just relax. You can trust me. I'm not going to do anything stupid."

She felt safe with his hands on either side of hers, but was still all giddy and nervous on the inside. Riding a four-wheeler at night—how cool was that? *Alone with Austin on that four-wheeler?* She shook her head. *Enjoy the ride, girl.*

They started slowly, driving across the pasture behind his house toward the trees. He leaned forward and spoke in her ear. "You okay?"

"Yeah, this is fun."

"I'm going to go a little faster. Tell me if it's too much."

"I'm ready for a little excitement."

"Atta girl." He rotated the handlebar grip and sped across the ground. Now *this* was fun. The wind against her face, flying across buffalo grass and cow poop—this was a Facebook worthy experience.

When they reached the end of the pasture, he slowed the machine and followed a trail through the trees. They climbed a steep hill, but she felt safe with his chest against her back and his arms around her. It was almost dark when he stopped the four-wheeler.

"It's just a little way from here."

"What?"

"You'll see." They climbed off the machine and he led her to a place where the trees opened onto a bluff.

She looked at the striped land below and the farmhouses dotting the landscape. "This is beautiful. But we're going to lose our view. It's almost dark."

"No. That's when the real show begins." He spread the blanket on the grass. "The sky is amazing out here." He sat and stretched out his legs.

A blanket in the middle of nowhere? She told herself nothing was going to happen—she wouldn't let it. Kelsey sat with her knees tucked under and pulled her dress over her thighs. "Don't forget, I have to be home by eleven."

"Not a problem. I'll set my phone alarm." He plinked on his phone and set it on the edge of the blanket.

They sat a few inches apart, close enough to touch, but they didn't. Kelsey's heart raced anyway. She stretched her legs out, crossed her ankles, and leaned back on her elbows. She dropped her head back and took a deep breath. "Smell that?"

He sniffed. "What?"

"It's clean."

He sniffed again. "I smell dirt. What are you talking about?"

She laughed. "Well, I'm not smelling city. It's grass and wildflowers." She looked at him. "And you."

"Me?" He bumped her with his shoulder. "What about you?"

"What about me?"

"You smell like pretty things."

"Pretty things?"

He looked into her eyes. "Yeah, like flowers and stuff."

Kelsey laughed and dropped to her back. "Look. The stars are coming out."

Austin lay back too, and looked up. "The sky is so clear out here it's like you could reach up and touch them. Keep watching."

"For what?"

"That." Austin pointed at a bright streak screaming across the sky. It was gone almost as soon as it appeared.

"Oh my God. I've never seen a shooting star before. How'd you know we'd see one?"

"It's the Perseid meteor shower. It happens every August. We learned about it in sixth grade. I come up here a lot at this time of year."

"Aren't you supposed to make a wish or something?" Kelsey searched the sky for another streak.

"Yeah, I think so. Go ahead, what are you going to wish for?"

"I can't tell you. First rule of wishes—it won't come true if you don't keep it a secret."

He laughed and said, "Close your eyes and make your wish."

She squeezed her eyes shut and wished time would slow just a bit. When she opened them, Austin was propped on an elbow looking at her. "What?"

"Nothing. It's just—I like seeing my world for the first time."

"What?"

"Everything is so new to you, it makes me appreciate what I take for granted."

She reached up and glided her fingers through his hair. She hadn't intended to pull him toward her and she wasn't really sure she had, but he lowered his mouth to hers and stars burst in her head.

They kissed long and slow. When the kiss broke, she turned on her side to face him. Their gazes locked and she felt eagerness mixed with hesitation and fear. Guilt lingered somewhere in the distance. *Not now.* She wasn't going to deal with that now. She tilted her chin just enough to reach his lips.

As they kissed, he pulled her against him and ran his

hand down her spine to just below the small of her back.

She rolled back, bringing him with her. He broke the kiss and supported his weight on his forearms. "Kelsey…"

She stared into his eyes, breathing so hard and fast her head was spinning. She couldn't think.

He kissed her softly and said, "I promise I won't…"

She nodded.

He kissed her again and she wrapped her arms around his waist and pulled him tight. His kisses were harder this time. Then he trailed soft kisses up her neck until he captured her mouth again. His hand drifted to the hem of her dress, but instead of plunging beneath it, he smoothed it over her thigh.

Every second he was with her, she wanted more. More kisses, more touches, more everything.

He pulled away and stroked her hair. "You are so beautiful—we have to stop—or we're not going to be able to stop."

She nodded and barely squeaked, "Yeah."

He rolled on his back and scooted so close their shoulders touched.

She tried to watch for more meteors, but then he turned his head to look at her and she couldn't resist tasting one more kiss. As soon as her lips touched his, she was gone again—kissing and touching him—losing her mind.

And then, his phone alarm sounded.

She broke the kiss. "I have to go."

*

Austin stood and helped Kelsey up. He gave her another little peck on the lips and pulled away. He stretched his arms above his head and stood on the edge of the bluff. The breeze had kicked up again—just what he needed to cool down.

It had been stupid to bring her here. As much as he'd like to tell himself shit happens, this was premeditated. He'd come up with the idea when they'd decided to leave the coffee shop. He shouldn't have flirted with her.

He took the folded blanket from her and kissed her again. "Ready?"

"No, but my parents get freaky about missed curfews." She straddled the engine box and he climbed on behind her. He nuzzled her neck before starting the engine and heading back through the trees. He wanted to pull her against his chest, but he knew he had to back off and calm things down a little. He just hoped he hadn't screwed up their friendship.

But it wasn't like he'd forced her to kiss him. She'd been more than willing. Thank God he'd set that alarm. Things had been close to getting out of hand. He'd never do more than she wanted, but he had the feeling she was in willing now and regret later mode. If things ever went that far with them, he didn't want her to regret it later. Hell, he didn't want her to regret tonight either, but he wasn't sure that wouldn't happen. He had to back off, leave her alone.

Yeah. That idea lasted about two seconds. As soon as they parked the four-wheeler and stood in the carport, he kissed her again. And it wasn't a sweet little peck. It was a long, hungry, *I can't get you effing out of my mind* kiss.

Kelsey pulled away first. "We'd better go."

Austin nodded. "Yeah." They held hands as they walked to his truck.

He figured she'd want to talk about things on the way home. He dreaded the *I have a boyfriend* talk. He didn't want to think about the fact that because of him, she'd cheated on prick-boy.

But the words never came. He glanced at her a couple of times. She just sat there with her hands in her lap staring out the windshield with a little fake smile on her lips. And he knew he'd just majorly effed up.

He parked in front of her house and turned to her. "Kelsey, are you okay?"

"Yeah, I'm fine." But instead of looking at him when she said it, she dropped her gaze to her hands. It was a gesture that screamed shame and guilt.

He walked her to the door. He wanted to hold her hand or put an arm around her or something, but things had gone all wonky and awkward. So he followed her up the steps at a respectful distance.

At the door, she held his hands, looked into his eyes, and bit her lip before speaking. "Look, Austin, tonight was amazing…"

"But…?" *Here it comes—I have a boyfriend—he's a douche but he's mine…*

"I cheated on Drew."

"I know. I shouldn't have…"

She popped up on her tiptoes and gave him a quick kiss. "Shut up and listen. It wasn't just you. Like I said, it was amazing. But I cheated. And—I'm not sorry."

"Okay. And…?"

"I don't know. I'm so mixed up."

"What's to be mixed up about? I'm here. We're here— together. He's there. We're amazing, he's—there. Kelsey…" He kissed her again. He wanted her to think about him tonight, not the guy she cheated on. He was the guy she belonged with.

The kiss ended and she backed up a couple of steps. "I can't keep kissing you. It's not right."

"So break up with him."

"I can't do that."

"Sure you can. You say, 'Dan…'"

"Drew."

"'Drew, I've met this amazing guy in Texas. So it's over between us.' Problem solved."

"Look, don't pressure me right now."

Austin took a step back and held up his hands. "Okay, no pressure. Do you want me to pick y'all up in the morning?"

"Of course. This doesn't have to change anything."

"Sure. Hey, you'd better get inside. I'll see you

tomorrow." He kissed her on the cheek and opened the door for her.

He cranked the music up on the way back to his house. What kind of game was she playing? *I love kissing you, but I'm not breaking up with prick-boy.* Why couldn't she see that she belonged with him? They were so much more than what had happened tonight.

When he rolled into his driveway, Hannah and Shelby were pulling out. He lowered his window and shouted, "Hey. Y'all okay?"

Shelby answered, "Yeah. It was pretty boring. I guess everybody was at Latte Da. Oh, but just before we left, Courtney and her crew showed up. Sabrina told everybody how Justin would have beat your ass if your Yankee girlfriend hadn't brought my car around."

"Seriously? What a loser."

Hannah yelled, "What really happened?"

"Justin jumped me in the parking lot. All he did was knock me down. The guy is too big a wuss to know how to fight."

Shelby said, "Be careful, Austin."

"I can handle Justin. Be careful going home."

They said good-bye and Shelby pulled onto the highway.

Frustration and anger swirled around inside Austin. Kelsey was sweet poison. He couldn't stay away from her, and this *kiss me—no don't* scenario of hers was killing him. Between that and having Justin go psycho on him pretty much made the evening one big ball of suck.

He kicked a rock as he walked up the gravel path to the steps leading to his door. He understood why Justin hated him and if things were reversed, he might feel the same way. But as much as he wanted to, he couldn't change things. One thing was for sure—if Justin jumped out of the bushes at him now, he'd beat the crap out of that sonofabitch.

*

Kelsey crawled under the sheets and tried to untangle her thoughts, but her mind was going in a thousand different directions. She couldn't blame Austin for what happened. She wanted to forget she had a boyfriend waiting for her. She'd come on to him, flirted with him, wanted to make out with him. She knew what she was doing—and it was great.

More than great. It was mind-blowing. She closed her eyes and tried to relive one kiss after another. She felt little pings of excitement as she thought about how his lips felt against hers. She'd dated Drew for eight months and not once had they made out like that. Oh, they'd kissed a lot, but not like that. Their time together was so… civil.

Austin's kisses were raw and passionate and if the alarm hadn't gone off, she might have taken a walk in Ryan's shoes. Not all the way, but closer than with Drew.

But that last kiss had been the scariest. It was demanding. It was a *you're mine* kiss. It was a kiss that reminded her she was already somebody else's. And when the kiss had broken, guilt loomed large in her mind.

She texted Drew.

Kelsey: Are you up?

She'd hoped he would be too busy to answer, but a reply dinged instantly.

Drew: Yeah. What are you doing?
Kelsey: Getting ready for bed, you?
Drew: Missing you.

Before she could think of a reply, her phone signaled a Facetime request.

Crap, she'd already taken off her makeup. She had to answer. She didn't have an excuse not to. "Hey."

"Hey, beautiful."

"Beautiful? I'm not wearing makeup."

"You look great. I miss you, Kelsey."

"I miss you too." Seeing him reminded her how much. He was so hot. Blond hair parted on the side, perfect skin, perfect face. *Nothing redneck about him.*

"Something wrong, Kelsey?"

"No." *Why? Do you see guilt in my eyes?* "I'm just tired. You know, with school starting and all."

"I wish I could come down. Mom and Dad are freaking out about this being my senior year. They're adamant that we spend the rest of the summer at the lake house. They didn't do this when Elliot was a senior."

"But he's not the youngest. I've spent more time with my family since we moved here than probably my whole life. It's kind of cool."

He flashed his bleached white smile. "That's why you're so good for me. You keep things in perspective. I can't wait until the gala."

"Me either. I finally have enough money for the tickets."

"Which is insane. I could have paid for your airfare."

"You know my dad…"

"Yeah. It's got to blow working in that diner."

"I'm getting used to it."

"What did Zoe say you called it—a trailer trash hangout? Just don't turn trailer trash on us."

"Never." She tried to stifle a yawn, but it came anyway. "Can I talk to you tomorrow? I have an early day."

"Sure."

"Drew?"

"Yes?"

"I miss you too."

"When you come, we'll do whatever you want. Get some sleep. I'll talk to you tomorrow."

"'Night." How could she have doubted her feelings for him? Everybody loved Drew. He was just like his kisses—sweet, even tempered, and predictable. He was perfect.

Thoughts of Austin niggled back into her mind. She couldn't help but give a deep, satisfied sigh. What was she going to do about Austin McCoy? She closed her eyes and mentally kissed him again. Nothing sweet about those. Drew might be the perfect guy for her, but Austin set her world on fire.

Her phone dinged a text. It was from Drew.

Two words.

Love you.

21

In Texas, any man caught wearing a suit in public after midnight can be arrested for vagrancy.

Austin had trouble sleeping, but by the time he pulled up to the Quinn house the next morning, two things were very clear. One, if Kelsey wanted him to back off, he had no choice but to oblige. And two, he was not going to give up. She'd said she wasn't sorry that she'd cheated on Drew and that meant there was hope. He was crazy about her and he had a pretty good idea she felt the same. Now all he had to do was make her see it too.

Kelsey and her sisters weren't as chatty as usual when they climbed into his truck. Kelsey looked like hell. Her eyes were puffy and the dark circles beneath them indicated she hadn't slept much. Good. He was glad she'd lost sleep and he couldn't help but rub it in.

He tried über cheerful. "Hey, y'all. Ready for day three?"

Three grunts replied.

"Okay, come on. It's not that bad. The rest of the week will fly by. We have our first home game Friday. Y'all go to many games in Chicago?"

Ryan answered, "We weren't really into football."

"Oh, that's gotta change. You haven't lived until you've gone to a Hornet game."

"I'm going with girls from the PC." Ryan looked at her sister. "How about you, Mackenzie?"

"Maybe."

Kelsey stared out the passenger window. Austin's stomach tightened. Things were already awkward between them. He couldn't let that happen. "What about you, Kelsey? Are you going to the game?"

"I'm going with Hannah and Shelby." She turned to face the back seat. "Mackenzie, you can go with us if you want."

Mackenzie shrugged. "Maybe. It's bound to be better than sitting at home."

Austin smiled. "Definitely better than sitting at home."

The rest of the way to school was pretty uneventful. The rest of school was uneventful. He didn't see Kelsey again until lunch. She sat a few people away from him talking to Hannah and Shelby. At one point, he heard the name Drew and wanted to puke. So had she decided after a sleepless night that Drew was the one?

He thought about how she'd kissed him the night before. Those weren't *I miss my boyfriend and you'll do* kisses. Those kisses were full of passion. They'd had chemistry almost from day one, and last night that chemistry ignited something beautiful and magical. He'd be damned if he was going to let her go. But this time he was going to move slower. Let her come to him.

He didn't see her again until after school. She was on her way to the pick-up line and he was hurrying to football practice. She hesitated as though she wanted to talk, but he just smiled, waved, and kept going. Perfect. She could just think about what she was missing.

Thursday and Friday were a clone of Wednesday. Nothing new, nothing exciting, just a struggle to keep his distance from Kelsey. On the upside, Justin seemed to have taken a vacation from Crazyville. He hadn't exactly befriended Austin, but he wasn't jumping him from dark corners either.

By game time on Friday, Austin was focused on one thing and one thing only: football. As soon as the team suited up, they huddled near the exit of the field house. On Coach Peterson's direction they took a knee, and Coach prayed for a safe game and then went into a pregame speech. Nerves played in Austin's gut as he listened to Coach blather on about how this was their time but they were playing for those who'd gone before them. Yeah. Yeah. Not that Coach's words weren't inspiring, but he'd heard this same first game speech for four years. He just wanted to get onto the field and play.

When Coach finished, Travis started the Hornet hum. "Zzzzzzz." The rest joined in and bounced together in the rhythm to their buzzing.

Coach moved to the center of the hornet's nest and yelled, "Who are we?"

The team yelled back, "The Hornets!"

"What time is it?"

"Game time!"

"What time is it?"

"Game time!"

"Hornets!"

"Fear the sting!"

"Now get out there and do your job." Coach swung the door open and the team ran to the tunnel and waited to be announced onto the field. They joined hands and someone started the buzz.

As they bounced and buzzed, adrenaline coursed through Austin. The announcer's voice echoed across the stadium. "Let's hear it for the Hillside Hornets!"

The team ran through the cheerleaders' spirit sign and onto the field. The crowd screamed and whistled like they were rock stars. This was it—Austin's senior year. His last season to play football. Nothing would stop him from making it his best.

*

Kelsey walked between Hannah and Shelby as they made their way to the student section. What was Austin doing right then? Was he nervous? Excited? She shook her head to dislodge Austin-thoughts.

It had been weeks since she'd asked Drew if he loved her. How weird was it that he'd decided to tell her the exact night she'd cheated on him? They'd talked every night since. He'd described Italy and how someday he'd take her there. It sounded way more romantic than early mornings feeding chickens and shoveling horse poop. She'd taken a ride on the wild side, but she was trained for the Junior League. Drew was her ticket to that life, not Austin.

She looked at her friends. She would leave them behind in a few months, but they'd been good to her and although she wouldn't allow herself to get attached, she would play along. Go to their games, hang out at the coffee shop, whatever. She'd never be one of them. She was just a tourist on an extended visit. And in a few months, she'd return to her world and Hickville would be stored away in the Fond Memories section of her brain.

Hannah turned to her. "What do you think about your first Texas football game so far?"

"I can't believe how many people come to these things. It's like the whole town is here." Kelsey scanned the stands. "One question?"

"Okay."

"I get the whole idea of everybody wearing the same shirt. It's pretty impressive to see how many people are supporting the Hornets. But why black shirts with gold letters? I mean, it's still like ninety degrees."

Shelby laughed. "Yeah, but since the Hornets on the

shirts look more yellow than gold, they probably figured it was better than having a stadium full of pee yellow."

Kelsey nodded. "Valid point. I guess *black out the stands* is better than *yellow out*."

They climbed to the area where most of the seniors hung out. Ryan and Macey stood several rows behind them. They wore the same five-dollar black T-shirt as the rest of the crowd, but Macey somehow made it look less fashionable than pretty much everybody else in the stadium. She wore black shorts, but they bagged on her super-skinny legs and her skin was so fair it almost created a glare. Kelsey was used to seeing pale skin in the Chicago winter. But here, in hell's oven, everybody had some color.

Poor Macey had more than just super-white skin going on. The black T-shirt and huge white-rimmed sunglasses she wore just emphasized her lack of color. Kelsey shook her head. Who'd have thought her sister the artist would hang out with a girl who needed some serious fashion first aid?

Kelsey spotted her parents making their way toward the stands one section over from where she sat. She waved at them, but they didn't see her. "I'll be right back," she said to Hannah, and climbed down the bleachers.

"Hey, guys."

They smiled when they saw her. It was weird to see her dad in a T-shirt; he was a collared shirt kind of guy. He reached for his back pocket. "How much do you need?"

Kelsey shook her head. "Nothing. I'm just saying hi."

Her mom was definitely in Junior League mode. The sleeves of her T-shirt had a crisp crease down the center and were rolled in a neat cuff. She wore the shirt tucked into a pale khaki skirt with a wide black belt. Her hair was pulled back in a low ponytail and she wore gold hoop earrings.

"Mom you look fabulous, even in the Hornet football fan uniform."

"Thank you, sweetie. I'd like to know who thought it was a good idea to wear black shirts in this heat, though. So, are you having fun?"

"Ehh." Kelsey gave a shrug. "I didn't realize you guys were coming."

"Oh yes. We're Hornet boosters now." Her mom's words held a hint of sarcasm. Poor Mom. Kelsey might be leaving in a few months, but her mom was stuck here forever.

Dad pulled a five from his wallet and handed it to her. "Just in case."

"Thanks, Dad." She looked at the five on the corner of the bill and was again reminded that in her other life, he'd have given her a couple of twenties. Of course, back then, she wouldn't have been caught dead at a football game.

Uncle Jack hollered from the stands, "Tom! Tom Quinn."

Her dad looked up and headed toward his brother. "Hey, Jack."

Kelsey's mom said, "Call me if you go anywhere after the game."

"Oh, I think we're going to Pepperonis."

"Okay. Be home by twelve."

Mom turned to follow Dad and Kelsey watched as pretty much the entire section shook hands or hugged her dad as though he was some kind of hometown hero. Didn't they know the only reason he'd returned was because he'd failed in the real world?

Kelsey returned to her friends and tried to watch the game. She yelled when the rest of the crowd yelled, but she really had no idea what was going on beyond scoring points.

Her attention was drawn to potential drama where her parents sat. Her uncle left his place next to her dad and some lady sat down and started chatting him up like they were best friends. Could this be the infamous Cassidy Jones—the girl who'd somehow ended her dad's football career? She had short tabby-cat hair and an abundance of lipstick, mascara, and blush. Not that her makeup looked bad, it was just sort of *too much* for a football game. But then, so was the huge, blingy cross she wore around her neck.

Even from where Kelsey sat, she could see her dad's face light up as Tabby-hair spoke to him. The strange woman placed her hand on his arm or knee several times, as if to emphasize a point. Kelsey's mom nodded and smiled at the women's rambling, but her hands were folded together in a white-knuckled clasp and with each of the woman's touches, her smile became a little tighter.

Aunt Susan's demeanor was less subtle. She sat on the other side of Kelsey's mom with her arms crossed, looking like she'd sucked on a Sour Patch Kid. She darted her gaze toward Kelsey's dad and muttered something. Whatever she said seemed to break the tension. Kelsey's mom laughed and batted at Aunt Susan's knee in a *stop it* sort of way.

Uncle Jack returned carrying a cardboard tray full of drinks. Tabby-hair gave Kelsey's dad a too long, too tight hug and headed down the bleachers. Uncle Jack sat next to her dad and her mom turned toward Aunt Susan, basically turning her back on dear old flirty Dad.

Kelsey heard "McCoy draws back..." boom across the stadium and looked just in time to see Austin launch the ball down the field. The other guy caught it and ran it across the goal line. Everybody yelled like crazy and even non-football-fan Kelsey could see he was a pretty good quarterback. He rocketed the ball down the field all through the game. Every time he made a pass or gained yards, Kelsey yelled as though she knew what was going on. She was caught up in the hype along with the rest of Hillside. And in the end, when they beat the Jackrabbits twenty-one to fourteen, she screamed and hugged Shelby and Hannah.

*

Kelsey and her friends were some of the first to arrive at Pepperonis. Apparently, it was a long-standing tradition to go to the pizza parlor after the game, and the restaurant was prepared for the onslaught of fans. The party room was full of gold and black balloons. Rows of wooden picnic tables were shoved together end-to-end to accommodate the crowd.

As soon as the girls sat, Kelsey's phone dinged. When she saw the text was from Austin, her whole face broke into a smile. The kind that was too big, but impossible to tone down without her face fighting her and morphing into some weird contorted shape.

Hannah elbowed her. "So what'd he say?"

Kelsey felt heat crawl up her neck to her face. Yeah, the red surely looked awesome with the weird gargoyle expression stuck on her face. "Who?"

Shelby answered, "Yeah, right. We've seen that look before. So what'd Austin say?"

"Oh, just that he and Travis are on their way and want us to save them a seat." She tapped out *Okay* on her phone and tried to refocus her emotions. She didn't want to break out in a spontaneous grin when he texted. She didn't want to feel all jittery when he was around, and she sure didn't want to feel as though something was missing when he wasn't. She didn't want to fall for Austin McCoy. The night of kissing was over. It had been fun, but they were just two friends who'd let loneliness get the better of them.

She flipped to a picture of Drew just to remind herself where her heart belonged. Somehow looking at him didn't cause uncontrollable facial movements, but she wasn't going to think about that now. Instead, she shoved her phone into the back pocket of her jeans.

Shelby stretched her arms across the table and wriggled her eyebrows. "I wonder if Caleb James will be with them."

Hannah shook her head. "He's liable to see you and run the other way."

"No, he won't. It's like a game. We flirt. I flirt more, he squirms."

Hannah turned to Kelsey. "She's totally obsessed. He's too nice to tell her to get lost."

Shelby added, "I'm not really sure I still like him, but I know I like flirting with him."

Kelsey shook her head. "What about other guys? Do you date?"

"Yeah. But I hardly get asked out." Shelby shrugged, "We've all grown up together."

"That's why we look at Spring Creek guys," Hannah interrupted.

Kelsey said, "You know, if all the guys here know about your Caleb obsession, they're not going to be too excited to ask you out anyway."

Hannah said. "That's what I told her. I think she does it because she's afraid to put herself out there."

"That's so not true. Besides, there's all that Spring Creek talent we're getting to know."

Hannah shook her head. "Not true. You talked about Caleb when we were with those guys Tuesday."

"Really?" Kelsey rocked back on the bench. "Okay, girl, you've got to change your strategy."

Shelby leaned forward across the wooden table. "What do you mean?"

"If you really want to see Caleb squirm, let him go."

"What?"

"Stop flirting with him and talking about him. And you have to go cold turkey. It will drive him nuts."

Shelby rubbed her hands together. "I love it. I can't wait to tell everybody I'm over him."

"*No,*" Kelsey almost shouted. "You can't tell anybody, you just do it. If you announce it, it will have less impact. You want to broadside him."

Hannah grinned. "I can't wait to watch this play out. I don't think she can do it."

"I can too. Just watch."

A waitress set a couple of pitchers of soda on the table, followed by three glasses of crushed ice. She looked at the girls and asked, "Three buffets?"

Kelsey checked her purse before ordering. With the five from her dad and what she had left over from Latte Da, she had enough money to order the buffet. She hated living like this.

They nodded and the waitress handed them a stack of plates from her tray. Kelsey saved a couple of places by setting plates in front of their seats. She looked at the other rows of tables filling up. "Looks like nobody wants to sit here anyway."

Shelby smiled. "That's because this is pretty much the jock table."

Great, now we look like football groupies. "Then why are we sitting here?"

"Because you sat down first," Shelby said. "Don't worry about it. We're sitting with Austin anyway."

When the players began to arrive, Kelsey caught a few looks as the jocks sat on the other end of the row. But it wasn't like Kelsey and company were the only girls. The other players had girls sit with them. Kelsey just wished Austin would hurry so they wouldn't look so desperate.

By the time he arrived, there were just a few places left beyond the ones she'd saved. When he walked in, the entire room clapped and whistled. His face turned crimson and held a huge grin as he made his way to her.

"Good game." She stood and hugged him tight, or tried to.

He gave her a half-hug back and said thanks before taking his seat.

Wow. His hug had no feeling. It was less than a friend pat. But it was her fault. She'd insisted he back off, and he had. So while she'd jumped up and gave him an *I'm special to you* hug, he brushed her off like she was Britney Boyd. And she felt stupid. She choked the feeling down and focused on her friends.

Kelsey had to give Shelby credit; she didn't flirt with Caleb. Of course, it could have been because she'd turned her attention to every other guy in the place.

When they were in the buffet line, Austin leaned over Kelsey and asked, "So, are you having fun?"

"Yeah. I am. This is pretty cool." And she was, but the feel of Austin so close and the faint scent of his aftershave teased her senses and made her want to forget her commitment to friends-only status. God, what game was her heart playing? Drew loved her and she loved him. Her obsession with Austin had to be purely physical—they were just too different for it to be anything else. He was the country mouse and she was the city mouse. He was farm animals and football. She was high heels and romantic dinner dates.

Still, to her huge disappointment, he didn't offer to take her home. When he finished his pizza he said to Travis, "I'm beat. I've got to be at the feed store early to help unload. I'm going to take off." He spoke to Travis. Travis! Not Kelsey.

He stood and patted her on the shoulder. "I'll see you later."

As she watched him leave, she wanted to yell, *Wait a minute. What about me? You're supposed to give me a ride home!* But this was the way it was supposed to be. Besides, Hannah would give her a ride. But all of that knowledge didn't take away the awful void right in the middle of her chest.

After Austin left, Kelsey tried to have fun. As amusing as it was to watch Shelby struggle not to flirt with Caleb, the room felt empty and cold without Austin. Shelby was spending the night with Hannah and they'd asked Kelsey to join them, but she wasn't in the mood. They dropped her off around ten-thirty—an hour and a half before curfew.

It was official. Her life sucked.

When she walked into the house, she found her parents sitting on opposite ends of the couch watching TV. Normally, she'd find them all snuggled up and she couldn't help but wonder if the encounter with the tabby-haired lady had caused some tension. "Hey, guys. Everything okay?"

Her dad turned down the volume. "You're home early."

"Yeah, I'm tired."

Her mom picked up a package from the coffee table and handed it to Kelsey. "This came for you today."

It had an Italian return address. Excitement poured into the empty space in her chest. She sat on the couch next to her mom and tore the wrappings off. Carefully, she lifted the lid of the box and unfolded the tissue paper. A silk multicolored scarf lay next to an aqua cashmere sweater. She held the V-neck sweater against her chest. "This is beautiful."

Her mom rubbed the sleeve between her fingers. "Very nice."

Kelsey said, "Do you think it will ever get cold enough here to wear it?"

Her dad said, "Yeah. It may be November, but it gets cold."

Kelsey picked up the package wrappings. "I'm going to go call Drew." As soon as she was in her room, she punched his number.

"Hi, Kelsey."

"Drew, I got the package you sent. Thank you so much! It's beautiful."

"You just got it? Anyway, I thought the color would look amazing with your eyes."

"It's so sweet." She laid the sweater on her bed and draped the scarf across it. He'd shopped for her while she flirted with Austin. "I so don't deserve you."

"Don't say that, babe. You're perfect."

If he only knew. "You're sweet."

"Hey, in a few weeks we'll be together again and I can show you just how perfect you are."

Guilt made her cringe. "I can't wait. As soon as I deposit my check, I'm going to buy my tickets."

"It's ridiculous that your dad won't let me buy them."

Kelsey sighed. "You how my dad is." *Can't you just*

drop it? "Besides, it's not that bad working at the diner. It feels good to earn my own money."

"Well, once you're in Chicago, I'm paying. We'll do whatever you want—you decide."

"You know I'm staying with Zoe, right?"

"Yeah, but I'm going to pry you away from her every chance I get. I'm lonely without you, Kelsey."

"Me too." The words sounded so fake—she was such a liar—but he didn't seem to notice.

She heard someone was talking to him in the background. "Hey, Kelsey? I have to go. I'll call you tomorrow."

It wasn't until she was leaning over the sink to spit out her toothpaste that she realized he hadn't said he loved her. In fact, he hadn't mentioned those words since he'd texted them.

She padded across the hall to her room and crawled under the sheets. Should it bother her? She hadn't said the words to him either. She scrolled through his texts until she found the one. She read the words and squeezed her phone to her chest. She imagined Drew holding her and saying that he loved her. But the memory of Austin kissing her kept invading her thoughts.

What was wrong with her? She could tell herself that night with Austin had just happened, but the truth was, she'd wanted it to happen. She'd been a more than willing participant.

One thing was for sure, she'd totally effed up their friendship.

Tears burned her eyes. When she'd hugged him after the game he felt a million miles away and when he left, the pat he'd given her was cold and empty.

Drew. Austin. How had her life gotten so complicated?

22

It is illegal to throw rubber balls or confetti in Borger, Texas.

Austin slapped his alarm off. Five seemed earlier than usual. He stretched and felt the impact of last night's game. He'd taken a couple of big hits, but it was part of the game and by the time he finished heaving feed bags, the soreness would have worked itself out.

He grabbed his laptop and clicked on Kelsey's Facebook page. She'd posted: *Chicago here I come!*

He clicked on Comments.

> *Zoe: The Magnificent Mile awaits your return.*
> *Katie: Do you still have all of your teeth?*
> *Lizzie: I get a dollar for every time you say "y'all."*
> *Emily: I've missed you girl, can't wait.*
> *Kelsey: Can't wait to get out of Hickville.*
> *Austin: The chickens are gonna miss ya.*

He scrolled through her pictures. This wasn't the first time he'd clicked on her photo album. He wanted to know what her perfect life had been like in Chicago. He rolled the cursor over the pictures and named the faces before the tags appeared. Zoe, Katie, Emily, Lizzie, and Drew.

Kelsey looked plastic in those pictures. She was beautiful, no doubt, but not like she was now. In those pictures, her makeup masked the freckles sprinkled across her nose. Her eyes were the same amazing deep blue, but the mascara was so heavy they almost looked stuck open. Her lips were sexy as hell no matter what she painted on them. That night at the bluff they'd been pouty red—begging to be kissed. He closed his eyes for a second and let out a deep, long sigh. He hated the taste and feel of lipstick, but for her, it was worth it.

She looked happy in the pictures, but there was no mischievous sparkle in her eyes. And something else was missing. He studied her smile. It was there, but so different. It seemed tighter—not forced, just not carefree.

He checked out a picture of Kelsey and Drew. He could see how they'd wound up together. They were Barbie and Ken. But now? Ken looked like the kind of guy who would consider her life on the farm her "dark years." Austin couldn't imagine pretty boy getting his hands dirty.

He clicked on the pictures of Kelsey sitting next to him on the edge of the pool. Frustration burned deep. Kelsey wasn't the same girl now as the one who'd blown in from Chicago. In this picture, she wasn't wearing makeup. She was sitting so close that their arms touched. They were watching her sister flip off the board and she was laughing. She wasn't just happy; she was joyful.

He clicked away from her profile, stood, and stretched his sore muscles. Who was he kidding? Kelsey hated living in the boonies. He wanted to believe she was happier here, but seriously, going from riches to rags couldn't be her desired life path. She was making do until she could blow this town. College-boy could give Kelsey her old life back.

Not that Austin didn't want to go to college, but he didn't have the luxury of having school paid for him. As much as he loved being the quarterback of the Hillside

Hornets, college football was not likely to be in his future. Austin's plans consisted of a couple years' stint at Spring Creek Community College and hopefully Texas A&M.

He sighed. If Kelsey wanted her old life back, he wouldn't be the one to give it to her. His future was pretty much the same as his past. He'd had a job at the feed store since he was twelve.

He padded into the kitchen to find his mom sitting at the table. She took a sip from a mug of coffee. "You're up early?"

"Yeah, I told Mr. Quinn I'd help him unload a truck this morning."

"Good game last night."

"Thanks."

"How is Ms. Kelsey Quinn?"

Great. Twenty Questions time. "She's good." He grabbed a bowl of cereal, poured a cup of coffee for himself, and topped off his mom's mug. "She's all excited because she's getting to go back to Chicago in a couple of weeks."

"Coming to Texas must have been a huge change for her."

"Oh yeah. It upsets her to see her friends luxing it out while she's stuck feeding chickens. It'll be good for her to get to do all that stuff again. She won't want to come back."

His mom smiled behind her cup. "You never know. She might find some things in Texas she just can't get in Chicago."

"Or she'll resent this life more than ever. It's got to suck to be rich and lose it all. At least we don't know what we're missing."

His mom laughed. "Yeah, but I wouldn't mind having a little taste of knowing."

Austin leaned back in his chair. "Mom, have you ever wanted to do anything besides work at the diner?"

"Of course. We all have dreams. I wanted to go to nursing school. I almost did once, but your dad wouldn't have it."

"So what's stopping you now?"

"I'm too old to back to school now."

"People your age go back to school all the time. I could help pay for it."

"Absolutely not. You save your money for your education." His mom rose and headed toward her room. "I told Donnell I'd take her shift this evening, so I won't be home until ten. Don't stay out late tonight—I want to go to early church."

"Yes, ma'am." He stood and washed his bowl. Was this a glimpse into the future—stuck in a minimum-wage job wishing he'd gone to college? No. He may not have school handed to him, but that wasn't going to stop him.

*

Austin heaved another bag onto the cart, kicking up a puff of dust as the bag slammed down.

"Hey there, cowboy."

Kelsey stood a few feet away from him wearing shorts and a tank top and smelling like spring. "Hey. What are you doing here? I thought you were working at the café."

"I don't go in for a while and I thought you could use some help. Are you ready for a break? I brought doughnuts. They're on the table in the kitchen."

"You're awesome."

Austin followed Kelsey to the beat-up wooden table that served as the feed store's kitchen. He grabbed a Dr. Pepper out of the fridge and a couple of doughnuts.

Kelsey sipped her coffee. "Do you want to sit outside? It's a really nice morning."

"Sure."

They sat and let their legs dangle off the edge of the loading dock. The smell of sweet feed and fresh-cut grass wafted over them. They sat next to each other without talking. It sucked, but it was better than not being around her at all. He demolished a chocolate-covered doughnut in two bites.

Kelsey set down her drink. "Austin, I think we need to talk."

"About?"

"That night on the bluff... I'm so confused."

Crap, he didn't want her to feel bad about it. It wasn't her mistake. "Kelsey, I knew what I was getting into. If anything, I owe you an apology. I know you have a boyfriend. I shouldn't have taken you there, I shouldn't have kissed you." He wanted to look her in the face and read the thoughts behind her expression. But he was a coward. So he stared at the tips of his scuffed boots.

"We both let it happen. The thing is—I have a lot of fun with you. You're my best friend. I don't want what happened to make it weird between us. I mean, I understand if it does, but does it have to?"

Austin put his arm around her and pulled her next to him. "Look. What happened, happened. Let's just move forward. Best friends. Drew doesn't ever have to know. And God, Kelsey, don't beat yourself up over it."

"Thanks." She stood and stretched. "I can't believe I'm going home in a few weeks."

Austin stood too. "Yeah, me either. So, are you here to feed me or to help me?"

"Okay, I'm coming."

Austin returned to heaving sacks onto the flat cart, only now Kelsey worked next to him.

"Dang!" He looked up and saw Kelsey sucking on her finger. "I broke another nail."

"Poor baby." He grabbed her hand and felt the calluses across her grip. "These aren't the hands you came here with."

"Yeah. Tell me about it. I remember the first time I unloaded bags, it took Ryan and me together to unload just one." She flexed her arm. "Check out these babies. Think anybody back home will notice?"

"Trust me, they'll notice." What would Drew think about the roughness of her hands? He doubted the guy would appreciate how hard she'd worked to earn those calluses. "So you've earned enough money to go to the thing?"

"The gala, yes. Now I can quit the diner."

"You're quitting?"

"I'm working today, but I'm going to talk to your mom. I'm only working on Saturdays right now anyway."

"Oh."

"What does that mean?"

"Nothing."

"You said it like it meant something."

"It was just a response. What do you want me to say?" His tone had more bite than he intended, but not as much as he felt.

"I don't want you to say anything. It just sounded like you were judging me."

"Because I said *Oh?* Seriously, Kelsey? I don't care if you work or not. It doesn't affect me one way or another." But it affected other people, like his mom. But Kelsey didn't think about the people who'd come to depend on her. Maybe she was just a dishwasher, but it freed up his mom, T-bone, and the other waitresses to do their jobs.

Austin loaded the last bag on the cart and straightened. "Mr. Wilson is going to back his truck up to the loading dock. I'll get these. He usually helps anyway."

He pulled the cart to the end of the dock and waited for Mr. Wilson. Kelsey followed. But he didn't want her there. He had a lot of anger in his gut. Not just about the job, but about everything.

As much as he pretended otherwise, he was mad as hell about the bluff. If she was so in love with Drew, why'd she make out with him? He sure as hell hadn't forced her. She'd kissed him first.

He didn't look at her when he spoke. "I thought you

were going to do something else."

"No, I'm here to help you, remember?" She said it with fake cheerfulness and it set his teeth on edge.

"I've got it, Kelsey."

"But I want to help." Her voice was a little strained.

"Look. The whole freaking world doesn't revolve around you and what you want."

"Okay." She turned and walked back inside the store.

As soon as the words left his mouth, he wished he could have them back. He knew up front that the only reason she'd taken that job was to get back to Drew and her rich friends. It pissed him off that after she'd got what she wanted, she had the luxury of being able to quit.

And what did that say about that night on the bluff? He wasn't going to go there, he wasn't ready to acknowledge that question.

He didn't wait for Mr. Wilson to help him unload. As soon as the truck was at the dock, he tossed the first bag onto the bed. When he finished, he hurried back inside to make up with Kelsey—except he couldn't find her.

He waited for Mr. Quinn to finish ringing up a customer and then asked, "Have you seen Kelsey?"

"She just left for the diner."

"Thanks." He pulled his phone out of his pocket and headed to the back room.

*

Kelsey was proud of herself for not losing it in front of Austin. She wanted to run to the bathroom and cry, but she wouldn't give him the satisfaction. She walked straight to her dad and without so much as a hint of a tear in her eyes, told him she was going to work. It wasn't until she started the engine of the clunker truck that the tears came.

As she drove to the diner, the words he'd said looped through her brain. *The whole freaking world doesn't revolve around you.* Where had that even come from? He'd said he wanted to be friends. He'd told her not to feel guilty about what had happened between them. God, he was such a liar.

Her phone dinged. She thought about Austin's freak-out about texting and driving. "Well, the world doesn't revolve around you, either." She picked up the phone and read the text.

Austin: I'm sorry.
Kelsey: Whateve…

One word. She couldn't get one word out. She looked up and realized the car in front of her had stopped at a light. She slammed her foot on the brake, but the old truck slid into the back of the Ford anyway. The rest of the scene unfolded in slow motion. The car in front of her was pushed almost to the center of the intersection. Tires on a red car squealed as it slid through the intersection and clipped the front end of the car she'd hit. The sound the cars made as they collided was not at all what she expected. There was no drawn-out metal crunching, it was just sort of a muffled pop. And then everything went still.

She got out of the truck and hurried to the other cars, where the other drivers were getting out too. "I'm sorry, it's my fault. I didn't see you stop. Are you hurt?"

A middle-aged woman stood next to the car she'd hit and shook her head. "No, I'm fine. Do you have insurance?"

"Yes. Can I call my dad?"

"I think you'd better."

The woman from the red car said, "I've already called the police."

Kelsey wasn't sure her dad would have his cell phone on him, but she knew he'd answer the store phone. She punched the number.

"Feed Store."

"Austin, can you get my dad?" She managed to keep

from blubbering into the phone, but it was obvious she was about to cry.

"Kelsey?"

"Just get Dad."

Tears fell while she waited for her dad to answer. She pressed her fingers against her lower lids, as if that would stop them.

"Hello."

"Daddy…" That was all she could say before she dissolved into sobs.

"Kelsey, what happened?" He used his business voice, not mean or *you're in trouble*, just *tell me what I need to know*.

Kelsey took a deep breath. "I had a wreck."

"Is anybody hurt?"

"No."

"Can you tell me where you are?"

His calmness helped her focus enough to answer his questions. "At the corner of Pecan and Maple."

"I'm on my way."

Kelsey stood by the two strangers while she waited for the police and her dad. "I've never had an accident before. I've never even had a ticket."

The woman from the car that had taken the double hit surveyed the damage and shook her head. "At least nobody was hurt." The words were clipped, as though it was all she could do to keep from saying more.

As they waited, the adrenaline coursing through her settled and was replaced by dread. She was in big trouble, and if her dad found out that she'd been texting, she was going to be in bigger trouble.

Her dad pulled up to the scene behind the police. When she saw him, all worries about being in trouble were suspended, and she ran to him. But he didn't open his arms to her, so she stopped short, in front of him. "Are you okay, Kelsey? What happened?"

She wanted to throw her arms around his waist and cry into his shirt, but instead she forced herself to tell him what had happened—without revealing the texting part. She'd barely finished her story before he started inspecting the cars.

The left side of the front bumper of the truck dragged on the ground, but otherwise, it looked unscathed. The car she'd hit was smashed on both ends, and the red car had a pretty messed-up front end.

Her dad shook his head. "Have you told work you're going to be late?"

"No. You expect me to go to work?" *Is he crazy? I just had a wreck!*

He folded his arms across his chest. "You're not hurt. If we can't get the truck drivable, I'll drop you off."

No room for argument. Just forget that you've been traumatized and go wash dishes. He had no heart.

"Okay." She tapped the number on her phone and tried to bite back tears. Sandy answered. "Hi. Umm... I'm going to be late, I had a wreck." As soon as she said the word *wreck*, the tears she'd been holding erupted.

"My word. Are you hurt? Is anybody hurt?"

She could hear concern and sympathy in Sandy's voice and hoped she'd tell her to skip work today. She managed to calm herself enough to say, "No. Just shook up."

"Do you need some help? Is your momma there?"

I wish Mom was here. She'd understand. "Dad is here."

"Okay, take your time. We'll handle things until you get here."

Wait. You didn't say don't come in. She'd barely ended the call when her dad motioned her to him. He stood between the policeman and the women from the other cars. Kelsey gave her statement to the police, apologized again for causing the wreck, and the whole time felt like she was watching the scene through a computer screen or something.

While the other women gave their statements, Dad inspected the truck again. He determined that the radiator was busted and the truck had to be towed. He made a few calls and then turned to Kelsey. "The tow truck has to come from Spring Creek, it's going to be a while. You need to get to work. Mom and Aunt Susan are on their way. They'll drop you off at the diner. I'll wait for the tow."

She wanted to shout at him. Couldn't he see how upset she was? "I'm really sorry, Dad."

"I'm sure you are. I don't know how this is going to affect our insurance. I just hope they don't drop you."

The officer walked over to Kelsey and her dad. "Young lady, I'm going to cite you for the accident. The woman driving the red Honda said she thought you were texting. Is that right?"

Kelsey's heart thudded in her chest and tears flowed again. Her throat was too constricted to talk, so she just nodded. She looked at her dad. The endless stream of tears may have blurred her vision, but not enough to miss the flat line that his mouth formed.

The officer shook his head. "You're lucky no one was hurt. Two years ago, I worked the worst accident this county has ever seen. Three girls about your age lost their lives because they were texting."

She signed the ticket and he ripped the yellow portion from his pad and handed it to her. He spouted something about her having the right to appeal or claim deferred adjut-a-something. She took the ticket, and he left.

23

An armadillo is a flat animal that sleeps in the middle of the road.

Kelsey expected her dad to yell at her after the officer left. But he didn't. He didn't even look at her. He just stood next to her with his arms folded across his chest. When Aunt Susan's car pulled up to the intersection, he walked to the car while Kelsey followed a few feet behind.

Her mom didn't even get out of the car. She talked to Kelsey's dad through the open window. "Don't worry about the store. The girls and Austin are doing fine. I'll head back as soon as we drop Kelsey off."

Her dad opened the back door and Kelsey crawled in. "I don't know how long I'll be here waiting on the tow. All three cars are going to have to be moved."

Kelsey leaned forward and looked at her dad through her mom's window. "I'll stay, Daddy."

"No, you need to get to work. You're going to have to pay for this."

Pay for this? I thought insurance did that. She nodded and sat back in her seat.

Her parents said good-bye and her mom handed her a

packet of Kleenex. "Here. Wipe your face as best you can."

"Mom, do I really have to go to work?"

Her mom looked over the seat to her. "Yes, Kelsey. You have a responsibility. You're not hurt, and you need to earn some money. We're not paying for this."

"I thought insurance covered everything."

"There is a deductible. We'll pay it up front, but you're going to pay us back."

"How much is it?"

"A thousand dollars. I'll take the money you earned for Chicago as a down payment."

Crap. They were going to take her airline money. She'd planned to purchase the tickets after work. The money was in the bank. All she had to do was make a simple transaction. If she waited much longer, the ticket prices would go up.

"Mom, I know you're angry with me, but just listen. Promise you'll listen."

"I'm listening."

"I'm trying really hard to be responsible. I got a job, I don't complain about chores or work. I have the money for the tickets now. If I can just go to the gala, I'll pay you and Dad back for the wreck. I promise. I'll even pay you back with interest. Will you at least think about it?"

Her mom parked in front of the café and looked at her again across the seat. "When you're off, let us know. You'll have to wait a few minutes, but someone will pick you up."

"Mom?"

"We'll talk more tonight."

"Will you think about it? Please."

"Don't push it, Kelsey."

A thousand dollars. She was going to have to bus a lot of tables to earn that kind of money. She climbed the steps to the sidewalk feeling so sticky, sweaty, and dirty she could almost feel zits forming on her face. The last thing she wanted to do was clean up other people's gross messes. She opened the door to the café and wanted to cry.

The place was full of people. Sandy and another waitress, Jenny, were running around like crazy and empty tables were piled with dirty dishes.

No time to feel sorry for herself. Kelsey put her purse away and grabbed an apron from the hook on the wall. She needed to clear dishes from the tables, but there was nowhere to put them. She rinsed and loaded dishes as fast as she could. About the time she'd get caught up enough to clear tables, more would appear on the stainless counter.

Things didn't slow until after three o'clock. She'd been on her feet for hours. Her hands were raw from the hot water and her stomach had given up begging for food hours ago.

T-bone stuck his head around the corner. "Lunch is up."

He never asked her what she wanted, but it was always good. Today it was chicken fried steak and mashed potatoes. She hadn't had this dish since the day they'd arrived in Hillside.

She sat at the bar with Jenny and Sandy. Jenny was younger than Sandy, but Kelsey couldn't tell her age. She was a single mom with a four-year-old and a six-year-old. If the dark circles under eyes were erased and the haggard look softened, she would be pretty. Kelsey felt sorry for her. She was sweet, but always seemed so sad. So it felt a little odd when she reached out and touched Kelsey's arm. "Honey, are you okay? Was anybody hurt?"

"I'm good. Nobody was hurt but the cars. I was distracted and slammed into a car at the light."

Sandy said, "I'm sure glad you weren't hurt. We were drowning before you came in."

"I'm sorry." *In more ways than you know.* If she couldn't earn extra money, she could kiss the trip to Chicago good-bye. "Sandy, do you think I could work extra?"

"Like when?"

"After school."

She yelled over her shoulder, "Hey, T, come here."

He appeared from the kitchen wiping his hands on a

towel.

Sandy looked across the bar at him. "What do you think about Kelsey working after school?"

"She can work four to seven. I don't want to be responsible for interfering with her studies." He walked back into the kitchen, and that was that.

Sandy faced Kelsey. "There you have it. The man has spoken." She stood. "Do you have a way home?"

"Yes. I texted Mom. She's on her way."

Sandy retreated to the back room and T set a plate of food on the counter and took her place on the stool. "Rough day?"

He'd probably said less than a dozen words to her since Kelsey started working. When he spoke, she almost fell off her seat. "Yeah."

"Makes you strong."

She nodded and wondered why today had to be the day he'd decided to talk to her. T-bone was a mystery. "Hey, T? Did you know my dad in high school?"

"Played with him. I was a receiver."

Kelsey toyed with her paper napkin. "Do you know why he quit?"

"Got his heart broke." He held his fork suspended over his mashed potatoes and looked her in the eyes. "Women are poison for quarterbacks."

His words bored through her straight to her heart. Was he talking about her or her dad? And what could she say? She just nodded and cleared her plate. *Wow, women are poison for quarterbacks?* Well, at least now she knew. Cassidy Jones had broken her dad's heart.

She rinsed her dishes and placed them in the washer. It was a good thing she and Austin had cooled it. She didn't want anybody thinking she was poison for Austin.

But then she turned and he was there. Austin McCoy, quarterback, stood in the doorway to the office with his arms opened to her. "Kelsey, I'm sorry."

She shouldn't have fallen against his chest, wrapped her arms around his waist, or reveled in the feel of his hands on her back. But the sympathy she needed from her parents had never materialized. For them, she had to handle the situation with maturity—and that didn't include hugs.

He stroked her hair and rested his chin on the top of her head. "When I heard that you had a wreck…"

Kelsey nestled against his chest and let tears fall. She felt safe in his arms. She felt something else too. Something bigger, deeper, scarier.

"I'm sorry I said those things."

She moved her hands to his waist and pushed away from his embrace. "I know." His words had cut deep, mostly because there was some truth to them. She had taken the job for the sole purpose of earning money for her airline tickets. She hadn't given a thought to the people she worked with. Imagine, the "trailer trash" waitress had not only became her boss, but her friend too. She'd even grown fond of T-bone's surly attitude.

"Kelsey, your mom's here." Sandy's voice sounded from outside the office. They both dropped their hands and took a step back.

Kelsey moved around Austin. "I've got to go."

"Kelsey?" He stood still, not facing her.

"Yeah?" She hesitated, but didn't look back.

"Are we still friends?"

"Of course." She said it as though he'd asked the stupidest question in the world, and that's the way she meant it. She hurried from the office and away from all the emotions that swirled in the air there.

When she reached her mom waiting in the dining room, she was relieved to find a smile on her lips—even if it did seem a little forced.

"Hey, Mom. I have good news."

"We could use a little good news. What is it?"

"T-bone said I could work four to seven during the

week."

Her mom took a seat on one of the counter stools. "Okay. But we need to figure out transportation. The truck is out of commission for a while."

"I can bring her home after football practice. It's practically on the way." Austin stood next to Kelsey. Her friend, supporting her, no matter how big a jerk she'd been.

"That's nice of you, Austin, but she still has to get here from school." Her mom rubbed her forehead as though the gesture would help her make a decision. "I guess I could drop you off here when I pick up the girls after school. It's not that far from the store."

"Thanks, Mom. Umm—did you think about my idea to pay you and Dad back after the gala?"

"Yes. We talked." This time she smiled for real. "You've worked really hard. We're going to let you buy the tickets, but you'll have to pay us back for the repairs with interest. Sound good?"

Kelsey had to suppress the urge to squeal and do a few spontaneous jumping jacks. "Sounds wonderful." She turned to Austin and pointed at him with both hands. "I'll see you Monday morning."

*

She practically skipped out of the café with her mom, and Austin was left scratching his head. T-bone took a spin on the stool to face him. "What's wrong with you?"

"I just offered to give her a ride so she could earn more money."

"Yeah, so why do you look like she just sold your favorite filly?"

"Because she's earning money to go to some dance with her boyfriend in Chicago."

T-bone hunched his shoulders and shook his head. "Well, what'd you go and do that for?"

Austin mimicked T-bone's expression. "Cuz I'm a dumbass. If she asked me to piggyback her to Chicago so she could see her boyfriend, I'd probably at least consider it."

"Boy, you got it bad. Is she worth it?"

"It doesn't matter. We had the *let's be friends* talk."

"So that's what you're gonna do?"

"Yep."

"Women are poison."

"Yep."

24

It is illegal to bathe in the streets of Amarillo... during business hours.

Establishing friends-only status with Austin was the greatest and worst thing ever. They rode to school together, walked side by side to classes, and sat next to each other at lunch. When he brought her home after her shift, he usually stayed to swim, watch TV, or hang out on the front porch. He teased her sisters like they were his, and there was no guy-at-the-dinner-table awkwardness.

It was so easy to be around him. She didn't worry about perfect makeup or flat-ironed hair. He didn't seem to notice her freckles or the curls that refused to be tamed. He was her friend and he liked *her*, not who he expected her to be.

And that was the bad part.

Because after all those weeks of chemistry between them, after an hour or so of serious make-out time, and one post-wreck hug—boom, nothing. They were friends, nothing more. If he had any residual feelings for her, he didn't show it. The ugly truth was, Kelsey wanted him to. She wanted him to keep flirting with her, to "accidentally" touch her, but it just wasn't happening.

So she focused on her trip while the rest of Hillside focused on Homecoming. Technically, she could do both. Homecoming was the weekend after the gala. But she was about to step back into her old life, and following the glamour of the gala with a football homecoming dance just seemed messed up.

To the town, Homecoming must be the biggest thing ever. The storefronts were decked out in gold and black and there were hornets everywhere. Ryan even painted a huge hornet on the feed store window with the words FEAR THE STING across the top.

Every organization in school, the flower shop, and even the grocery store sold something called Homecoming mums, and apparently, the bigger and gaudier the better. The Monday before Kelsey was to leave for Chicago, she rode with Hannah and Shelby to Spring Creek to pick up their mums.

While they waited for Hannah's and Shelby's mums to arrive from somewhere in the back of the store, Kelsey toured Texas Mums Etc. Braided ribbons, glitter ribbons, gold, black, white, green, and probably the colors of every other football team in Texas hung across a wall. Jingle bells, miniature cowbells, silver footballs, basketballs, soccer balls, and megaphones filled baskets lining the floor in front of the wall of ribbons. On one side of the store, white, brown, and black miniature teddy bears sat on shelves from floor to ceiling. Next to the bears hung bear-sized cheerleading and football uniforms in various color combinations. Just beyond the bear section, goats, hawks, rams, bulldogs, and hornets formed an array of toy mascots that filled the shelves.

The racks in the center of the store held single, double, and triple mums. Kelsey lifted a triple mum—three silk crysanthemums attached to a kind of heavy poster board.

Shelby walked over. "See, you start with the base and then pick out ribbons and stuff."

"Is yours this big?" Kelsey held the thing out and tried to

imagine why anyone would want to wear the monstrosity.

"Oh yeah. Are you kidding? We're seniors."

"And?"

"It's sort of an unwritten tradition that seniors get the biggest and baddest mums. Are you sure you don't want to order one? You're only a senior once."

"Thanks, but I'll pass. I'm not going anyway."

Hannah flashed giant cow eyes at her. "I wish you'd change your mind."

Fortunately, before Kelsey had to think up excuse number two thousand and two, a middle-aged woman appeared from the back room carrying two breastplate-sized mums hanging from coat hangers and wrapped in dry-cleaning plastic. "Here we go, girls. Did you order garters too?"

Hannah replied. "Not this year."

"Then I think you're all set."

Kelsey looked at Hannah. "Garters?"

"For the guys. But since we're single, we didn't have to shell out the cash."

The lady handed the girls their prizes and they held them up for Kelsey to inspect. Hannah asked, "What do you think?"

Three silk mums were clumped together with a giant hornet stuck in the middle. White ribbons cascaded from the flowers. Silver glitter letters spelled out HORNETS HOMECOMING across one ribbon and SENIORS down another. Tinsel curly ribbon and jingle bells fell between the folds of the satin strips. Shelby's matched Hannah's, except that instead of a hornet she had a bear in the center of hers.

"Wow, that's amazing. And you pin that thing to your clothes?"

"Oh, we don't pin them." Shelby turned the mum around. "See, there's a cord that slips over your head."

"Seriously?"

Shelby nodded. "Feel how heavy it is."

Kelsey held the thing suspended from one hand. "This thing weighs a ton. Doesn't it hurt your neck?"

"After a while. But it's totally worth it."

"But how do you dance with one of these things on?"

Hannah shook her head. "You don't wear them to the dance. They're for the parade and game."

"You know school is out the Friday of Homecoming," Shelby said.

Kelsey smiled. "Yeah, that's another thing that'd never happen back home."

Shelby led the group out of the store. "It's awesome. The parade starts downtown and goes down Main Street to the old high school. Then there's a pep rally. It's been a tradition for like forever. The whole town shows up. Pretty much the only thing open during the parade is Wal-Mart."

Hannah unlocked the doors of her car and climbed behind the wheel. "All of the school clubs have some sort of float, then there's the Cub Scouts, Girl Scouts, the Kiwanis clowns. You're going to love it."

"I can't wait." She tried to sound excited, but the words came out flat.

Sarah turned to Kelsey. "I know your brain is totally on seeing Drew. So when are we going to meet him?"

"I don't know—he's so busy." But she wasn't sure she wanted him to come to Hillside. Not because she didn't want him to meet her friends. She didn't want her friends to meet *him*. She was afraid he'd use the same condescending tone he used when he poked fun at Hickville.

The tone she'd been guilty of until a few weeks ago.

Hannah pulled onto the highway heading back to Hillside. "Well at least he's not too busy to take you to— what's this thing?"

"It's a gala that my old school hosts to raise money. It's bigger than prom. It's not just for students either. It's for students and anybody else who has deep pockets."

Hannah glanced at Kelsey in the rear-view mirror.

"Wow. What are you going to wear?"

"Surely you have dresses as fabulous as the rest of your wardrobe," Shelby said.

"I have what I wore last year."

Shelby shook her head. "You can't wear that."

"Yeah, and I can't buy a new one. Zoe said she was going to get my friends to bring their dresses over and see what we could figure out."

"That's a great idea," Hannah said. "We'd bring our old prom dresses for you try on, but you'd drown in them."

Shelby laughed. "Especially mine. But my little sister is tiny like you, Kelsey. She had a beautiful one last year. I can see if she'll let you try it on."

"Uh, okay. I can give it a try." But judging by their taste in mums, she doubted very seriously she was going to wear a Hickville hand-me-down.

Hannah dropped by Shelby's house before taking Kelsey home. They waited in the car while Shelby ran in to get the dress. In less than five minutes she returned carrying a dry cleaning bag full of coral fabric.

"Here's the dress. Take it and see if you like it. If it doesn't work, I'll pick it up later. No big deal. She said she was going to donate it to this organization that gives prom dresses to underprivileged girls anyway."

Kelsey Quinn and *underprivileged*—words she'd never thought she'd hear together. "Thanks. It's really nice of you—and your sister."

Shelby handed Kelsey the dress and slid back into the front passenger seat. Hannah pulled out of the drive and returned to their favorite topic, Homecoming.

Kelsey looked at the dress lying on the seat next to her. A year ago, she would have shopped Saks for a dress. Sue Wong, BCBG Maxazria, Tadashi—those were the designers she loved. And now? She was officially reduced to a charity case.

Hannah turned down the long drive leading to the

farmhouse. The Infinity looked out of place in front of the weathered farmhouse. The contrast between their old life and their now life was once again brought into focus. Kelsey loved the remnants of the nice things they had. She could hang on to *then*. Anger at her dad burned in her again. How had he screwed up so badly that he'd lost everything? Dads weren't supposed to do that.

Once inside the house, Hannah and Shelby sprinted up the stairs to the bedroom while Kelsey trudged up behind them and slipped into the bathroom. She didn't want to try on the dress any more than she wanted to embrace the life her dad had forced her into. But Shelby and Hannah didn't deserve the disdain she held for her situation, so she tried on the dress and stepped into the hallway to show the girls.

She took two steps and heard a soft whistle followed by, "Damn. That Drew is a lucky man."

As soon as Kelsey heard his voice, her face broke into that too-big smile and warmth spread through her. She turned to face him and hoped she could keep her voice casual. "Hey, I didn't know you were here."

"Just got here," Austin said. "Is that what you're wearing to the thing?"

"I don't know. Just trying it on. It's Shelby's sister's." She spun in a semi-slow circle. "What do you think?"

"Beautiful. And the dress is pretty too."

"You're funny."

Austin looked past Kelsey. "Hey, you two."

Hannah and Shelby had stepped into the hall. Hannah said, "I thought that was your voice we heard."

Austin nodded. "Yeah, but I need to go there." He pointed to the bathroom. The girls backed toward Kelsey's room to allow Austin to pass. Before he got to the door, he stopped and turned toward Shelby. "By the way, Caleb asked me if you were okay. He said something about you not being around lately." He headed into the bathroom and the girls retreated to Kelsey's room.

Shelby closed the door and fell against it. "Did you hear? Oh my God, Kelsey, you are a friggin' genius! I can't wait to see him tomorrow."

Hannah shook her head. "I don't want to be a buzz kill, Shelby, but you can't chase him now."

Kelsey nodded. "She's right. He has to come to you. He's worried and that's good. If he didn't care, then you'd know you didn't have a chance. Obviously, he does care."

Shelby fanned her face with her hands. "Okay. Okay." She drew a long, deep breath and blew it out slowly. "But for Homecoming, I want to make him wish he was mine."

Hannah smiled. "Just make him come to you."

Kelsey said. "You've got this, girl."

"Yeah. I've got this. So—Kelsey, what do you think about the dress?"

"I haven't really looked at it. The bathroom mirror is so small."

Hannah pulled Kelsey to stand in front of the full-length mirror next to the dressing table. "Look at yourself, girl. You're gorgeous."

"The dress is gorgeous." And it was. The coral chiffon fabric fell from the empire waist in soft pleats. The bodice fabric rippled across her breasts and was held by rhinestone spaghetti straps. The beauty of the dress was in its simple elegance.

The coral color somehow made her skin glow and it was awesome with her hair. But the crazy curls and minimal makeup sort of ruined the effect. "I look like crap from the neck up."

Shelby plopped on the bed. "I don't know where you get that. You never look like crap. Girl, if I had your curls I wouldn't even own a flat iron."

"Drew loves my hair straight. I used to straighten it every day. But it's just easier to let it curl. Besides, I'm not trying to please anybody here."

Shelby cocked her head. "Please anybody? Girl, I'd wear

my hair however it suits me. Screw the rich boy if he can't handle it."

Oh God, same song, different accent. "It's not like that. I care about Drew and want to look my best for him. I don't think he really cares if I don't straighten my hair, I just know he likes it better that way. Does that make sense?"

"No," they both said.

"I'm going to change back into my shorts. Thanks for the dress, Shelby."

After Kelsey changed, the girls ran downstairs to grab a snack. Austin, Ryan, and Mackenzie sat on the sofa shooting imaginary guns at the TV. Austin bumped shoulders with Ryan and said, "Dang, girl. Are you even aiming at the screen?"

"Yes. But you and Mackenzie are faster at blowing stuff up."

Mackenzie grabbed his shooting arm and pulled it away from the TV. "Now's your chance, Ryan."

A brief wrestling match ensued, and for an instant Kelsey wished she could trade places with her sister. But then she remembered he was just a friend. Her boyfriend was waiting in Chicago.

25

In El Paso, it is illegal to throw faded bouquets in the trash.

Kelsey woke up giddy with excitement. Her dad was actually letting her check out of school at noon to give her plenty of time to get to DFW airport. She couldn't believe it was really happening. She was going home.

Those first four hours of school dragged by. When the lunch bell finally sounded, Austin waited outside of her classroom. "Hey, can I walk you to the office?"

"Sure. Can you believe I'm going home?"

"Yeah. You worked hard for this. I'm really happy for you, Kelsey." He looked at her as though he was appraising her. "You look beautiful. Drew won't know what hit him." He veered to the right a couple of steps, increasing the space between them.

"Thanks." This new non-flirty Austin was what she'd asked for, but it wasn't what she wanted. She missed their play fights and the way he made everything Texas sound bigger than life.

"So what are your plans for Chicago, besides seeing Drew?"

"There is so much I want to do. Mostly, I want to see my

friends. But I have to admit, I'm dying for some real Chicago pizza."

"Our pizza isn't good enough?"

"There are some great things about Texas, like the barbecue, but your pizza sucks."

Austin slapped his hand across his heart. "I'm hurt. What's so great about Chicago pizza?"

"You gotta taste it."

"Yeah, well, I don't see that happening."

That was a conversation killer. Kelsey tried to think of something to dispel the silence that filled the space between them, but came up empty.

Austin stopped just outside the office and turned to her. "Well, here we are. You're going back to the life you love."

She chewed on her lower lip. "Austin... there is so much I want to say to you."

"Like?"

"If it weren't for you, I'd have gone crazy here."

"You'd have been fine."

"No. I wouldn't have. I mean, yeah, I'd have survived. But you made it fun."

"We'll still have fun."

"I'm only going back to Chicago for a weekend, but..." She studied her hands. "I know this is a turning point for us."

He nodded. "Hey, you are going to have an awesome weekend." He gave her a hug and she wanted to melt into it one more time. But he released her and held her at arms' length. "Have fun at the gala. I'll see you when you get back."

"Thanks."

Her dad opened the glass door to the office. "Come on, Kelsey. You need to sign out so we can get on the road."

Although the old truck was back from the shop, her dad had picked her up in the Infinity. How appropriate that she was riding in style on this first leg of her journey back to her old life.

Dad had suggested they hit a drive-through in Spring Creek and pick up lunch. Kelsey was starving and wasn't sure her stomach was going to make it twenty minutes down the road. But when they passed Latte Da, all she could think about was that night on the bluff. Regret filled her. It had been a huge mistake to kiss Austin. That night had forever changed their friendship. Things would never be as carefree as before those kisses.

*

Kelsey leaned her head against the tiny oval window of seat 10F. The moment she'd dreamt about was finally here and all she could think about was that walk to the office. Austin had become a part of her family—especially in the two weeks since she'd told him she was going to Chicago for the weekend. Even if they hadn't said it, they both knew it was the beginning of the end. It was like she was building memories of something that would never be.

The captain advised the flight attendants to prepare for landing and Kelsey tucked away the thoughts swirling in her mind. She was minutes from being home. Minutes from Drew. She checked her makeup and refreshed her lipstick as the plane began its descent.

It seemed like forever before they were allowed off the plane. She received a text from Drew that he was waiting at the baggage claim. She couldn't get there fast enough. Her heart pounded in her chest. This day was really here. She was really back in Chicago.

When she saw Drew, all thoughts of Texas and Texans flew from her mind. She resisted the urge to run to him, but walked as fast as her two-year-old Kate Spade heels would carry her.

He stood with arms folded across his chest, wearing a broad grin as he watched her come to him. When she was close, he reached out and grabbed her hand. He gave her a half-hug and a quick kiss. "Welcome home."

A tall cowboy ducked his head and said, "Excuse me," as he scooted around them to grab a bag off the carousel.

Seeing the cowboy hat, the boots, and the jeans with a suit coat brought Texas flooding back. She didn't mean to stare, but she must have because Drew laughed and said, "Hey, you left Texas behind. Come on. Chicago is waiting."

"Yeah. Sorry." She shook her head as though the gesture would dislodge thoughts of dusty hats and beat-up trucks. "So fill me in on everybody. I want to hear everything."

They walked hand in hand to his car, and she listened as he told her stories about their friends. She couldn't wait to see everybody, but her thoughts kept going to how awkward her hand felt in his. She remembered walking through the parking lot of Latte Da with Austin and how naturally his fingers had laced with hers.

Drew must have sensed something, because when they reached his BMW, he pulled her against him and kissed her long and slow. When the kiss broke, he rested his forehead against hers and breathed, "I missed you." Then he released her, but it wasn't slow, as though he wanted the feeling of her to linger on his fingertips. He just let go, almost like he'd said what needed to be said and now everything was good.

As they pulled into Zoe's parents' drive, he grabbed her hand and smiled. "I have a surprise for you."

She gave a little squee of excitement.

He'd barely stopped the car when Zoe ripped the door open. Kelsey scrambled from the seat belt and into Zoe's arms. "Oh my God, I've missed you." They hugged, cried, and hugged some more. Finally, Zoe held Kelsey at arms' length and said, "Wow, you're so tan."

"Yeah. That's what happens when you live in hell's oven."

"You look great."

Kelsey flexed her biceps. "Check out these babies."

"Are you going to a gym?"

"Yeah. It's called Hillside Feed. We do pull-downs and curls with fifty-pound bags of horse feed."

Drew cleared his throat. "Zoe, let's show her our surprise."

Zoe hooked arms with Kelsey. "You're going to love it."

It felt good to be back. To pretend her life was as carefree as it had been a few months ago. She loved the sound of her heels on the marble tiles in the foyer, the airy feel of the high ceilings, and the luxury that surrounded her. She barely had a chance to take it all in before Zoe's family met her with hugs. Zoe's dad whisked away her bag and her mom offered her a soda.

Zoe shooed her mom away. "Drew and I want to show her the surprise."

Her mom laughed. "Okay. Don't keep Kelsey waiting."

They ushered her upstairs to Zoe's room. She thought maybe the surprise was a gathering of her friends, but why would they hide there? So now, she was totally clueless.

Zoe pushed open her bedroom door. "Ta-da!"

Kelsey wasn't sure what she was ta-da-ing about at first. Then she saw it. A white ball gown stretched across Zoe's bed. "For me?"

Zoe nodded. "I helped Drew pick it out. It's a Sue Wong."

Kelsey stepped closer. It was strapless, with a fitted bodice and a poufy skirt. Clusters of pink flowers were embroidered across an over-layer of white tulle, with sparkly sequins scattered between the flowers. "It's stunning. I don't know what to say." She smoothed the skirt of the dress with her hand. "I feel like Julia Roberts in *Pretty Woman*—without the whole prostitute thing."

Drew stood behind her and ran his hand along her back. "I want this weekend to be all about you."

Kelsey turned and wrapped her arms around his neck. "Thank you. Thank you for everything."

He pulled her close. "Welcome back to our world." The

doorbell sounded from somewhere in the house, and Drew released her.

"The girls are here," Zoe announced.

"This is my cue to leave." Drew walked toward the bedroom door.

Kelsey followed. "You're leaving?" The girls' excited voices drifted upstairs.

Drew stopped in the doorway. "I know how much you've missed your friends. Have fun with them. I'll see you tomorrow."

Zoe folded her arms. "Not so fast, Skippy. We have salon appointments tomorrow."

"Okay, I'll pick her up for breakfast."

"She has to be back by nine."

"That's too early."

"Then she can't do breakfast. You'll have to wait until you pick her up for the gala."

Kelsey stood between Zoe and Drew. "Wait a minute."

Drew stared at Zoe. "Then you'll have her tonight and most of tomorrow."

Kelsey tried again. "Guys!"

They both looked at Kelsey and Zoe asked, "What?"

"Neither one of you has custody of me. Zoe, what time is the appointment at the salon?"

"Ten-fifteen."

"Fine. Drew, pick me up for breakfast at eight?"

"Okay." He flashed an *I won* look at Zoe.

Zoe looked at Kelsey. "Tonight is girls' night. Come on—they're waiting."

Kelsey turned to Drew. "Do you want to hang out with us?"

Zoe snapped her gaze at Drew. She didn't say anything, but it was obvious to Kelsey she was letting him know he wasn't welcome.

Drew returned the look to Zoe, but then he faced Kelsey and the hard angles softened into a smile. "You need a night with your friends. I'll see you in the morning."

Zoe turned her back on Drew and hooked her arm in Kelsey's. "Come on, the girls are downstairs."

When they reached the foyer, Kelsey was mobbed. After she hugged everybody at least twice, Drew stepped up beside her. "I'm going to take off. Have fun tonight."

"Wait, I'll walk you out." To her friends, she said, "I'll be right back."

When the door closed behind them, Drew put his arms around Kelsey and kissed her. She waited for the fireworks to explode in her mind or at least for a squiggly feeling in her stomach, but there was nothing.

He ran his hands down to the small of her back and pulled her tight against him. But instead of melting into him, like she had with Austin, her muscles tensed and she backed away from the embrace. When their lips parted, he kissed the base of her neck. "I've missed you, Kelsey."

"I missed you too." She leaned away from him. "But the girls are waiting…"

"Let them wait." He moved his hands up her back and kissed her again. She wanted to enjoy the kiss. But his mouth was open too wide and his tongue reminded her of a lizard's, the way it darted in and out of her mouth. When she didn't think she could stand any more, she broke the kiss. Drew heaved a heavy sigh. "I know, I know, your friends are waiting. I'll see you in the morning."

"Thanks for understanding."

He kissed her again and thankfully it was a short one, because she had sort of a sick feeling in her stomach. Amazingly, as soon as she crossed the threshold into the bevy of her girlfriends, the feeling went away.

It took them about ten minutes to decide they needed to order a pizza. An hour later, Kelsey nestled into an overstuffed chair in the basement and bit into a slice of Chicago's finest. She chewed slowly, relishing the mixture of spices and crust.

Emily and Lizzie laughed about Stephen Hartwell totaling his BMW just one month after he got it. Katie filled her in on the latest shopping trip and showed off her three-hundred-dollar Cole Hahn sandals. Kelsey nudged her scuffed Kate Spade heels under the coffee table and laughed in all the appropriate places. But after having been away from that life, it seemed outrageous that they'd laugh over crashing a car. She'd been working her ass off to pay for her wreck. She couldn't blame them, though; she'd been just like them—probably worse.

When the conversation lulled, Kelsey look at her friends and said, "It's so good to be back. I've missed you guys so much."

Zoe said, "Welcome back to the simple life."

They all laughed and Kelsey added, "I'm going to soak in every bit, before I have to return to Hickville."

Lizzie smiled. "Speaking of Hickville—we have a surprise for you." She looked around the room. "Girls, I think it's time."

Zoe pointed to Kelsey. "Don't move. I'll be right back."

She ran upstairs and came back with a large purple gift bag. She set it in front of Kelsey and said, "This is an homage to your life in Texas."

Katie reached into the bag, pulled out a hot pink cowboy hat with a tiara glued to the crown, and placed it on Kelsey's head. Next, she handed her an oversized T-shirt with a picture of the front of a diner painted on it. *Early Bird Café* was painted in the window and above the picture was printed *Trailer Trash Palace.* The girls laughed wildly and insisted she wear it. She pulled it over her blouse and tried not to feel guilty for making fun of the café. The next item was a sash with the words *Trailer Trash Queen* spelled out in sparkly silver letters.

She laughed with them and told them about T-bone and Sandy. Only she didn't explain how T-bone always made her a hot lunch, or how Sandy worked extra shifts so Jenny could spend more time with her kids. Instead, she mimicked Sandy's drawn-out twang and the way T-bone scrunched his face when he was chopping vegetables.

"Oh, and you guys have got to hear about Homecoming. They wear these ridiculous mums, they're huge. Like, they cover the whole chest."

"No way." Emily pulled her phone out of her pocket. "I'm searching it."

Kelsey said, "Look up Texas Mums Etc. That's where my friends got their breast plates of flowers."

As soon as she pulled up a picture from the website, the girls passed the phone around and broke into fits of laughter.

Somewhere, she was aware that pictures were being taken, and sort of suspected that one of the iPhones might be videoing the event. But she'd slipped fully into her old world, and wasn't about to let a little thing like a conscience stand in the way of having a good time.

After they'd made fun of most of the sites and people of Hickville, Katie cocked her head at Kelsey and said, "Of all the people you've talked about, there's one person we know nothing about. Who's the hottie sitting next to you by the pool in that Facebook picture?"

"Austin. He's my best friend in Hillside."

Zoe raised her brows. She didn't say anything, but Kelsey knew Zoe suspected there was more to the story than friends.

Emily rubbed her hands together. "Best friends, or best friends with benefits?"

Kelsey shook her head. "Just friends. But enough about Hillside, I want to know more about what's going on here." The conversation returned to St. Monica's gossip, but Kelsey's focus remained on the cowboy she'd left in Texas.

After the girls left, Zoe turned to Kelsey. "Do you want to try on the dress?"

"Of course." They grabbed a soda and went upstairs.

After Zoe had helped her squeeze into the dress, Kelsey

looked at her reflection in the full-length mirror. She twirled and the skirt billowed around her. She stopped and stood in front of the mirror. Kelsey Quinn of Saint Monica's Catholic Prep. Pretty. Rich. Popular.

And a total lie. That Kelsey Quinn no longer existed.

Zoe fluffed the skirt. "Kelsey, you look like a fairy princess."

"This is a fairytale. In a couple of days I'm going back to a life of dirt and sweat. I'm an impostor in this dress. Help me out of this thing."

Zoe unzipped the bodice. "But nothing says you can't enjoy the good stuff for a couple of days."

Kelsey stepped out of the dress and slipped her blouse over her head. "The good stuff? Let me show you something." She plopped the suitcase on the bed and pulled out the coral gown. She held it up for Zoe.

"Nice, but it's not Sue Wong."

"Exactly."

"Okay, I'm lost. Are you saying you like this dress better?"

Tears stung Kelsey's eyes and she nodded.

Zoe picked up the Sue Wong and smoothed it onto the bed. "What's really going on?"

"This is all wrong. I mean—not you—Drew. I have the boyfriend I've always wanted. I've dreamt for months of going to the gala with him, and… I cheated on him."

"Austin?"

Kelsey hugged the dress to her. "I mean, we didn't *do it,* but we made out."

"So, why are you still dating Drew?"

"The night I was with Austin, Drew told me he loved me." She gave a half-shrug. "Well he didn't tell me, he texted me."

"*Texted* you? How romantic. So let me guess, you felt guilty and talked yourself into deciding you were in love with Drew."

"Something like that. Zoe, Austin is the best thing that's ever happened to me. He doesn't care if I wear makeup or my hair is perfect. We just have fun together. I've never felt so *me* before."

"What are you going to do about Drew?"

"Get through the gala with him and then hope Austin will take me back."

"You have breakfast to get through first."

26

In Texas, you may not use a feather duster in a state building.

Kelsey sat across from Drew sipping coffee. She hadn't straightened her hair for him; instead, she'd let it fall in soft curls around her chin. Her makeup was so light that her freckles screamed imperfection across her nose and cheeks. She didn't care. Her mind was on the guy she'd left behind.

"Are you okay, Kelsey? You seem distracted."

"I'm sorry. I'd forgotten how wonderful this place is." She scanned the restaurant. An ice sculpture of a seahorse glistened in the center of a table surrounded by shrimp cocktail, oysters on the half shell, crackers, cheese, and fruit. In the corner of the room, a couple of chefs prepared omelets, French toast, and Belgian waffles to order. Servers wearing gold jackets, black slacks, and white gloves hurried around the room pouring coffee and juice.

Drew leaned back in his chair. "Do you miss this?"

"I did at first. But when your days consist of feeding chickens, cleaning the coop, slopping the hog, and shoveling horse poo, you sort of forget about leisurely breakfasts at the country club."

He curled his upper lip into his nose as though he'd just

smelled horse poop. "It sounds horrible."

"Nah. It ain't so bad." Kelsey threw a little Texas twang into her words.

Drew winced and looked around as though he was afraid someone might overhear her. "Wow, you do that hick voice well."

"Maybe I am one." She stretched the words out and made the "I" sound like "ahh."

Drew smiled and set his juice on the table. "Very funny. I promise there will be nothing rural about this weekend."

Kelsey cradled the coffee cup just below her mouth. "What if I like rural?" She didn't mean to be picking a fight with him. It just ticked her off that he assumed she didn't want anything to do with the country.

He leaned back in his chair with a swagger that she found annoying. "Do you really want that, Kelsey? Slopping hogs? Be real. Are you making any real money working in that diner?"

"No. But what I make, I've earned. What have you done to earn money lately?"

"Don't look down on me because I'm not poor. I know how fortunate I am to have the life I have."

"But you see, Drew, that's the problem. You think I'm not fortunate. You feel sorry for me because I can't spend money on things I don't need."

"That's not true." Drew shook his head. "You're full of crap, Kelsey. Tell me you don't miss this. You can wear your hair in curls, and stop wearing makeup, but you're still one of us."

She sat her cup on table and breathed. "Sure, I miss being able to spend money without a second thought." The words almost choked her as she spoke them. "I miss wearing designer clothes. I miss eating fancy food. I miss driving an expensive car." She stopped and tears dripped down her cheeks.

Drew handed her his napkin. "Don't be so hard on

yourself, Kelsey. Everybody wants to live like this."

Visions of the weeks spent sweating in the sun, shoveling manure, and working in the dusty feed store flared in her mind. She saw Austin sitting in the dirt holding his bleeding thumb to his chest, and thought of the way he made sure everybody in school knew she was his friend. And then there was the night on the bluff.

"But I've found something better. I'm sorry. I don't want to be with you anymore, Drew." She stood and grabbed her purse. "I'll call Zoe to pick me up." She ran from the room before he had a chance to speak.

She stood in the foyer of the country club and punched Zoe's number. She knew breaking up was the right thing to do, but actually doing it was harder than she'd imagined.

Drew walked up and gently pulled the phone from her hand. "I'll take you back." The words were soft, not harsh and angry, as they should've been.

She nodded and chewed her bottom lip as they waited for the valet to bring his car. They didn't speak until Drew pulled into Zoe's drive. He turned off the engine and sat back in the seat. Kelsey waited for a couple of breaths before reaching for her seatbelt buckle.

"Wait." He turned toward her, and she sat back with her hands in her lap. "I've been trying to figure out what I did to make you want to break up with me."

"It's not you. I'm not the same girl."

His gaze rolled over her. "Seriously, you're giving me the *it's not you, it's me* speech?"

She looked him in the eyes and nodded. "It's true."

"Maybe, but something has really bothered me." His eyes narrowed. "One question. Did you cheat on me with that guy?"

She looked away and swallowed hard.

"Get out." He spat the words and Kelsey felt as though she'd been assaulted and all at once, the anger she'd been harboring broke loose.

"I'll get out, but first you're going to listen," she hissed. "I kissed him, and I'm not sorry. You strung me along giving me bits and pieces of your affection, making me feel like I was useless without you. Do you know how much time I spent looking perfect for you? It wasn't until you saw the picture of me and Austin—"

"Austin and me."

"Shut up, Drew. *Me and Austin*, that you said you cared."

"I said I loved you."

"You *texted* it. Who does that?" She unbuckled her seatbelt and opened the door. "I'll take back the dress and have Zoe drive me to the airport on Sunday."

"Keep the dress as a reminder of who you used to be the next time you're shopping at Wal-Mart."

"You're a real prick, Drew."

"And you're a hick."

"Thank you. You finally got it right." She got out of the car and slammed the door. He squealed the tires as he pulled through the circular drive.

Zoe must have heard Drew speed off, because she opened the door before Kelsey had a chance to ring the bell. Kelsey didn't have to say a word. Zoe hugged her tight and let her cry.

Finally, Kelsey pulled away and wiped her eyes. "I don't know why I'm crying. I wanted to break up."

"Well, now it's done and we have a salon appointment."

"I can't go to the dance. I don't have a date, remember?"

"So what? The rest of us are going as a group. Come with us. It'll be more fun anyway."

Kelsey took a deep breath. "Okay."

"Besides, you already have the dress."

"I'm not going to wear the Sue Wong. I'm going with the other one. I have other plans for the Wong."

*

Kelsey waited for the rest of the passengers to find their seats and thought about the weekend. Other than the whole breaking up with Drew drama, it had been perfect. She'd been able to spend time with her friends. She'd worried briefly about seeing Drew at the gala, but he hadn't even been there. In the end, everybody danced with everybody and she'd had a blast.

In some ways, Sunday had come too soon. She hated to say goodbye to Zoe, but she was excited to get back home.

Home. Hillside *was* home now. And Austin was there, and she couldn't wait to see him, to be with him, to feel his kisses…

Her phone dinged a text.

Ryan: Check your Facebook page.

She clicked to her page and her heart stopped. There she was, in cowboy hat, T-shirt, and sash. The caption below the picture read: *Queen of the double wide.* Below the picture was a series of videos. The first one was of her making fun of Austin's mom and T-bone. In the next one, she explained Homecoming. The last line of this video was her calling Shelby and Hannah's mums *breast plates.*

Shit, shit, effing shit. I can't fix this.

She called her sister. "Ryan, can everyone see this?"

"You're tagged in it, so I think so."

Kelsey deleted the posts, but they'd been up since the night before, so no telling who'd seen them. She had two hours and thirty-five minutes to think of a way to fix her Facebook *faux pas.* And during that time, one phrase circulated her brain: *They'll never forgive me.*

Ryan and her mom met her at the baggage claim. Her mom gave her a warm hug, but Kelsey hung on. She wished her mom could make it all go away. But this was her mess, and she had to clean it up. She let go of her mom. "Did you see my Facebook page?"

"Yes."

"What do I do?"

"What can you do? Apologize and hope for the best."

While they waited for her baggage, Kelsey called Austin, but it went straight to voice mail. Shelby's and Hannah's phones did the same. She turned to Ryan. "Have you heard from anybody?"

"Yeah. Austin said he couldn't take us to school this week."

"I've ruined everything."

Her mom pulled her bag from the carousel. "Give it time, honey. You'd be surprised what the heart can forgive, given enough time."

That took her back. She looked at Ryan, but her sister gave her the *not now* look.

Mom blinked and looked for the exit. "Let's go, girls. Tomorrow is another day."

Kelsey hung back from her mom as they walked to the car so that Ryan fell in step next to her. Kelsey whispered, "What's up with her?"

"They had a huge fight. I don't know anything else, but Kenzie thinks it was about Cassidy Jones."

"Crap."

"Yeah. Crap."

By the time they reached the car, Mom seemed to be back to herself. Ryan and Kelsey exchanged worried looks, but neither said anything else. Instead, Kelsey focused on the mess she'd made of her life.

She texted Austin several times on the way home, but he didn't reply. The third time she texted Shelby that she needed to talk to her, she got a reply that said, *Sorry, I'm getting my breastplate ready for this weekend.*

As they neared town Kelsey turned to her mom. "Can we stop by the café? Just for a minute. I just want to run in."

She could see her mom's raised brows reflected in the

rear-view mirror. "Are you sure?"

"Yes. I have to try."

Her mom parked close to the café and Kelsey ran up the steps and hurried through the door. Fortunately, the place was almost empty. Sandy sat at a table rolling silverware in paper napkins.

"Hi, Miss Kelsey." The warm smile she usually offered was gone, but at least she'd spoken.

"Sandy. I came to say I'm sorry."

"About the video?"

"Yes. It was stupid. You're wonderful. T-bone is wonderful. I don't know what happened."

"Austin tried to show it to me, but I didn't watch it." She pulled out a chair. "Have a seat."

"Mom's waiting in the car." Kelsey glanced at the door, but took a seat anyway.

"I can guess what happened. Your friends were making fun of us because we're different and you got caught up in it."

"Yes, that's exactly what happened. I would never have said those things otherwise."

"Really? Because I don't think you stuttered when you called my place the Trailer Trash Café." T-bone joined her at the table.

Tears filled Kelsey's eyes. "I'm sorry." She dabbed her eyes with one of the napkins.

T-bone let out a laugh so gravelly that at first Kelsey thought he was wheezing. "Hell, girl, my feelings aren't hurt. I do kind of scrunch my face when I chop."

Sandy laughed too. "We've teased you about that for years." She turned to Kelsey. "We're pretty thick-skinned. I know you didn't mean to hurt anybody. But your friends aren't going to be so forgiving."

"What should I do?"

"Give it time." She rolled the last napkin and stood. "I will see *you* tomorrow after school."

*

School. It was worse than horrible.

Austin refused to acknowledge her existence, even in class. After a few misses, she cornered Shelby and Hannah in the hall. "Please listen to me. I'm so sorry. I didn't mean anything by it. I was being stupid."

She thought that at one point Shelby might have been about to cave, but then the five-minute bell rang and she and Hannah walked away. During lunch, she found an almost empty table at the back of the room. She could have cried when Ryan joined her.

Every day that followed was like the day before. She was in the hell she'd created while the rest of the town counted down to Homecoming.

Homecoming. That gave her an idea that might soothe hurt feelings. On Wednesday, she left work early and headed to Spring Creek. She was going to have to spend money she needed to save. But if she could get back in the good graces of her friends, it would be worth it.

27

"Once you are in Texas it seems to take forever to get out, and some people never make it." —John Steinbeck

The schools and pretty much all the businesses were closed on Friday for the Homecoming events. Fortunately, a cool front moved in and dropped the temperature to a pleasant eighty degrees. Perfect for a parade. Austin doubted even Kelsey would complain about the heat, not that he cared.

The football players wore jeans and game-day jerseys as they sat on a flatbed trailer and tossed bubblegum to the crowd. When they pulled up to a large parking lot, the trailer served as a platform for speeches and cheers. As Austin waited to make his quarterback speech, he studied the crowd and thought about Kelsey's video. She was right—the girls did look ridiculous in the humungous mums, but he loved seeing them. It was part of the Homecoming tradition. Hannah and Shelby probably had the biggest mums this year, although he had heard that some girl got one that actually wrapped over her shoulder to her back.

He scanned the crowd again, and saw her—the girl with the enormous mum. She had dark hair that fell in soft curls around her face and he was pretty sure he could see freckles sprinkled across her nose.

When his turn came to speak, he stood in front of the microphone and shouted, "Hey, y'all. I don't know if y'all heard, but we got a football game tonight." The crowd went crazy yelling and whistling.

And then, she moved to stand front and center. Kelsey Quinn, the girl with the most ridiculous mum he'd ever seen, was looking up at him and smiling. It would have been so much easier to stay mad at her if she hadn't been so pretty.

He waited until the noise quieted. "This game falls early in the year… but the team has been working hard…"

A familiar voice from crowd shouted, "Yeah. Kick their ass!"

Austin ignored his dad and continued, "This is our turf! This is our time! This is our game!"

His dad made his way to stand next to Kelsey, and Austin could tell he'd been drinking. *Why now? Why here?* It was time to end the speech before things got out of hand. "Go Hornets! Fear the Sting!"

The crowd clapped and a few people whistled. Austin took his place sitting on the edge of the trailer with his legs dangling over the side. Coach Peterson started his speech and Austin tried to figure out a way to motion Kelsey away from his dad. The man was in confrontation mode and that meant trouble.

His gut clenched as he scanned the crowd for his mom. Maybe he could give her some kind of warning and she could help out. He didn't think his dad would do anything too stupid in the middle of a crowd, but any interaction with the man was too much. He spotted his mom standing with the Quinns and let out a breath. At least she was safe. When he looked back for Kelsey, she'd disappeared.

The band played the school song after Coach spoke and then the whole thing was over. Austin hopped down from the trailer to find Kelsey.

His dad walked toward him. "Austin. I need to talk to

you."

Austin ignored him and kept moving toward the Quinns.

He had taken about two steps when his dad moved in front of him, blocking his path. "I said, I want to talk to you."

Austin didn't acknowledge him. Instead, he focused on the people behind the man.

His dad jabbed him in the chest near the shoulder. "I'm talking to you, boy." Austin's muscles tensed and he tried to step around his dad, but the old man countered, stopping him.

"Go away, Dad."

"I just want to talk, son."

"Leave us alone."

"I'm your dad."

"I don't have a dad." He'd barely got the words out when a fist crashed into his cheek. The man was strong even when he was drunk. Austin dropped to his hands and knees and spit blood onto the blacktop. He heard scuffling above him and he was sure he was about to be kicked in the ribs—it wouldn't have been the first time. He braced for the impact, but it never came.

He heard Mr. Quinn yell, "What the hell do you think you're doing?"

His dad yelled back, "This ain't none of your business."

Austin sat on the blacktop and cradled his cheek. The whole side of his face throbbed from the impact. His mom knelt next to him. "Are you okay?"

Austin worked his jaw. "Yeah. Just stings."

Mr. Quinn and Coach Peterson stood in front of his dad. *Great, now the coach is involved.*

Jimmy Davis jogged toward them with his hand resting on his sidearm. "Are you okay, Austin?" Austin nodded. Jimmy pulled handcuffs from his belt and looked at Austin. "Son, do you want to press assault charges?"

"Hell, yes."

The officer cuffed his dad and read him his rights.

"I'll bond out before the game, you son of a bitch."

Austin pulled himself up to stand. "Stay away from us. Stay away from Mom."

"What are you gonna do, boy? Try to kick my ass?"

He wanted to do just that. Austin moved inches from his dad. He imagined how good it would feel. Each impact would represent all the times his dad had knocked him around. He was stronger than his dad now. Overpowering him would make up for the times he'd shoved his mom around. His hands closed into tight fists. His entire body revved for a fight.

Then, he took a step back and relaxed his hands. "You're not worth it."

The officer led his dad away and Austin rolled his shoulders as though he was dumping weight. It felt good. But his cheek hurt like hell and he worried about his mom and wondered where the heck Kelsey had gone.

He held out his phone to text her, but then he remembered the pictures, the video, and Drew. She'd said her trip was a turning point in their relationship, and she was right. He put his phone back in his pocket and decided to forget about Kelsey Quinn, which probably had something to do with his game that night.

He threw three interceptions in the first half. He managed to get it together better in the second half, but if it hadn't been for Travis's amazing ability to catch the ball, they'd have lost the game. As it was, they won by a field goal. The whole freaking stand screamed with excitement, but it should never have come to a field goal. They were playing a crap team. It was Homecoming—it was supposed be an easy win.

After the game, everybody went to Pepperonis. All Austin wanted to do was put ice on his face and fall into bed. But like a good quarterback, he went along with the rest. He smiled, talked crap with the guys, flirted with a few girls, and hated himself for wishing Kelsey was there.

When Saturday night rolled around, he wanted to skip

the Homecoming dance. But Travis and Caleb were both nominated for Homecoming King. Not that he gave a rat's ass who won, but he felt it was his duty to be there to give both of them a load of crap for even being nominated. He refused to wear the suit his mom had had dry-cleaned. Instead, he wore jeans, boots, and a suit jacket.

*

Kelsey's plan had almost worked. Well, it kind of almost worked. Hannah and Shelby saw her at the parade and burst out laughing. Shelby gave her a hug and said, "Girl, you look ridiculous."

"Really, I love it."

Hannah gave a slow smile. "Very classy, Kelsey Quinn."

Kelsey shook her head. "Those girls didn't mean anything by making fun of that stuff. And I'm sorry I hurt your feelings. I love you guys. After all, you've made a Texan out of me."

Shelby laughed. "Then drop the *you guys,* girl."

Hannah turned to Kelsey. "What about Drew? What happened in Chicago?"

"It was great seeing my friends. But Drew and I broke up."

Shelby have her a sideways hug. "I'm sorry."

"I'm not. I should've broken up with him before I had the first kiss with Austin."

Hannah and Shelby said together, "I knew it!" Shelby practically jumped up and down. "Have you told Austin?"

"No. He won't talk to me."

Hannah looked at Shelby. "We have a mission."

Shelby nodded. "We will get you two back together."

So step one was for Kelsey to show Austin the huge mum, sort of as an act of contrition. But then his dad showed up. The man reeked of alcohol. When he stood next to her, Kelsey was afraid to move, afraid of him. Hannah and Shelby swooped in and guided her away. They'd heard the scuffle between Austin and his dad, but Kelsey didn't want to embarrass Austin by being there, so they took off.

She'd gone to the game with the girls, but Pepperonis' just didn't seem like a good place to confront Austin. Besides, Shelby was still in her avoid-Caleb mode. So step two was to wow Austin at the Homecoming dance.

*

Kelsey fluffed her hair and lightly brushed pink across her freckles. "What do you think?"

Hannah stepped back to appraise her. "Fabulous. But if you don't wear that gown you brought back from Chicago, I'm going to cry."

"I told you I wanted to donate it to Project Prom."

Hannah sighed, "They're all gently worn gowns. So gently wear this one and then donate it. Besides, think of the irony. A beautiful gown at a Hickville Hoedown."

Kelsey looked at the girls. "Should I, really?"

"You're an idiot if you don't wear it." A mischievous smile formed on Shelby's face. "Besides, you want to get your man, right? Wear the trap."

So Kelsey squeezed into the Sue Wong. Shelby and Hannah looked equally elegant in their dresses. And they all giggled as they descended the stairs to the room with the coffee-pot wallpaper.

Kelsey's dad whistled. "You girls look mighty pretty."

"Thanks, Dad." He tossed Kelsey the keys to the Infinity. "What's this for?"

"I thought it might be easier to get in and out of than the truck."

"Thanks, Dad."

The girls jammed to CDs all the way to the school. Kelsey parked close to the gym and turned to her friends. "Are *y'all* ready?"

They laughed at the way she emphasized *y'all*. Shelby pulled the handle on the door and said, "Let's go."

Which was just when Kelsey's cell rang. "Hello."

"Kelsey, this is Sandy. We've got a problem. I'm running a fever and Jenny's sitter can't get to her house until nine. I know it's Homecoming, but is there any way you can help out? I wouldn't ask if there were any other way. As soon as Jenny gets there, you can leave."

Her heart sank. Of all nights... "Sure. I'll be there in a few minutes."

"You'll be waitressing. Don't worry about the dishes, we'll figure that out."

"Okay. Don't worry, I have it handled." She punched End and dropped the phone in her purse. "Well, girls, I have to go to work. I should be back around nine-thirty."

Hannah said, "Work? But it's Homecoming! Tell her no."

"I can't. There's no one else. Austin's mom is sick and the other waitress can't come in until she gets a babysitter. As soon as she shows up, I'll be back."

Shelby looked like she was about to cry. "That *so* sucks!"

Hannah shook her head. "What about your dress?"

"I'm going to see if Mom can bring me some clothes. I'd better go."

The girls crossed the parking lot to the gym and Kelsey climbed back behind the wheel.

She held her tears, but just barely. She owed it to T-bone, Sandy, and Jenny not to let them down. She tried to call her mom a dozen times on the way to the café, but it always went to voicemail. When she got to the café, she didn't have time to worry about her clothes. The place was slammed.

T-bone was having everybody write their own orders and yelling at them if he couldn't read them. Kelsey managed to tie an apron around her gown and grabbed an order pad. After an hour of running around like Cinderella on crack, she got an incoming call from Jenny.

She leaned against the wall and answered it. "Thank God, it's you. Are you coming early?"

"No. I'm calling because my babysitter just quit. I'm trying to find somebody else. I'm sorry, Kelsey. I probably won't make it tonight."

Kelsey felt her chin quiver, but refused to give in to it. "It's okay. We're handling it."

"You're a doll, Kelsey."

Kelsey texted Shelby.

Kelsey: Won't make it to the dance. Have to work until close. Call if you can't get a ride home.

If there was ever a time to feel sorry for herself, this was it. But the crowd kept coming and T-bone was ringing the order up bell.

*

Austin looked for Kelsey in the crowd and told himself it didn't matter that she wasn't there. But as soon as he saw Hannah and Shelby, he made his way to them and shouted over the music, "Is Kelsey coming?"

Hannah answered, "She was, but she had to work. Your mom got sick and the other lady doesn't have a sitter."

Shelby bounced with the music and shouted, "Hey, can you give us a ride home?"

"Yeah, but I'm leaving as soon as they announce the king and queen."

As if on cue, Mrs. Bettis stood in front of the microphone and cleared her throat. "Could I have everybody's attention? It's time to announce the Homecoming King and Queen. Could I have the nominees on the stage, please?"

Caleb, Travis, and a band nerd named William stood on

the stage, followed by Courtney, Shelby, and some girl named Cheyenne wearing a hot pink cowboy hat.

Mrs. Bettis opened an envelope. "This year's Homecoming Queen and King are... Caleb James and Shelby Cox!"

The crowd clapped and whistled while Shelby and Caleb were crowned. The music played and the royal couple stepped onto the dance floor. Caleb smiled into Shelby's eyes and held out his arms. About halfway through the dance, the space between them seemed to shrink as Caleb wrapped his arms around Shelby's waist and held her against him.

Hannah looked at Austin. "I guess we'll find another ride."

Austin didn't waste any time getting to his truck. He called his mom to make sure she was okay. He'd planned to text Kelsey next, to tell her he was coming, but by the time he got off the phone with his mom, he was almost to the café.

He couldn't believe how packed the place was. He had to park behind the dumpster. The inside of the restaurant was sort of an organized chaos. In between orders, Kelsey had been washing dishes. She wore an apron over her dress, but the part that was showing beneath the apron had a few stains.

He barely said hello as he shed his coat and rolled up his sleeves. He grabbed an apron and headed to the dishwashing area. It was nonstop washing, serving, and cooking. Nobody spoke, except to give and receive orders, but they managed to catch up and stay slightly ahead of the mayhem.

The café normally didn't close until ten, but at nine-thirty, T-bone emerged from the kitchen and flipped the Open sign over. He looked at Kelsey and groused, "We're out of chicken-fried steak. Time to close."

Kelsey looked too tired even to thank him. Instead she just nodded. Thankfully, the café was emptied by ten. T-bone cleaned the grill and grabbed a bucket to help Kelsey clear the last of the dishes. She shook her head at him. "We've got it, T."

"It's my place, I'll help."

Austin stacked plates in Kelsey's tub. "Seriously, man. Let us take care of it. This is the last load, anyway. You've got to be here early tomorrow."

T-bone set the tub on an empty table. "You know how to lock up?"

Kelsey smiled. "Yes."

"All right. I'm calling it a night." T-bone left through the back door.

After the dishes were washed, Austin plinked quarters in the jukebox and watched Kelsey wipe the last of the tables. "I'm sorry you missed the dance."

Kelsey smiled. "Me too. But this was more important. There's no way T-bone could have handled that crowd alone."

A slow song came on and Austin held out his hand to Kelsey. "Want to dance?"

She stepped into his arms. "Austin, I'm sorry about the stupid Facebook stuff. I shouldn't have said those things."

He gave a half-smile. "They weren't that bad." He guided her between the tables. "So—you're back. I guess this is our own homecoming."

She smiled. "I guess so."

He looked into her eyes. "And Drew?"

"I broke up with him."

Relief, joy, and hope spread through him all at once. "And?"

"And this." She rose on her tiptoes and kissed his cheek.

It was all the encouragement he needed. He lowered his mouth to hers.

*

When their lips touched, warmth consumed Kelsey like a hot August day in the Texas sun. He kissed her long and slow, stirring embers that had been smoldering since that night under the stars. Flames ignited inside her, making her want to feel his body against hers. He pulled her tight and she wished they were back at the bluff. All the fear and sorrow over what she'd lost seemed like a distant memory.

He'd made a Texas girl out of her after all.

Epilogue

The town of Batson held a Batson Round-Up in 1903 when all unmarried women were brought to the town square and auctioned off as wives.

Kelsey's dad had told her not to worry about chores the next day, but apparently all those weeks of getting up at the crack of dawn had reset her internal clock, because she was up anyway. And after being away for a couple of days, she was ready to get back to her chickens. She dressed and headed downstairs for a cup of coffee.

She heard her parents' voices on the front porch. When she stepped out to join them, her face broke into a wide grin. Her mom and dad sat snuggled together in the glider. Whatever was up with them must have been over. Mackenzie sat across from them. But the source of Kelsey's smile sat in the rocker with a mug cradled between his palms.

"Morning, Kelsey. The chickens are fed. Relax and have your coffee."

"Thanks, Austin. I believe I will." Kelsey took the seat next to him. She didn't worry that her face was makeup free and probably had a sleep line or two stretching across it. She was going to enjoy the morning sitting on the porch with her family and Austin. Life just didn't get much better than this.

She looked at her sister. "Kenzie, have you already run this morning?"

"No. I'm taking today off."

"Almost all of us are here together—that never happened in Chicago. Where is Ryan, anyway?"

Kelsey's mom answered, "She spent the night with Macey Brown."

Kelsey shared a look with Mackenzie. Her sister said, "Macey's not likely to throw a crazy-wild party."

"You're right." Kelsey sat back and propped her feet on the coffee table.

"I see the worry between you two," her mom said. "Just so you know, I spoke with Macey's mom. She seems very nice and guaranteed me it was a girls-only sleepover."

"I'm not worried," Mackenzie said. "Are you, Kel?"

"No. I've seen how Macey dresses."

A black Chevy truck rumbled down the drive, catching everybody's attention. Austin stood. "What the—"

Kelsey stood next to him. "Who is that?"

"Justin Hayes."

The truck pulled up to the house and Ryan slid from the cab. She turned toward Justin and Kelsey saw *Hayes* across the back of the football jersey she wore. She gathered her stuff and said, "Thanks. I'll talk to you later."

By the time she reached the bottom step of the porch, her mom was standing in front of her and her dad was next to Justin's truck door. "Son, we need to talk."

Mascara was smeared beneath Ryan's eyes, and her hair had the just-rolled-out-of-someone's-bed look. Her Homecoming gown was wadded up in her arms, with her shoes balanced precariously on top. Water dripped from the dress and plinked onto the porch step.

She looked at her mom. "It's not what you think."

THE END

Thank you for joining the Quinn sisters as they settle into small town life. I hope you enjoyed Kelsey's story. And now, to find out what really happened to Ryan Quinn, here's an excerpt from book two, *Hickville Confessions*.

Hickville Confessions

Book Two In the Hickville Series

By Mary Karlik

1

Nobody asked the Purity Club girls to dance.

They stood in the corner looking like painted-up losers and Ryan Quinn was smack dab in the middle of the group.

Relax. New beginning. New town. New group.

New me.

If this had been her old school, she'd have put some fire into this party—

Not true. If this had been her old school, she'd have ditched the party for… no, she wasn't going there. Being a member of the Purity Club was the perfect way to atone for the sins she'd committed then. As long as her past remained secret, she'd handle being ignored at the dance.

After the king and queen had been announced, the PC girls were ready to leave. That was fine with her. She was bored out of her mind. Things probably weren't going to get any more exciting at the PC sleepover, but at least she could shed her gown for Soffe shorts and a tank top.

She lagged behind as they crossed the parking lot to Macey Brown's mom's Tahoe. The girls whispered, followed by a round of giggles. Were they laughing at her? Nah. She was just being paranoid. They'd included her in all of the pre-Homecoming stuff. She was the one who'd held back, not sure she was ready to open herself up to a new group.

Once they were in the SUV, Macey cranked up the radio—and it wasn't the Christian rock she usually listened to. They drove around town and sang along to the radio and for the first time, Ryan almost felt like she fit in. Macey parked in front of the courthouse fountain.

"Come on, girls, let's go."

Macey and Katie McDonald exchanged one of those looks that said they had a secret. All the girls laughed—they were in on it too. Uneasiness wafted across the hairs on the back of Ryan's neck. She reminded herself she was being stupid, and forced a grin. "What's funny?"

Macey flashed a plastic smile. "You'll see. Ladies— shoes." They kicked off their heels and climbed out. Katie grabbed a plastic grocery sack with a bottle of dish soap sticking out of the top.

We're going to soap the fountain. PC girls committing minor vandalism? This was not in her change-my-life plan. She didn't need this crap. She should've gone for loner status. But that was easier said than done, and being a fringe member of a marginally popular crowd was better than no group at all.

Macey called out to her, "Come on, Ryan. Let's have some fun."

So they were soaping the fountain. Even if they got caught, how bad could it be? Harmless fun. This was not Chicago. These were nice girls. And as far as they knew, she was a nice girl too. *Stop holding back. Give them a chance.* Ryan slipped from her strappy sandals and drew a deep breath.

All in.

The girls held up the hems of their dresses and climbed into the fountain, squealing and giggling as the cold hit their legs. Ryan stepped over the stone wall into the water, ignored the cold chill that shot from her toes to her head, and joined in the splashing and giggling.

Macey waded over to her. "Ryan, I have to confess that

we brought you here for a purpose."

The girls moved close to Ryan.

She smiled, but wariness eased its way into her mind. "What? Is this an initiation?"

Katie McDonald and Carle Davis each grabbed an arm.

So, they're going to dunk me. Relax.

Macey looked back at her with cold black eyes. Her sweet Southern smile was replaced by a sneer. "On your knees."

I can deal. They're just having fun. She dropped to her knees, and sucked in a breath as the cold water hit her torso.

The other girls closed in. Britt Stern pulled plastic scouring pads from the bag and passed them to the girls. Macey pulled the cap open on the soap. They had crazed looks in their eyes and despite her bravado, the hairs on the back of Ryan's neck screamed that this was not good. "What are you doing?"

"We discovered you've been a naughty girl."

Shit. Shit. Shit. She tried to laugh but all that came out was a nervous giggle. "What do you mean?"

"I'm talking about abusing the temple God gave you. You've abused and shamed your body with sex and drugs."

Her captors tightened their hold. Ryan's heart raced and she tried to pull away, but then it seemed like a thousand hands were on her. They poured soap over her and scrubbed. She screamed and they pushed her under. When they let her up, she coughed soapy water.

Scouring pads scraped across her skin. She twisted and kicked to get away, but they held her down. Macey straddled Ryan and screamed, "You are soiled by the workings of the devil!" She ran the pad above the scoop neck of Ryan's gown. Soap bubbles foamed in the water. "You're evil and unclean." She scrubbed the pad across Ryan's face.

The first pass felt like sand, but she kept working that damned pad. Over and over her cheeks, across her lips, down her neck. It felt as though fire raked across her with each angry stroke.

She's gone batshit crazy. She turned her face to get away from the torture, but Macey clamped a hand on her chin and dug the nylon deeper into Ryan's skin with each stroke.

Britt yelled, "Stop it, Macey. That's too much!" The hold on her right hand was released and Ryan fought to push Macey off. But the other girls were quick to pin down her arm again. A knee dug into the inside of each bicep. They held her legs by putting pressure on her kneecaps. She fought, but they kept her pinned.

Britt yelled again. "Macey, she's bleeding. Let her go."

Macey released her chin and looked down on her. The whites of her eyes glowed in the lamplight, giving her a crazy, detached look. She held the scouring pad above Ryan's face and squeezed.

Soapy water mixed with blood showered down. Ryan clamped her eyes shut and prayed the torture would end.

Macey dropped her voice an octave. "I command the darkness in you to come out."

A low, deep growl sounded from somewhere. The girls released her and squealed. She heard splashing as they scrambled to get out of the fountain. Ryan's body shook as she sat up and tried to wash the soap from her eyes. Before she could open them, she heard splashing.

Somebody was slogging through the water toward her.

ABOUT THE AUTHOR

Following a career as a nursing instructor, award-winning author, Mary Karlik earned an MFA in Writing Popular Fiction from Seton Hill University in Pennsylvania.

A native Texan, Mary loves horses, dogs, cats, and small town diners. Although she has recently relocated in northern New Mexico, her heart remains in the Lone Star state.

AVAILABLE NOW
Welcome to Hickville High
Hickville Confessions
Horseplay

COMING SOON
Hickville Redemption

Made in the USA
Lexington, KY
20 September 2015